JUNGLE LAB TERROR

GUSTAVO BONDONI

SEVERED PRESS
HOBART TASMANIA

JUNGLE LAB TERROR

Copyright © 2020 Gustavo Bondoni

WWW.HARDCOPYGAMES.COM

ISBN: 978-1-922323-44-6

CHAPTER 1

Something landed on the floor of the hut with a wet thud. Philippe dragged his maimed leg behind him, shuffling over to have a look. He bent down and picked the item up.

It was a wet paperback whose cover depicted a muscular man with his shirt almost completely torn away. Philippe smiled and turned to the creature that had dropped it there. "Good work, Chiffon," he said. He patted its head and turned back to his visitors. "She brings me gifts, you see."

Two men occupied the only chairs in the shack. They looked on impassively, staring blankly at Philippe and at his creation. The smaller of the two, an Asian man with a round face and tight eyes, spoke first. "Impressive. It clearly has some reptile in there. Also some cat genes. But what else?"

Philippe replied proudly. "Some elephant, though you can't tell from looking at it, to improve intelligence, as well as a small amount of penguin."

"What for?"

"Penguins are good at adapting to wide temperature variations. You could take this one with you to Siberia, and it would function just as well there as it does here in the jungle."

The Asian man's name was Park Sun-Lee, and Philippe didn't like the predatory way he was looking at Chiffon. Philippe tried to change the subject. "But this one is just a pet, a tame toy. If you'll accompany me to the farm, I can show you some of the bigger specimens. Those will truly impress you."

Sun-Lee held up a hand. "Wait." He turned back to the door and shouted something in Russian that Philippe couldn't understand. Two men dressed in black from boots to balaclavas walked in, threw a net over Chiffon and pulled the creature away.

Philippe's heart sank. In the jungle, everything from the mosquitoes to the jaguars wanted him dead in some way, shape or form. Now, these men were taking his only friend.

But he dared not contradict them. He could build another pet. An army of pets. One thing he couldn't do was to revive himself if these men took things the wrong way. And he certainly wouldn't escape if they decided to tell the French government where he was. Death would be preferable to that... the French had been after him for a long time, and wouldn't be in the mood for niceties if they caught up to him.

Sun-Lee watched him as if to see how he'd react. The Korean seemed disappointed when Philippe just shrugged.

"As I said, there are more impressive creatures out back. Come this way."

They spent three hours among the cages and pens. Sun-Lee selected a few of the more easily transported creatures, which were sedated and placed in crates. A pyramid of cages awaited the return of the helicopter.

Once done, they returned to the relative coolness of the hut.

"What you've done here is quite impressive," Sun-Lee said. "But I have to admit that I'm also disappointed. The reports I read about your work hinted strongly at the use of human elements in the mix."

"I... I don't do that anymore."

"Ah. The trouble with the authorities?"

Philippe said nothing.

Sun Lee continued. "It must have been quite traumatic, what happened to you in Paris. Men coming into your house to arrest you in the middle of the night." He shook his head and tsked. "From all reports, you barely made it out alive. And then, in Gabon. There were rumors that you continued along those lines. But, again, something happened, didn't it? Dragons in the swamp, a little she-goblin. Strange stories these Africans spread, aren't they?"

Anyone could tell Sun-Lee didn't care about the answer. Even the question was just a way to strut his knowledge, to tell Philippe that yes, they knew all about him, and that the source of the information wasn't the French government because, if it had been, Philippe would already have been snatched by the C.O.S., to await trial in a high-security cell in Paris.

He wanted Philippe to know that they had power over him.

"What do you want?" Philippe asked when the silence grew too heavy.

"Nothing. The animals you've given us will help our own lines of research immeasurably. In fact," he turned to the man beside him, an impassive pale blonde man who'd stayed silent throughout, "Anton has brought you a gift."

"I don't need anything."

"No. You don't. From what I've seen of your setup, you are perfectly prepared to continue as you've been doing and creating the hybrids you like. You might need a fourth generation CRISPR editor soon, but other than that, your equipment looks good for another five years."

"Then what..?"

"Anton has something you might be able to use, if you like. It's a machine that allows you to copy a human mind onto... well, onto whatever brain you might have lying around. We could use it to put a different mind into your own head, memories and all."

"What would happen to me if you did that?"

Sun-Lee shrugged. "We don't know. Our labs are in Russia. It's a wonderful country, where, if you have the right people behind you, you can act with remarkable freedom. But it's not perfect. Even Russia has its limits, and experimenting on human minds... it's still beyond that limit, I'm afraid." He looked around the hut. "But here, in the Darién gap, in the middle of a jungle? Who's going to come enforce the law? The Panamanians? I doubt it. They love the money you're giving them from your exotic pet trade... yes, we know about that. The Colombians? They won't send police in here in case it starts the drug war again. No. This is the perfect setup."

"I don't experiment on humans," Philippe said. It was weak. They held all the cards, and if they wanted him to experiment on humans, that is what he would end up doing.

But Sun-Lee surprised him. "Of course not. The tech is way too experimental for that. We would be grateful if you didn't, in fact." The Korean let a significant pause develop before continuing. "Of course, we'd be equally grateful if you'd try it out on a few of the larger-brained animals you build. Just to see what happens. And if you could send us an update every once in a while, that would be excellent."

So, he had his marching orders. "What kind of machinery are you talking about? It will need to be pretty robust to work here."

Anton pulled a small black suitcase from beneath his chair and opened it. Under a mass of diodes was a dark black plastic item. "The battery should last for a hundred applications," Anton said. His accent was Russian, perhaps giving credence to the Korean's words about their operations. "You just place the diodes against the skull the way it shows in the manual—it's in English—and you press the red button. No need to turn it on or off or anything."

"And that will put a human personality into one of my creatures?"

"Yes. Memory and all. It has the added benefit that the person loaded inside is experienced in switching to different brain architecture."

"I thought you said you couldn't test on real humans."

"I only said," interjected Sun-Lee, "that the political climate in Russia doesn't permit us to do so now." He shrugged. "The dead past, as you say, is a different country."

Philippe looked at the suitcase in distaste. "Who is he?"

"What?"

"The man you've got locked in there. Who is he?"

"Just someone who annoyed me. A man named Luca." Anton's gaze held no mercy. "But if you must know, he consented to having a copy made of his mind, so you shouldn't feel too bad about it. Besides, the original is living a happy life somewhere in South America. He became a very wealthy man thanks to this."

"Yeah, whatever. Leave it over there."

The roar of a jet engine and rotors above their heads signaled the end of the conversation. Boxes were winched onto a black helicopter, followed by Philippe's visitors themselves.

He watched them go and returned to the dingy hut.

Automatically, he opened a can of cat food, product of the small trade he did with Panama, before he remembered that Chiffon was on his way to probable dissection in Eurasia.

"Damn."

He sat heavily on the chair vacated by Anton and stared at the suitcase. It looked like something out of an old movie, a shiny black hard-shell case with chrome accents. Somewhere inside was a human mind and memories, just waiting to be transferred to an animal brain… all for what?

He didn't know, of course. Sun-Lee and his ilk didn't go around gratuitously sharing their plans. They just wanted the data, and the samples they'd already taken. And if something went catastrophically wrong, they'd send a team in to collect what data they could. His life meant little more to them than stealing his pet had.

That reminded him of the book Chiffon had brought. He stepped over to the countertop where he'd left it.

His first impression had been right. It was a trashy romance novel in Spanish, still soaked from being dragged through the marshes around Philippe's camp. Mud trailed across one edge and what appeared to be blood fouled the spine.

Philippe smiled. Chiffon could be a little aggressive in acquiring gifts for her master. He just hoped the lizard-cat had chosen to steal this particular book from one of the Colombian peasants that shared these woods and not from the Panamanian border patrol. Neither would incommode him in the long run, of course, but if she'd decided to rob the soldiers, there would be tedious questions.

He looked at his bookshelf, a meter of novels salvaged from the jungle. How had Chiffon understood his love for books? He didn't know. Maybe the elephant genes had allowed her to crack the pattern. Maybe there was something unknown in cat DNA or even penguins. He was pretty sure the lizard material was pretty much useless in that sense.

He smiled wistfully. That was the nice thing about art. When you started, you never knew what you'd end up with.

And he'd have to start again. The jungle would be lonely without Chiffon to keep him company. Maybe this time, he'd try a monkey gene... no. That hadn't gone well last time. Maybe dogs. Yes, dogs were loyal and useful. And he'd always wanted to see how far spider genes could scale up. That was a start. The rest would come to him once he started working.

Of course, he would also need to think about the abomination in the black suitcase. Not trying it was out of the question. The Russians had given him a very clear message: we found you once, and we'll find you again if necessary. Running was no use, and it might just result in another nighttime visit from the French.

He would have to think about that, too.

But first things first. The book. It would be of no use until he cleared off the mud and dried it out. But simply applying heat to the moist volume would not serve. The paper would end up wrinkled, obviously having been wet. Ruined.

No, the only choice was to freeze-dry it. That would leave it as good as new.

Then he could read it, savoring the pages of a new and unknown volume.

It certainly wouldn't replace his beloved copy of *Pride and Prejudice*, lost in a mangrove forest in Gabon a lifetime ago, but it was a book.

And, until the forest threw up a copy of Austen, it would serve.

CHAPTER 2

Max Cipreyes woke, every sense alert. He reached under the jacket that served as his pillow and pulled out a long-barreled .45 ACP, lovingly modified for him by a gunsmith in Cartagena who only worked with the most select clients.

The man would no longer consider Max a select client, but the gun remained. He pushed the tent flap open with the barrel and looked out into the post-dawn jungle.

"What's wrong?" Serena asked sleepily.

"Shh. I heard a noise in the trees," Max replied.

"So what? There's noise in the trees every minute of the day and night."

"This was different."

She leaned in to kiss him. "Max, you need to relax. There's no one after us. There hasn't been for months."

He was about to tell her the news from Bogotá, the announcement that the resistance would be taking up arms against the Colombian government once again, rekindling the fire that had been smoldering under suffocating peace treaties, but that would never go out as long as there was anyone alive in the country who understood how capitalism crushed the spirit and destroyed entire cultures.

But there were more pressing issues. His followers would learn of the new state of affairs when they needed to. He peered into the foliage, trying to remember who was supposed to be on guard. Liliana, he remembered. She'd volunteered for the dawn watch, since she was usually awake by then anyway.

So, if whoever was making the noise was hostile, they'd already gotten her. She wasn't the kind to miss something big.

Max crawled out of the tent, keeping his belly low to the ground and snaking behind a bush that offered a little cover. He focused his attention on a couple of small trees between the clearing and the stream they used for water. The sounds were emerging from there.

He raised the gun and charged through.

And checked himself just in time as three alarmed faces turned his way.

"Max," Emilio Vázquez said. "You scared the shit out of us."

"Yeah. Well you shouldn't skulk around that way."

"I heard a sound in the trees."

"It was just us coming back," Emilio replied.

"They called out before coming in," Liliana said. Then her eyes moved down from his head and to his bare crotch. She smirked.

Max paid her reaction no heed. She'd seen him naked before, and she hadn't been smirking then. Of course, he still wasn't forgiven for having replaced her with Serena, but as long as she was loyal, she didn't need to be forgiving.

"All right," he said. "So if there's no problem, what's with all the noise?"

"Have a look."

Pablo and Emilio moved aside to reveal the carcass of an animal the size of a sheep. It had four legs and its head was shaped like a dog's, but it was covered with white down from its clawed feet to about hip height. The animal's back was bare of feathers, scaled like a lizard.

"What is it?" Max asked.

Pablo smiled. "Breakfast," he said, pulling out a wicked tactical knife and burying it into the animal's side.

"Ugh. Make sure you clean it well," Max replied. But he didn't make any objections to the food itself. Meat was meat, and you got it where you could. People always thought the jungle was full of food, and it was true that fruit could be found if you knew where to look and what trees to climb, but large meat animals... not so much.

He returned to the tent just as Liliana was emerging, dressed in green pants and a tight t-shirt, hair in wild disarray. He took her by the waist.

"We've still got some time before breakfast is ready," he told her. "And I'm pretty worked up after that tension."

He kissed her roughly. She returned it and allowed herself to be pulled back into the tent, already unbuttoning her pants as she moved.

***

7

"It tastes like chicken," Coca said. His real name was Pablo Escobar, a common enough combination, but one that, thanks to the famous 1980s drug lord, came with all sorts of narcotics-related nicknames. Hence, Pablo became Coca, short for Cocaine.

Liliana tasted it cautiously, lip curled in distaste. She had her black, frizzy hair tied back in a pigtail, out of the way of her face. "Yes, it does. Kind of." She chewed carefully, thinking hard. "What was that thing, anyway?"

"How should I know?"

"Max, do you know what it is?"

"No clue. Good though." It was. A little fire-blackened, perhaps, but the meat was white and just fatty enough that it tasted fantastic. "If we had some arepas and cheese… heaven."

Liliana wasn't done, though. She crouched on a rock, her dark features screwed up in thought. "I mean it. Over the last few weeks, we've shot a bunch of animals none of us had ever seen before. Why?"

Max shrugged. "We're in Panama now. Different wildlife."

"Don't be silly. It's the same jungle. The same goddamned hills. All the other animals, the ones we used to see in Colombia, are the same. Why would there be creatures we've never seen before? They can walk through the jungle just as well as we can. Better, probably."

Coca interrupted her between mouthfuls. Whatever his shortcomings, being squeamish about strange food wasn't one of them. "This one wasn't very good at moving through the forest. Tried to climb a tree when he heard us coming and he fell straight out. I almost felt pity for it." He laughed. "Then I shot it. Boom. Right between the eyes. So we can't eat the brains, I guess."

"Ugh," Serena said.

"Don't say those things," Liliana said. "Can't you see the little princess is squeamish? We don't want her indisposed to perform her special and important duties, now do we?"

Serena didn't reply, simply staring daggers at the other woman and drinking her coffee. Liliana shrugged. "Anyway, we shouldn't have things here in Panama that we haven't seen a million times in Colombia."

Max cut her off. "Maybe the Panamanians have laws protecting some of the bigger animals. Maybe they're migrating from further north because of global warming. Just leave off already. It doesn't matter."

"No need to get angry. I just think they're weird, that's all. I mean are they mammals? Birds? Some kind of lizard?"

"They're probably a mix, like a platypus. Do you know what a platypus is?"

"Of course."

"There. At least these things don't have beaks."

Liliana didn't look convinced, but she knew enough not to make Max angry. "Whatever."

"Besides," Max went on as if she hadn't spoken, "we're moving out today."

Groans met this. The campground was perfect. Colombian patrols never crossed the border and the Panamanians didn't care they were there. There was food—and it was tasty, even if it was occasionally weird— sunshine and water. Even when it rained, the place would dry out reasonably quickly and be pleasant again the next morning.

And any moving around meant hiking over the hilly terrain and through the dense forest that had made the Darién Gap one of the least populated places on Earth.

Max held up a hand. "Yeah, I know. I'm not looking forward to lugging the tents around either, but we've got a job to do."

Emilio spat into the fire. "A job? Who do we work for?"

"The same group we always worked for: the downtrodden Colombian poor."

"Ah… so they're back on the agenda…"

Max kept his cool. Anyone else questioning their dedication to the underprivileged of his country would have taken a bullet, but not Emilio. His father was a hacendado, and Emilio had run from a life of comfort and riches to be there. He knew more about socialist theory than anyone else in the group.

"I got a call last night."

The half-smile disappeared from Emilio's face, and everyone else sat straighter, the food momentarily forgotten.

Max basked in the feeling of honor and wonder that he was the leader of this little cell and of the foot soldiers—the peasants and field hands who formed the backbone of the army but weren't privy to the discussions of the intelligentsia who knew the theory and guided the movement— camped a few hundred meters downstream. "The Captain has taken up arms again."

The thrill of excitement that ran through his comrades was palpable. There were no cheers here, no unseemly exultations, but seeing the sense of purpose, of hope, return to the gathered visages was inspiring.

"Bogotá has gone too far. They think that, just because there was a treaty in place, they can do whatever they like. Well, the Captain has decided that they can't. We will remind them that, much like they don't feel they are obligated to make concessions, we are not obligated to submit to their policies."

"And what's going to happen now?" Serena said. She looked frightened, the only one who did.

"We are going to act. Our orders are to move towards the coast. Twenty kilometers from here, a group of American scientists is studying the effects of climate change on native ant populations."

"So? They aren't dangerous, are they?"

"Of course not. But the Captain has decided that, in the next phase of the war against the government, we will need hostages… Even if we have to take them in Panama."

Emilio nodded with a grim smile. "We should have been doing this long ago. They'll feel safe in Panama."

Max shrugged. "They're just academics. Even if they were on their guard, how long do you think they could hold out against Coca's men? Three minutes? What could they do? Run off into the jungle?"

"Don't all Americans carry guns?" Serena asked.

Max laughed. "Only in Texas, my dear. And these aren't those kinds of Americans. These are the ones in universities. They pretend to love the poor and hate the other Americans, the ones with the guns. They're soft."

"But if they love the poor, should we still take them? I don't understand." Serena's earnest look almost made him laugh, but he saw contempt for her flash across Liliana's face, and that angered him to the point where he could forgive his lover's ignorance.

"They're Americans. They pretend to care about the poor, but if you try to take away their air conditioning, or their cars, or their fancy coffee, they'll scream for the Marines. They don't actually care about the poor outside their country, it's just fashionable to say they do. They're the worst kind of hypocrites." He let his smile widen. "And that makes them the best kind of hostages because if one or two of them should get damaged, we won't shed too many tears."

Emilio laughed.

"So, I wanted to make sure we were all on the same page. Liliana, I'm putting you in charge of getting our camp packed. I want it done in two hours. Coca, can you lend her five men from the main camp as porters?"

"Of course. They'll be happy to help."

"Good. How long do you think the men will take to get ready? Would it help if I came over and gave a speech?"

Coca nodded. "They'd like that."

"All right. Let's go."

Ten minutes later, they entered the main camp. It wasn't too big— attrition had been high over the past few months. They hadn't suffered combat losses, but troops had wandered off in ones and twos, rejoining the families they'd left behind, losing the fear of the warlord's power or simply becoming bored with the whole thing and striking out for something else. Men who had nothing to lose.

But fourteen still remained, ranging from old José, who'd joined one of the cartel's enforcement arms when he was little more than a boy and still walked the trails forty years later, to Esmeralda, seventeen years old and who carried a year-old baby in a sling. She'd joined with a boyfriend who'd disappeared into the jungle when she told him she was pregnant. The rest of the troops, all men, had rallied around her, supporting her and helping to care for the child when it was born. In Max's mind, that represented what they were all about: even in the middle of the jungle, where they had nothing, his people had gone all out in support of the member of their tribe who needed help.

It pained him to force the most important members of his strike team to dwell under the trees, in a damp hollow that never got enough light, but they couldn't risk being seen. A small camp like the one that held the leaders would be ignored by the small planes holding Colombian government spotters, but a dozen men? They'd be raided immediately, arrested under suspicion of drug trafficking... Even the Panamanians wouldn't ignore a direct request from Bogotá.

So the leadership had to be separated from the rank and file. The leaders needed to stay sharp—it was one thing to replace a strong set of arms, but quite another to replace the central knowledge necessary to keep an army like this one, scattered across tens of thousands of square miles of jungle, focused on its goals. Even Serena, innocent as she was in the true ways of the world, had studied political science in Caracas. She might be the proverbial babe in the woods... but she had the theory down to an art.

He stood on a log and twenty-seven eyes—a man called David had lost one in some long-forgotten altercation—stared up at him with a mixture of respect and expectation. These were the true core, loyal not only when the war was sexy, but also in the hard times, the boring times, when nothing seemed to happen.

"Good morning, my friends. I know these days have been difficult for you." He looked around. "This hollow in the woods is wet and miserable. It's a symbol of how our fight has gone in these past few months.

"But we knew when we started that this was not a struggle we could win in just a few days. The road we were promised was a long one, and it most certainly has been long and slow. I applaud you for your tenacity in the days that have gone past, and," he fixed his eyes on the young girl, noting how pretty she was becoming. He smiled at her, "I will find a way to thank each of you personally."

He let them think about that.

"But most of all, I came to tell you that the waiting, the uncertainty, the feeling that the world has forgotten about us, that our cause is buried under everything else that's happening on the planet, is over. Today, we head out."

This time, there was a roar of approval from the troops. Not, perhaps, because they truly felt anything, but because they'd learned that the pauses after a big announcement were there for cheering. So they cheered.

"And we're not heading out on a training exercise. This isn't a political statement. We have a real mission, a combat mission."

Again he paused, again they roared.

"Best of all, the mission isn't against our own countrymen. Misguided as some Colombians might be, they are still our brothers. A complete victory is one where we can change their thinking, bring light into the darkness without hurting our own flesh and blood. This strike will be against foreign invaders!"

This time, the noise went on for some while.

"American invaders!"

The crowd was nearly wild with frenzy. Some of it might even have been sincere: these troops knew just how badly American interference had distorted Colombian politics.

"They are on Colombian soil." Technically, they were in Panama, but he didn't want to sow unnecessary confusion. The troops weren't privy to maps and GPS systems; why muddy the waters? "Spreading their influence in the jungle that, traditionally, foreign invaders never dared to enter. Why? Because they think we've grown complacent, they think our vigilance has lapsed." He held their gaze. "Should we teach them the error of their ways?"

Max waited for the cheer to die away, then gave them the reassurance their anxious faces craved. "The good thing is that the invaders are unprepared. So confident are they that they would find a submissive population, a Colombia open to being colonized, that they aren't heavily armed. They sent students and teachers to do the work when they should have sent their most heavily-armed special forces. By the time they realize they how stupid they are, it will be too late. Their little university mission will be in our hands.

"Now, time to work. Get this camp packed and be ready to move in two hours. I'll speak to you more when we arrive!"

The crowd dispersed and Coca caught his superior's eye. "That was well done. It should keep them happy until we get our hostages. After that, we will have no problems."

Max nodded his thanks. "And the girl... I'd like to meet her tonight, after we make camp. Preferably without the baby and far from the rest of them."

Coca raised an eyebrow. "And far from Serena?"

"Naturally."

"You're a pig." But the man's smile belied the words. Both knew that there would be no coercion. They both knew the girl worshipped the ground Max walked on, and she would make whatever contribution to the cause he requested. As the upcoming mission wouldn't require putting her life at risk, she would be more than willing to show her commitment in other ways.

"Men in my position need to find ways to relieve the stress."

"Of course. I'll take care of it," Coca replied.

Max had known he would. Unquestioned loyalty to Max personally, even in the face of unusual requests, was why Coca was in charge of the troops. He wasn't the most polished lieutenant in the Democratic Republican Commando... but he did his job. That was all one could ask, wasn't it?

"Oh, and don't forget to send us five porters for our gear."

"Of course," Coca replied.

CHAPTER 3

Professor Cora Gomez swatted at a mosquito, wondering if this was the bite that would give her the Zika virus. Apparently, no amount of repellent would convince Aedes Aegypti that she wasn't good to eat. Or maybe, despite the manufacturer's claims, she'd sweated away the last application.

"Damn," she said.

"What's up?" John Vincent was the Associate Professor of Plant Physiology. He didn't work directly in her department—Cora herself was head of the Ecology track, but not specifically employed by the Biology school—but had been the very first to sign up for the study. Two of the three grad students who'd come along were biology PhD candidates and former students of his. His light-blonde hair, nearly white in the dusk light, and pale blue eyes seemed uniquely unsuitable to the tropical conditions. As if to underline the point, he wore a pith helmet.

"I can't find the crate with the jars."

"You can't think of doing any collecting tonight, can you? We just got here."

"Of course not," she replied, hoping that her expression wouldn't tell him that that was exactly what she had been planning. "I just really want to look inside to see that the glassware survived the trip."

"Come on, I'll help you look."

The campground was a maze of wooden packing boxes. It was hard to believe that the huge pile of supplies was meant for just five academics and three jungle-savvy local guides; it looked like there was enough stuff there to equip a small army. Of course, since they were planning on staying for three months, most of the content of the crates was food.

Finally, he found the one they were looking for and pried it open. Inside, secured carefully so they wouldn't move around, were a series of smaller boxes, plastic ones. When opened, each of these revealed a foam-filled interior. Cylindrical holes had been drilled into the packing material, each large enough to hold one collection jar.

"Looks OK to me," John said.

"Thank God. Do you know what it would have been like to find glass jars in this place?"

"I think that would have been the easy part. Try keeping them sterile, though…" He chuckled at his own joke and they walked back to the campground, where the three grad students were attempting to erect their tents.

"Come on, guys," Gaar said. "We practiced this a bunch of times." His tent was up and looked like something that would have satisfied the toughest sergeant in the British Dragoons.

"That was on a lawn, and we had decent light," Amber Cross replied. She was a muscular woman in her late twenties with skin the color of coffee and cream, enormous almond eyes and uncontrolled curls. Her own effort sagged in the middle and, as Cora entered the clearing, collapsed upon itself. "This stuff on the ground… I don't even know what it is."

"Some biologist you turned out to be," the third grad student said. Stephan Gregoire was a statistician, and looked it. Pale, with short, dark hair, he looked even more out of place than John. But in his case, a pith helmet would only have added to the impression of tropical inadequacy. His tent was a pile of rods and cloth that didn't even make an attempt to get off the floor.

"Mr. Ching," Cora said with a smile, "I'd really appreciate it if you could assist your colleagues in pitching their tents instead of making them feel like idiots. It's their first time out in the field. The first time I ever went on a research trip, I almost had to sleep out in the open, as I'd never even seen a tent, much less pitched one."

"Hey, it's my first trip, too," Gaar replied.

"Help them anyway."

He grinned at her and walked over to Amber's tent. "So, where you went wrong is…"

"Are you going to be an asshole about this?" Amber asked. "Because if you are, I'm…"

The rest of her words were swallowed up by the jungle as Cora rounded a bend in the track the donkeys—the only way to get cargo this deep into the Darién forest—had made through the underbrush. The three Panamanian expedition guides they'd hired to accompany them already had a fire going, and had slung hammocks between the trees. They looked like they'd been there for months.

"Hello, Doctor," their leader, Joaquín, said. "Do you need any help?"

She thought of the students' pathetic attempts to get themselves set up and smiled, but shook her head. "No. We'll be fine. I wanted to speak to you about tomorrow's excursion. We're looking for ants."

"Yes. We know. You won't have to go very far. Here's one." The guy laughed like he'd said something enormously witty. Cora signaled her forbearance by not bashing him over the head with one of the fiery logs.

"These are a specific type of ant called brachymyrmex gagates, and we'll have to look around a little before we find a suitable colony. If we can't find one of those, we have two back-up species that are nearly as good for the purpose of our study."

He looked puzzled. "So what do you need from us?"

"We want to walk inland a bit, and find a thick forest with dark floors."

"That shouldn't be too hard."

"No. But we want it to be no more than a couple of hours' walk from the camp and easy to return from."

He shrugged. "I think you chose the right spot. It should be easy."

"Good. Do you need anything from the supplies?"

Joaquín looked around. "No. This is a good place," he smiled. "Also, an agouti came too close, so we won't need anything for dinner."

Cora swallowed and walked back to the main camp. Agoutis were rabbit-like rodents, probably delicious, but not something she would ever eat out in the bush.

***

Later that night, after much longer than it should have taken, they sat around their own fire, eating pre-prepared dinners that, rodent or not, smelled a lot less delicious than the agouti had.

"So," Gaar said during a lull in the conversation, "how did you manage to get the funding for this, anyway? Word around campus is that The Iron Lady has you in her crosshairs."

Cora smiled. This was the kind of thing every grad student always wanted to ask and which, back when she was one of them, would never have dared inquire of a senior member of faculty. Times had certainly changed. "Dr. Hillary can recommend cutting my programs until she's blue in the face, but unless the current board of governors decides to retire or resign, she'll never push it through."

"You have friends there?"

"Not so much friends as allies. The board is from a different era, and the current focus on identity studies as opposed to the hard sciences is pretty much a lost cause with them."

"Then how did Dr. Hillary ever make it to Chancellor?"

Cora shook her head. It was a question she often asked herself. "I think it was a question of hiding her true colors until it was too late for anyone to do anything about it. And, in her defense, she is a magnificent administrator."

"But she hates the natural sciences."

"Not as such. I think she just wants people to recognize other fields as equally valuable."

Amber cut in. "I'm in favor of anything that sheds light on the unequal nature of our society, but… how can anyone be so pigheaded as to remove funding from eco-programs in this day and age, especially at UCSD? We're like the first line of defense against global warming!"

Cora shrugged. "Politics, especially among academics, can blind people to the real world, sometimes. It's not a new phenomenon. Besides, as long as the board can control her, Hillary isn't my main concern."

"What is?"

Cora thought about trying to explain the stuff that kept her up at night to her students.

"Let's talk about something else. Like our strategy for finding the ants. Noda's research shows that these ants actually use rotting wood from fallen trees to…"

The night grew long as they discussed the project that had brought them to this particular virgin wilderness.

***

Something flashed between the trees.

"Did you see that?" Amber said.

"Yeah, some kind of animal," Gaar replied. Any excuse was good to stop walking around in the unbearable heat. Besides, he'd wanted to talk to Amber alone since they'd gotten on the plane. He'd never really paid attention to her on Campus—her specialty was mainly in fish, of all things—but he'd found her knowledge of entomology both broad and, when it came to the specific ants they were there to study, deep.

Of course, she was statuesque and beautiful in the most exotic of ways as well, but he knew he was above that kind of consideration. Having no illusions about his own looks, he hoped she would return the favor.

"A big one."

He shrugged. "The only dangerous stuff that size we might find in these woods are big cats… and they're rare as hell and also unlikely to be anywhere near humans. Your best bet is an escaped goat."

"So, it's not dangerous. But what is it?"

"I don't know. Wanna take a look?" Gaar wondered if Amber would allow herself to take a detour. Their guide looked on incuriously: whatever they decided, his face seemed to say he would be paid the same.

"Yeah. It should only take a few minutes, and we've been making good time."

They set out across the ground. Gaar had expected the going to be muddy and uncomfortable, but it was March, and the dry season was in its third month. So it was dusty and uncomfortable. Of course, the humidity in the actual air didn't seem to have gotten the memo, but you couldn't have everything.

"There!" Amber pointed to a moving bush, then to a shape— unmistakably an animal of some sort—running low across the tall grass in a tiny clearing.

"What the—"

"Come on." Amber grabbed him by the arm and they crashed after the creature, making more noise than a herd of stampeding elephants. Birds flew off the neighboring trees with indignant squawks and calls.

"That way!"

It was a playground scene, which, had they not been caught up in the joy of the chase, they would have sternly lectured anyone against. Everything about what they were doing was wrong: frightening a member of what was probably a rare and endangered species, running after an animal which might be dangerous, and just generally romping about destroying habitat in the world's most pristine rainforest.

But Gaar didn't care. He'd spent the last ten years locked up in classrooms, watching the natural world—consisting of squirrels in the trees outside the Muir Biology Building—through windows. This was the real deal, even if they were just running after… what was that, some kind of monkey? He knew enough about wild animals to know they'd likely never catch it, so these tantalizing glimpses were all that they would get.

"Cut it off over there!"

"No, not that way, it's going around the back!"

Eventually, Amber got lucky and zigged just as it zagged, and they got it between them. "Grab it!"

But, even cornered, the creature was too quick for them. It darted to the left, up a tree and then, apparently unfazed by the new elevation, jumped from that tree's upper branches to the next, causing the canopy where it landed to bend and distort alarmingly. But it didn't fall, and dashed away to lose itself in the heights.

Gaar and Amber had long since stopped watching, however. "What the hell was that?" she said.

He shook his head. "I was hoping you could tell me."

"No chance. It climbed like a monkey, but walks like—a lizard. And were those scales on the tail?"

"It looked like it to me. And the face was definitely a little aligatorish." They smiled at the technical term.

"But it looked like a monkey."

"It looked like some kind of tiny human."

"Except with an alligator face."

"Yeah."

They were both flushed, not just from the heat and the exercise, but from the excitement of that feeling that only a scientist can know. Neither of them dared to put it into words, however. That might jinx it.

Gaar broke first. "Do you think..?"

"I'm absolutely sure there's no description of anything like it anywhere. Not since the monster compendia that were so popular in the Middle Ages."

"I love those books."

"Yeah, me too. But I never thought they might actually be describing real things. Monkey-lizard-men of the Antipodes."

Another thought hit him, and he slapped his forehead. "We should have gotten a picture."

Amber looked into the trees and pulled out her cell phone. "We might be able to, still. Most primates would have gotten just far enough to feel safe and then turned around to see what we're doing." She set off into the underbrush at a fast clip.

Gaar paused just long enough to be certain the guide was following and went after her.

"So, you're leaning toward the primate family?"

"Of course. You saw how it climbed, and the tail was kind of weird, but it curled when it was climbing."

"The problem is that it curled to the side, not along its length. And it's shaped a lot more like a crocodile's than a monkey's. It looked like it was wide and flat where it met the torso. Speaking of which, that torso looked more like something meant for swimming than walking."

"If that were true, it would be spectacularly unsuited for climbing trees, don't you think? Yet it did so perfectly well. We may need to stop speculating until we get a specimen."

Gaar studied the trees. Too tall to climb, too thick to shake. "That might be easier said than done," he replied. "But what I'm mostly worried about are the scales. Did you see them, too? Mammals... well, they don't have scales."

"I'm aware of that, but it might just be strangely mottled skin. We didn't get a good look. It might be akin to a rhino's wrinkles, except in a regular pattern. We can't tell at this point. Besides, if they were scales..." she left the rest unsaid.

Gaar knew what she meant, though. Finding a new species would put them on the map. Finding an undiscovered class of animals... that was millionaire lecture circuit territory. It hadn't happened in the vertebrate sphere in a century. More. He couldn't even remember who the last person to do so was.

Lost in visions of glory and fortune, and with his eyes scanning the upper reaches of the trees, Gaar completely missed a fallen tree and went ass over appetite into the undergrowth, twisting an ankle in the process.

"Ouch. I hurt myself."

Amber rushed over. "Can you stand?"

"I... I think so."

She held out a strong hand and he clasped it. Halfway up, he felt her grip loosen and nearly toppled back. He had to scramble to stay on his feet.

"What was that?" he asked.

"Look." Amber was pointing to his feet. No, she was pointing to the tree trunk he'd fallen over. It was covered with ants.

"Are those..?"

She bent down and picked up a specimen, eyes crossed as she studied the antennae segments. "I think so. We'll have to check with Cora, but unless I'm missing my guess, we've got a winner." She smiled. "This is great. If we study this colony, we can keep our eyes out for anything unusual. We might get that Nobel after all." She motioned the guide over, carefully removed a jar from the pack and scooped a handful of ants into it. Then she pulled out a satellite GPS and marked the spot.

"They don't give you a Nobel for finding stuff by mistake," Gaar said.

Amber laughed. "That's the dumbest thing I ever heard. That's pretty much the only way to win a Nobel."

***

Later that night, when everyone was asleep, the flap of Gaar's tent opened and Amber climbed inside. It was a tight squeeze for two people. "Let me see," she said.

Gaar turned the notebook he'd been drawing on towards her. She studied the artwork. "That isn't bad at all. You've got hidden depths," she said.

He was speechless, flinching away from her slightly to minimize the contact between their bodies. If he reacted to her presence, the unaccustomed proximity of an attractive female in his tent, she would notice it, and he'd have to walk into the jungle and commit suicide— unless he died of embarrassment on the spot.

Amber didn't recognize his discomfort. She was peering at the drawing he'd made of the creature in the forest. "It should have a little more fur around the neck area, and I think you should make the tail look scalier."

"I thought you said it was like rhino skin," he mumbled.

"I said that would be a possible explanation... but it certainly *looked* like it was covered in scales, so you should show that."

He was sweating profusely now. He'd been perfectly cool and relaxed just minutes ago, drawing to his heart's content, and now he was covered in perspiration and his tongue was tied in knots. He'd expected her to have a noticeable smell after the long day in the woods—he knew he did—but the only scent she'd brought in with her was the soft fragrance of her perfume: the slightest hint of jasmine on the breeze.

"All right," he stammered. "I'll make those changes."

"Awesome."

She ducked back out into the night, leaving nothing but the jasmine behind.

Gaar was relieved to discover that he could breathe again, and picked up his pencil and eraser, and began to draw.

Birds and insects buzzed and cawed to themselves in the night.

CHAPTER 4

Three empty cages stared back at him accusingly. What bothered Philippe wasn't the fact that they were empty—plenty of cages in his enclosure stood uninhabited—but the fact that they'd been vacant for too long.

Animals always returned to places where food was plentiful. And animals like the ones he created were very unlikely to be distracted by things such as potential mates. They just didn't exist.

That meant his creatures, his beautiful, noble animals, were being killed out there in the leafy wastes. He glared out into the jungle and thought.

This batch of creatures were about the size of a large dog and, though they weren't particularly fast or agile—he was working on that—they were bigger than most of the predators in the Darién Gap's tropical forest.

The jaguars, widely scattered to begin with, that might have hunted larger prey had been all but hunted to extinction by the handful of people in the area. One could understand that. Most of the people around here were subsistence farmers trying to scratch an illegal living from poor soil, burning the forest where they could get away with it, which meant as far from the eyes of authority as possible.

The rest were the laughable guerrillas. Political activists who'd quickly discovered that society wanted no part of their utopian fantasy and had taken solace in the fact that groups would support them to stay in the jungle and cause trouble. They thought they were creating a worker's paradise, while, in fact, they were doing the bidding of the Medellín cartels. Morons in a moronic place.

Philippe seethed. Jaguars hadn't killed three of his creations. If just one was missing, he'd shrug it off as the cost of the jungle. But three? No. Too much coincidence.

Worst of all was that it probably hadn't been the farmers. They'd been around since before Philippe arrived, and attrition among his animals had been close to zero. That meant there was a group moving around in the forest that hadn't been there before. And they were nearby.

Their proximity didn't worry him particularly. He had an agreement with the drug cartels in much the same way as he had an agreement with the Panamanian government and any Colombian soldiers who might "become disoriented" and penetrate that far into Panamanian territory. Philippe made the right contributions, and he was, therefore, listed as an ally. The animals that he didn't keep around for himself were popular pets among those who either didn't care about laws or those to whom laws simply didn't apply. He had rich customers… yet another reason he felt safe.

So, though he wasn't worried for himself, he was furious for his animals. He lived in the most inaccessible piece of wilderness in the entire Western Hemisphere. There was nowhere on Earth that the creatures he released should have been safer from the depredations of humanity. That someone would kill them here was abominable.

Chapeau, the furry dog-monkey he'd vatted to replace Chiffon walked into the enclosure and looked up at him. It must have been feeding time, because Chapeau hated coming into contact with the larger animals.

"They're killing your brothers out there," Philippe told him. "This just won't do."

Chapeau cocked his head. The name, which meant 'hat' in French came from the mop of black fur that flew out from a ridge in the creature's skull.

"Come on. Let's get you some food and see what we've got in the files."

He opened a can of dog food—meat-based, as Chapeau wouldn't eat fruit and vegetables, which Philippe found strange, but also scientifically interesting—and limped to the lab area. His old aches were acting up that day, which added to his irritability.

After a couple of quick lunges into the plate, his pet followed.

The door to his lab was well camouflaged: a wooden gate roughly hewn together from the same local wood as the rest of the cabin opened onto a small, dark interior patio.

Beyond that tiny space was a second door: a sliding glass panel.

A whoosh of outgoing air hit them as the pressurized interior ensured that airborne dust and other contaminants stayed out.

Then he had to wait in the tiny cubicle between the glass he'd just crossed and another pane while the pressure between the two doors was lowered before the interior door finally opened. Another blast of air—this one smelling of several chemicals from the lab—rushed into the space he occupied.

He and Chapeau entered the lab. He smiled to think how well he'd designed the pressure valves to keep airborne contaminants out only to give the dog-monkey the run of the area. Still, it was better to sort what he could and use the rest as happy accidents. He'd found more viable combinations by mistake than on purpose, so a little bacterial DNA, or monkey-dog hair might be a welcome addition.

But he wouldn't be creating today. At least not yet. He was sure the design he needed nestled somewhere in his files.

"So," he said to Chapeau, "what do you think? Something big. As big as Harold, maybe? But not so smart. Harold had too much human in him, didn't he?" He scratched behind Chapeau's ears. "He joined that awful little Poupée and tried to kill us, didn't he, sweetie. No, we won't create another Harold."

He stared at the screen. Files—chromosome combinations and diagrams of what a creature would be expected to look like when it came out of the vats—scrolled past. "No. No. No. Hmm."

An elephant-based monstrosity, probably herbivorous, caught his eye. It had curled tusks based on Narwhal teeth and the sleek fur of a seal. Best of all, it had a small brain embedded in a thick skull. A Colombian peasant armed with an old Kalashnikov for which he didn't have much ammo wouldn't be able to take that beast down before it managed to bring the tusks to bear.

But it had problems. The most obvious were the fact that it was essentially an elephant in shape and size, which meant that it would be hard-pressed to navigate in the forest without making huge amounts of noise. It had also been designed for much colder climates, and might conceivably keel over in the stultifying heat… which would defeat the whole purpose of the exercise.

He could fix those with just a little work on the editor, but he admitted the elephant simply wasn't the elegant solution for this kind of landscape.

He sighed. "Looks like we're back at Harold after all. He brought up the file for his second-greatest achievement. This one didn't have sketches; it had photographs. Pictures of Harold right out of the vat. Harold at a couple of weeks. Then, from a safe distance, Harold at a month. By that time, he had adopted the mangrove swamp as his home and almost never came on land.

Except when it was time to murder his own maker.

"We don't want another Harold," he said to his attentive pet. "Harold would have swallowed you up in a bite. But maybe something that looks like Harold, but will remain loyal. And we should really get rid of the wings. I don't care if a dragon should have wings. They looked ridiculous. Wait." He held up a finger. "I think I have just the thing. Not in the computer, though."

He pulled out some yellowed papers, papers he'd had to bribe half the underpaid and eternally unhappy staff of the French criminal justice archive to recover.

"Here we go. Look." He showed Chapeau a sketch. The dog-monkey attempted to eat the yellowed paper. "Just a long snake with legs and a nice lizard head. Perfect for moving quickly and silently through the trees… and big enough to bite a man in half right out of the vat. Yes." He peered at the specs. "Oh, and I'd forgotten. Simian-level intelligence. A big brain, there. Hmm. Yes, this should do nicely. The guerrillas won't know what hit them." He shook his head. "Too bad about the farmers, but I guess you can't have everything, can you?"

He removed the entire sheaf of papers that referred to project HRL-2 and stacked them neatly on his desk. He stared at the dragons sketched on them for a few moments. There was potential in the design. Better still, once he proved the creature could function in a hostile environment and live at least a few months, the Chinese would go nuts over these, especially if he could redesign the scales to look as colorful as the ones on traditional parade floats.

Dragons would be dangerous, of course, but China, like every other country in the world, had citizens who would simply ignore the cries of their fellow citizens and order up a batch of these. For no other reason than because they liked dragons and because they could do whatever they felt like, laws and public outcry be damned. Simple as that.

Also, the Russian contingent would love receiving his notes about how well a flock of dragons would adapt to the Panamanian jungle. The info he'd been sending about the goat-sized hybrids had been met with lukewarm interest at best.

He was about to put the lid on the box of papers again when he stopped dead in his tracks.

"Oh," he said simply, looking at another diagram. This one looked humanoid in shape but, to his practiced eye, he could spot exactly which fish had given him the shape of the head and the gills and also which amphibians had given him the webbed hands and legs. "I'd completely forgotten about you," he told the drawing. "Let me see. Ah, yes, not too smart." Then he shoved the papers back into the box. "No. I really, really shouldn't."

But he knew he would. Even after he'd finished programming his first batch of dragons into the vats—they'd be ready in a couple of days—the box of papers with the bug-eyed, frog-fish-man remained exactly where he'd laid it.

Ready to be entered into the database. Ready for the necessary pieces of DNA to be printed. Ready for the strands to be spliced together.

Ready for implantation into the artificial eggs he'd grow in parallel.

Ready to walk an Earth that wasn't ready for them.

***

"Sked here," Brown said. The call had made it through several layers of security. Whoever was on the line had business with him. Even so, he used that week's codename. Anyone with legitimate business would know they had the right number. Anyone who'd dialed by mistake, or trying to spy on him would wonder where they'd messed up.

"We track you as on the ground in Panama."

"Who is this?"

"Marseille."

"Ah. Yes. I'm in Panama City."

"How long until you can reach the target?"

Brown exhaled into the receiver. "That's a loaded question. Getting into the jungle will be easy enough, but I can't just drop in on the target. I need to make the drop a few miles away to keep him from spotting me. Also, I can't drop in at night, so the earliest I can be in the area is tomorrow morning. Let's say contact with the target by noon. Are you sure you want him alive?"

The voice on the other end wasn't in the mood for discussions. "Yes. And his research undamaged. He needs to stand trial."

"And the files?"

"That isn't your problem. Just be sure they're in good shape when you leave the complex. We'll call your sat phone tomorrow at three PM your time. We expect you to have results by then."

The call dropped and Brown rolled his eyes. Whoever the bureaucrat on the other end might have been, he'd never been in the field. Anyone who knew what they were doing would have had *him* call *them* once the target was in custody. If things went wrong—and Murphy was *always* on the case in ops like this one—he'd end up with a vibrating sat phone in the middle of the most delicate part of the operation and no way to call his clients once the grab was done.

Morons.

He grinned at the immigrations guy who barely glanced at his passport and waved him through. Panama was one of the countries where American passports were a good way to avoid inconvenience. That was why he'd decided to come in this way instead of Colombia. Colombians always got hassled in the U.S. so they hassled Americans right back. His fake passport was actually genuine other than the information inside... but it still would have made him nervous to have it get inspected by angry border guards.

Panama City Airport always made him feel the same way: like someone with money had spent a lot of it to create a modern airport but had managed to miscalculate the number of people it would have to hold. It always seemed twenty percent too small, and consequently hot and crowded. It was a relief to get outside, where the air was even hotter, and humid to boot, but where people weren't packed like sardines.

He caught a yellow taxi outside the terminal and asked the driver to take him to a mall in Costa del Este, a suburb of the capital.

There, he met his pilot, a young, dark woman named Priscilla, who looked Panamanian but spoke with an American accent.

"This came for you," she said without preamble, and handed Brown a locked briefcase, a hardcase item of shiny plastic. A cursory glance told him it hadn't been tampered with; if someone had tried to force it without the right voice recognition phrase, an incendiary device within would have reduced the whole thing to molten slag.

They sat at a booth in a café and he ordered a local beer, not even catching the brand name the waitress said. She grimaced at his choice and asked for water.

"It looks like the weather tomorrow morning will be a little rough, so I recommend flying the next day."

He thought about the idiot who'd be calling him at three and chuckled. "Sure, that sounds fine."

"All right. Well, I'll need you to be at the airfield at five thirty, with anything you need to bring with you, but not more than fifty kilos."

"No problem." His carry-on bag, the backpack he'd be taking with him was eight or nine kilos. The contents of the suitcase—stuff you didn't want to carry on an airplane after 9/11, would add four or five more. That left him plenty of margin.

"The parachute you bought is in the plane."

"I'll want to re-pack it myself."

"Then you'll have to get there at five."

"I can pack a chute in fifteen minutes."

"I don't care. Be there at five."

"Fair enough."

They sat in silence for a few minutes and he studied her. Dark hair which looked a little greasy, as if it hadn't been washed in a week, fell lankly to her shoulders. The features it framed were delicate, with a pretty, upturned nose and big eyes. Unfortunately, a slight scowl marred what would otherwise have been a pleasing effect.

"What's wrong?" he said.

"Nothing. Everything is in order." She stood to go, taking the plastic bottle of water with her. "I'll just get going. I imagine you have many things to do."

"Wait. I'd like to talk to you for a few minutes."

"I need to get back to the airport. Besides, I'm paid partly for my discretion so the less I know about you, the more discreet I can continue being."

"Humor me."

She sat.

"Thank you. Now, I want to know why you've got a stick up your ass about this flight."

The profanity had little effect on her. He wasn't expecting it to—he knew that Priscilla had been a Coast Guard pilot out of Clearwater before she neglected to report a boatload of Cuban refugees and got caught. She was one of the guys.

"Fuck," she replied, as if to prove it. She called the waiter over and ordered a beer. A Budweiser. "It's not this mission. I just hate my life in general."

"Don't we all?"

"Well, you chose to get involved with the criminal elements. I always thought of myself as being on the side of the angels. Look at me now, ferrying... hell, I don't even want to know what it is you do. But I'm not dumb enough to think that the briefcase holds anything other than a gun."

"Full marks. Ammo, and a bunch of knives, too."

"Damn. Me and my big mouth. That's the kind of thing I didn't want to know. I didn't want to be a hit man delivery system for the cartels." Her beer arrived and she took a long pull. "But there comes a time when you take whatever work you can get. Anything to keep the plane maintained while you hope word of mouth gets around to the plutocrats who live in the city and they ask you to pull one of their advertising signs or hire you as their personal air taxi service. Meanwhile, I get to ferry hired guns. One of them, eventually, will need to tie up loose ends and come after the witnesses. I'm a witness, which is why I sleep with a twelve-gauge under my pillow."

"Well, I won't be the one who comes after you."

"You will if your hit goes sour."

"I'm not what you think. I'm actually working for a government."

She snorted. "Heard it before."

"I promise you that I'm not here to kill anyone. The man I'm after is going to stand trial."

"Why should I believe you?"

"Because it's true," Brown said. He didn't really think she'd believe him, but it was a way to build trust. If she felt he'd tried to make her feel better, she might drop him in a better spot. It was important to be on good terms with your pilot.

"I guess I'll read about it in the papers then."

"I hope so." He looked at her face. "You're still not happy."

"Well, if you're not a hit man, then I can say with all certainty that you shouldn't be jumping into the Gap."

"Why not? I've jumped into jungle before, and this time we're aiming for a beach anyway."

"Because the place is a shithole. No food, very little water, and most of the people in there wouldn't blink before they cut you to ribbons with a machete. That's why wanted drug lords hide in there." She gave him a significant look.

He looked down at the map spread out on the table. It was a topographical map clearly showing the hills and valleys of the tropical jungle below. Aside from the closely-spaced lines showing elevation changes, the map was pretty much entirely green, from northern Panama all the way down to Colombia. It was a busy-looing map, but one thing the target area didn't feature were little points denoting towns or lines showing the path of roads. In fact, quite a few roads ominously petered out just a few miles after they entered the area.

It was the kind of chart that screamed danger to anyone trained in what to look for. Hell, even a fourth-grader would have taken a single look at this one and suspected that something was very wrong with the lay of the land.

He smiled.

"I can take care of myself. I've been in dangerous situations before."

She weighed him carefully. "You don't look like a soldier. You'd be carrying around less mass around the stomach if you were. And more around the shoulders. Even an ex-soldier would look a lot harder."

"You're right. I'm a hacker."

"A computer guy?" She gave him an incredulous look.

"Yes. More important than the man I'm going in to arrest are the things in his databases. You can't just send some Neanderthal after delicate stuff like that."

She hung her head. "I knew I should have walked. You're so dead it isn't even funny."

"I told you. I can take care of myself." It was true. He'd been through special ops training… and this wasn't his first drop. Not looking the part was unimportant.

"The Darién Gap is like a trillion acres of jungle, with mountains and Colombian guerrillas in it. I've lived in Panama long enough to know one thing: when a stupid gringo decides to take a hike in there, you do anything you can to talk him out of it, and if that fails, you take a monkey wrench to his kneecap. He'll thank you for it later."

"You're just a box of sunshine, aren't you?"

"Can I go now?"

He laughed again as Priscilla walked away. She was probably right about the jungle, but he was only planning on being there a few hours. Once the computers were secure, the French would send in the helicopters and whisk everyone out.

He'd be fine.

CHAPTER 5

"It's Claudio, Max." Emilio looked troubled.

"What about him?"

"He's gone."

Max sighed. He thought the mission, the new sense of purpose, would galvanize his men and cut off the slow death of attrition, bleeding off his assets one by one. And yet, he still lost soldiers to the jungle. "Deserted?" The word tasted like ashes on his tongue.

"I... I don't think so. He wasn't the type."

"You always think that."

"But this time I really mean it. He was one of us. I know that his one dream in life was to help to push the revolution forward. He actually asked me once if it would be okay for him to go to university in Cartagena and then come back, so he could help lead from the front. That was what he said: 'lead from the front'."

"Maybe he was disappointed that you told him no."

"I didn't. I told him I'd break protocol and send letters to some friends in the university and ask them about it. I told him I'd have news in a couple of months. He was so happy."

"How long ago was this?"

Emilio shrugged and Max understood. Time became fluid when you were camped in the jungle; days flowed into an endless succession of sleepy afternoons and tasteless meals as tropical torpor sucked the purpose from even the most experienced troops.

"A couple of weeks. A month at most. He should still be waiting."

Max peered at him. "What were you planning on telling him when he asked? Of course you didn't send any letters."

Emilio laughed. "Of course not. I have no idea what I'd tell him. Maybe that the letters had gotten lost along the way. I would have thought of something." Then he turned serious again. "Really, Max. I don't think he ran."

"You think we should look for him?"

"Yes."

"All right. When was the last time anyone saw him?"

"Last night. He was going into the jungle to take a shit. He told Old José not to wait up. There's a set of tracks leading out of the camp, and then they go on for a bit past the latrine trench… then disappear. No trace of him doing his business, either."

"That means he took off into the woods."

"The strange part is that there's nothing missing. No food, no water. He didn't even take his gun. He's not stupid enough to try to survive without that."

"So aliens came to grab him when he was taking a dump?"

"I don't know. We should go out and see."

Max sighed. They were just a day's march from the university people, and this would delay the operation. But Emilio wasn't one to ask for silly things or jump at every shadow. "All right. The usual drill. Four teams. One each for you, Pablo, Liliana and Serena."

"You're not coming with us?"

"I'm useless at tracking through the forest. You know that."

Instead of rushing off to carry out the order, Emilio waited for the other shoe to fall. Damn, he knew Max way too well. "And that girl, what's her name… Esmeralda, that's it. She can't go either. It wouldn't be good for the baby. Tell her to stay in camp, and that I'll be around to see her a bit later."

Emilio grinned.

***

"All right. This is close enough," Max said. The coordinates put them an hour's hike from the Americans' campground. It was possible they might have moved, but if the expedition was the size that he'd been told they'd be easy enough to track. "We'll camp here and strike tomorrow."

The tents went up in record time. There wouldn't be separate camps that night. They were too close to the quarry, so everyone, leadership included, would be under cover in a damp hollow.

Food was served cold: the last of their energy bars. They could afford to be profligate because by the next day, they would be gorging on crates and crates of American food.

Their mood was somber, however. No one had found any sign of Claudio except for a single soft hat which José said he'd been wearing when he stepped away. Pablo's team had found the article of clothing atop a tall bush, well above head-height. They went over the entire area with a fine-toothed-comb, but found no other traces of his presence. No tracks, no signs of violence, not even the presence of other people, which might account for his disappearance.

It was as if he'd disintegrated, leaving his hat to fall to the floor.

Max called Emilio over. "Post two sentries in each shift tonight."

Emilio nodded, but again he stuck around. "How was she?"

Max shook his head. "Inexperienced. Eager, but not very skilled. She'll need a lot of teaching." He sighed. "To tell you the truth, I don't think she was worth the trouble I'm going to have with Serena over this."

"Maybe Serena won't find out."

Max laughed bitterly. "Want to bet?"

"Do I look stupid?"

"It was worth a shot. Go post the sentries."

They retired to the tents. Max couldn't really tell if Serena was being cold or just tired from the long march. Once they'd given up on Claudio, they'd made excellent time through the woods, but at a cost.

Whatever the reason, she rebuffed his half-hearted advances and was soon snoring softly. Max supposed it was for the best. Better to deal with any hysterics in the morning. Things that were easy to brush off in the day could drag deep into the night.

He drifted off, Serena's heat comforting even though the night was warm.

As always, Max dreamt of blood. He was leading the vanguard of the Comando Republicano Democrático across the plaza in front of the Casa de Nariño, Colombia's presidential palace.

Guards dressed in uniforms of the darkest blue with red accents and little black helmets raised their bayoneted wooden rifles. They were ceremonial troops, but Max knew that a bullet from them counted just as much as one shot by a real soldier. He brought his AK-47 to bear and cut them down. Blood sprayed through the air and onto his forehead.

He jumped over the first of the bodies, but landed on more of them. He had to make his way to the presidential palace over the corpses of fallen guardsmen. They covered the plaza and he wondered at their numbers—he'd certainly never suspected there would be so many of them. Enough, in normal times, to protect a dozen presidents.

But they hadn't reckoned with Max. He kept coming, over each of the men he killed, the blood pooling between the bodies.

Finally, leaving the corpses trampled by his boots behind, he reached the main entrance hall where he was accosted by another army, but this time, instead of rifles, they carried thick sheaves of paper. Bureaucrats. Gray-faced, pot-bellied, balding men and prim, humorless women barred Max's way, menacing him with their forms in triplicate. He didn't even bother to aim, and shot indiscriminately, blasting arms, torsos and faces. If anything, it felt even better than shooting soldiers; these were the true oppressors, the apparatchiks through whom the government controlled the heel upon the peoples' neck.

Blood flew. Max laughed.

The corridors grew darker and more opulent. Rich carpeting covered the floor, a tasteful maroon which went well with the dark wood paneling. Max had taken the tour of the presidential palace, of course, every schoolboy in Bogotá had done so, but he'd never been this far in.

Finally, the ministers and secretaries came out to stop him. He shot down Health and Education and blasted Economy in the groin. Several others fell so quickly that he couldn't identify their portfolios.

Finally, the Press Secretary appeared. She was the most famous of President Ramirez's close aides. A former Miss Colombia who was rumored to have murdered her ex-husband. She stood firm, unarmed. "I'm sorry, sir. The President isn't taking questions yet. You'll have to wait your turn."

He raised the Kalashnikov and took careful aim at her forehead. He didn't shoot her immediately, but gave her time to realize what was about to happen. He savored the way her eyes, those famous, sensual eyes, grew huge with shock. He reveled as her mouth formed an 'O' of surprise. And then he enjoyed the scream.

Something shook his arm.

"Max! Wake up!" Serena's fingernails gripped his arm hard to draw blood.

"What is it?"

"The scream. Did you hear it?"

"Yes, I heard it." Sadly, what he'd heard probably hadn't been Ramirez's Press Secretary.

"Go see what it was."

He was tempted to order her to go out and see for herself. He could do it; she was a soldier under his command, after all. But he didn't. If the scream he'd heard in the dream had happened in real life, he wanted to see what the hell was going on.

The camp was astir. Men with guns shone flashlights into the trees. Max stopped the nearest as he passed. It was Pablo Escobar. "What happened?"

"Have a look." Coca led him towards the tree line, where three of his troops were illuminating something on the ground.

"Is that an arm?"

Coca nodded.

Max peered at it more closely. The arm had been torn off just above the elbow. The fingers formed a half-closed claw. It appeared to be a man's hand and still wore the remains of a faded green shirt. Blood blackened the end of the cloth around it.

"Claudio's?"

Coca shrugged. "Your guess is as good as mine. I'm not going to touch it to take a closer look, either."

Max realized that everyone was keeping their distance from the severed appendage. Most pretended that it was because they were illuminating it with a flashlight but, really, how many flashlights did you need to light up one lost arm? He walked into the illuminated circle and, swallowing his distaste, picked it up.

The hand wasn't particularly clean. There was something under the fingernails. He tried to ignore the fact that his soldier had last been seen heading for the latrine and brought out the impurity.

"This looks like fish scales," he said. Every eye was on him, the way it was supposed to be. He smelled the arm. "It doesn't stink yet. This one hasn't been dead very long."

A voice emerged from the trees. "Is it Claudio?"

"No." He had no clue, of course, but still pronounced it with finality. "Who found this?"

"Esmeralda," Coca replied. "She was on sentry duty."

Max hid his smile. This was just another example of why Emilio was the perfect revolutionary: he didn't care if the girl had shared the commander's bed. She would do her duty and stand her shift at guard like anyone else. It was the way things were supposed to be. "Bring her here."

Esmeralda came and he saw that she'd been crying. The scream must have been hers. He gave her a comforting smile. "Are you all right?"

The young woman nodded, eyes big and red. "Yes, I'm fine. It just scared me so much. I thought I would die."

"What happened? How did you find it?"

"It almost hit me when it fell."

"It fell?"

The woman pointed upwards. "Out of the tree. I heard something moving up there. It sounded like a monkey, or something bigger. I wanted to see if it might be something we could eat." She broke down again. "But it must have been a jaguar. It ate him!"

She turned and ran into the trees. Max almost went with her, to comfort her. He knew how such comfort ended. But this wasn't the time.

"Coca, is everyone else accounted for?"

"I don't know. Emilio was counting heads. He should be back in a minute."

"All present," Emilio announced when he arrived. "And no one is missing an arm."

"Good." Max tossed the arm into the forest and turned back towards his tent. "This isn't Claudio, either. Claudio deserted, and he must be a hundred kilometers away by now, probably heading north. This was some poor farmer. He probably died of something else and then the scavengers got to him."

In his own mind, Max sang a different tune. This wasn't the work of an animal. Someone had killed one of his men, followed them across a vast expanse of jungle and dropped the arm into their midst as a warning.

Fury burned, but he had a job to do. Once he had the scholars in custody though, he would deal with whoever was responsible.

They would regret ever having been born.

***

No one felt rested the following day. The troops hadn't slept at all and Max had been tormented by nightmares of shadowy bureaucrats biting his troops to pieces. This time, the battleground wasn't a glorious attack against the presidential palace but the jungles. His jungles. The bureaucrats had no business here.

But they won battle after battle. They were obviously winning the war.

After that dream, he gave up. It was five in the morning, and dawn would soon appear over the horizon. Instead, he kissed Serena awake and began to undress her.

Neither of them enjoyed the lovemaking. Serena was still distant. He wanted to talk to her, to close the rift, but he knew she would never understand.

At one moment, he pulled away and said: "Forget it, go to sleep."

But Serena pulled him back to her. "No," she whispered.

That had no effect but to make him angry. If she was upset, why didn't she just tell him she knew what he'd done? That way they could have the fight. A decent fight was almost as good as making love.

Better than what they were doing now.

Finally, it ended. He left her crying softly in the tent and crossed the camp to find Emilio sitting on a rotting tree. "How soon can we move out?"

"Let them rest. The sun isn't even up."

"We'll catch the scientists unaware."

"Do you think the scientists will ever be aware? We can march in with a brass band, and they wouldn't be ready for us."

Max sighed. His friend was right. "All right. We'll give them another thirty minutes. Do you have any coffee?"

They drank in silence, then roused the leadership team. An hour later, they were on their way again.

***

The plane jumped around like a rabbit hit with a cattle prod.

"You okay?" Priscilla said.

"Yeah. But I hate these little planes."

"Tell me again how you can take care of yourself."

"I'll be fine once I get out of this deathtrap."

He pulled out the plastic briefcase and set the combination to three zeroes on each side. A small microphone popped out of a hole.

"The Pinzon brothers were a bunch of sailors," he said, enunciating carefully. He didn't stop to wonder who'd made up the ridiculous password. It was obviously secure, which was all that mattered.

The latches popped open to reveal an interior with several compartments. He removed a Sig Sauer P226 and three magazines, along with its holster. He also pulled out a silencer, a combat knife in a sheath.

"Going to war?"

Brown rolled his eyes. "My client seems to believe so, yes. The truth is that if I have to shoot the gun, my mission is already a failure. It's strictly there for intimidation purposes."

"Three magazines worth of intimidation?"

"Someone has a sense of the dramatic. The knife is a nice touch. I'm surprised they didn't include Malaria pills and an inflatable raft."

Priscilla chuckled, and Brown mentally scored one for him.

The scenery below them was beautiful but monotonous: dark green jungle rolled past, bordered to the west by a brilliant white stripe of beach. And then the gray-green roll of the sea, reflecting the clouds above.

He kept an eye on the coordinates. They were getting close, and he compared the scenery below to the map he'd studied exhaustively the night before. There. That slight outcrop was less than five klicks from the target zone.

He looked for signs of human habitation, somewhere he could strike out for if things went to hell… but there was nothing in sight but green hills. The intellectual knowledge of the conditions on the ground simply hadn't prepared him for the utter desolation. The tropics were supposed to be warm and friendly.

Those woods didn't look friendly.

"Circle around once," he said.

Priscilla complied. At least the jump wouldn't be too difficult. Though the sky was grey with cloud, the air was still as the grave. He wouldn't have to contend with gusts, and the beach was wide at the selected landing point.

"All right. Let's do this."

As he'd said, once out of the plane, he could take care of himself. He hit the beach exactly where he wanted to and, as he was gathering his chute—he'd return for it if he could—he waved up at the plane.

Priscilla wagged her wings and flew away, leaving him alone with the desolation. She wasn't paid to take him back.

After the initial pang of anxiety of being hundreds of miles from civilization with no exit strategy if things went pear-shaped, Brown calmed down.

He was in no immediate danger. His GPS was working perfectly and he was probably the only armed human for miles around. Animals would leave him alone.

He struck inland. Apart from the gear the French had sent him, which would likely be worse than useless, he'd bought something actually necessary. A big machete was the perfect way to slice through annoying underbrush.

The going was relatively easy. It only took him two hours to close within three miles of Philippe's complex—or at least to the coordinates where it was supposed to be.

That was when he discovered there was another group sharing this part of the forest with him.

No, he soon realized. There were two groups, one camped across a large area with supplies and equipment for a long stay.

The second group headed straight towards the first. These were armed to the teeth and dressed in ragged jungle uniforms. They seemed good at walking the jungle paths, but their surveillance was terrible.

Brown almost stumbled over the rear sentry. If the guy hadn't been looking up into the trees, he almost certainly would have been spotted.

He wondered what would happen when the two groups ran into each other. One was clearly a legitimate expedition of some sort, while the other was just as obviously—almost comically—one of the famous guerrilla bands that made the Darién Gap so infamous.

"I wonder if Philippe is having a party," he said to himself.

Then he chuckled and followed in the wake of the guerillas. His other business would have to wait; he certainly didn't want to leave armed insurgents at his back until he knew where they were going.

CHAPTER 6

It was almost ridiculously easy. The guides who'd been hired by the university team, and who had set up a camp about a hundred yards away from that of the main expedition, had been rounded up first, before dawn. Each of the three men woke to find a hand covering his mouth and a cold muzzle pressed against his temple. None had struggled.

The main camp presented a little more of a challenge, at least on paper. Max wanted the capture to be caught on film, which meant waiting for dawn. And he wanted everyone to be awake because their expressions when they realized what had just happened to them would be amazing propaganda tools: the helplessness of those who thought they were beyond reach of justice when justice descends. It was the perfect narrative for a glorious operation.

So they watched and waited.

About 8 AM, smoke and the irresistible smell of frying bacon signaled that the time had come. Max split his troops into four strike teams which surrounded the camp and awaited his signal.

Then he marched in at the head of his own mini procession, guns at the ready.

Initially, the three scholars around the fire didn't seem particularly worried to see them. It was a natural mistake, Max supposed. After all, they were in Panama, and Panama was a peaceful—or perhaps *pacified* was a better word—country.

Two young men and one young woman were eating breakfast. One of the men, an Asian who might have been thirty, but was in terrible condition, chubby and pale, stood and said, "Hello," in English. The bastard didn't even bother to address people in Spanish. Typical American.

Max fired a burst into the air.

The scientists jumped but seemed unable to process where the sound came from. Max enjoyed watching each head swivel around, searching for the source of the detonations before finally focusing on the gun he still held up in the air. Their double-takes were priceless.

Oh god, he thought. *Are people this innocent actually allowed to exist?*

He'd known this was a soft target, but never imagined it would be this soft. After years in a jungle occupied only by predators, he never imagined *anything* could be this soft.

"Sit down," he said, in English.

The Asian guy sat.

"Good. If you do what we say, no one will be unnecessarily hurt."

The other man, a blond guy, spoke now. He asked the obligatory question: "What the hell is this?"

"This is what you'd call a kidnapping. You are now guests of the Comando Republicano Democrático."

"Which drug lord do you work for?" the blond guy asked.

Ah, that was more like it. Max took four steps toward the man and smashed the butt of his rifle against his face. The blond guy sprawled out onto the floor with a cry, holding his bleeding cheek.

Max was disappointed. It hadn't been that much of a blow and, worse, the guy had just watched him coming up and done nothing to defend himself. His two friends, likewise, had remained motionless. It was like kidnapping a bunch of kindergarteners.

But at least it made him look decisive, and he hadn't had to fire a single shot at anyone yet. That would come across as merciful on the video one of his men was filming.

The rest of his troops entered the camp from all sides, all armed, all walking slowly. This appeared to affect the prisoners much more than the appearance of Max's original group. Somehow, seeing themselves surrounded made the situation seem real to them. Faces fell and their shoulders slumped—well, except for the blond man who was still writhing in pain. He hoped the cameraman had captured that crucial moment when hope faded.

Coca had entered from the north, opposite the main entrance. They met at the campfire, just a couple of meters from the prisoners. "Señor Escobar," Max said in Spanish for the cameras. "I turn the prisoners over to your care."

His lieutenant made a couple of gestures and revolutionaries with cable ties roughly brought the three scholars to their feet and bound their wrists behind their backs.

"Check the tents. This expedition consists of five scholars. Bring the rest of them," Max said, disgusted that they would still be sleeping at this time of day. His troops had been awake for more than three hours.

"This one's empty," one of Coca's troops called.

"This one too."

The rest of the tents proved to be uninhabited as well.

"They're not here," Coca said. "All five tents seem to have been used recently, but there's no one in them now."

"Dammit," Max said. "They must have been out in the jungle when we arrived. How the hell did you miss them?"

"They weren't out there where we came from. There's no way we wouldn't have seen them."

"I don't care. Get out in the jungle and find them. They can't be far."

He turned to the guy filming the proceedings. "And turn that thing off, you imbecile."

***

John Vincent was squatting behind a tree when a hand covered his mouth. "When I release you, you won't scream or make any loud noises, all right. If you do, you will die. Nod if you understand."

John nodded.

"Good." The hand moved away. "Now finish quickly. Turn around when you're done."

Obviously, the mood had passed and Vincent, business not even started, pulled up his pants and turned to his attacker. He expected to see a typical jungle guerilla standing behind him, but the man holding the serious-looking pistol resembled an accountant more than he did a desperate freedom fighter.

"Sorry to frighten you, but we've got a bit of a situation on our hands."

"What do you mean?"

"Come with me."

"Where?"

"We're going to save your boss."

"My…. You mean Professor Gómez?"

"How should I know? I mean the woman who seemed to be in charge of your expedition from where I was standing. Not too tall, dark hair."

"Yeah, that's her."

"Well, she came into the forest just after you did, probably looking for privacy as well. If we don't get to her before she finishes, she's going to walk into a very nasty situation."

"What situation?"

"We don't have time to get into that now. Just trust me."

For some reason, John found himself believing the man. Despite the handgun, he didn't seem particularly threatening. He seemed more of a man concerned and, somehow, in a hurry.

"All right. Which way?"

"This way. And quietly." John followed the man in a semicircle, staying far from the camp, and trying to keep off the main paths, which meant that they spent much of their time carefully pushing vegetation out of the way. At one point, the other fellow stopped dead in his tracks and held out a hand. John couldn't see anything, but he heard a faint rustling to their right. It passed and the man advanced, silently.

"She's over there," the man whispered. "Want to talk to her, or should I?"

John couldn't imagine the dignified Cora taking well to having a hand pressed against her mouth while going to the bathroom. He was about to advance to the spot where his companion pointed when, to his utter relief, the Professor emerged.

"I was looking for you," John said.

"It couldn't wait?" A raised eyebrow and the beginnings of a smirk made it clear that the timing was… inopportune.

John pointed to the man with the gun. "He insisted."

"I'm really sorry," the man said. "My name is Brown, and your friends are about to get captured by Colombian guerrillas."

"What? No." Cora made as if to charge into the clearing. The guy with the gun took her by the arm and stopped her.

"Where do you think you're going? I counted sixteen people with automatic rifles. I probably missed a few. What are you going to do against that?"

"I…"

"Let me tell you what. You will become a hostage, just like the rest of them, and make it onto the front page of newspapers all over the world. That's all. Unless you make them mad. Then they'll just shoot you and be done with it."

"My students… I have a responsibility."

"Yes, you do. So now, what you have to do is get out of here and tell the authorities exactly what happened. You should probably walk along the coast. Head north. There's a National Park station around somewhere. You might run into a boat."

"You're not coming with us?"

"Do I look like the US cavalry? I just stopped long enough to see what the guerrillas were planning. You guys just got lucky I spotted you. I have other things to do."

Shouts sounded in the forest behind them.

"Don't run," Brown hissed. "They're screaming to spook you into running and making noise. They know they have you outnumbered, so they want you to give yourselves away. They're utter crap at tracking people."

He led them deeper into the jungle. At every turn, it was like he knew exactly where he was going. The shouts and rustles faded into the distance. It was clear they were, slowly but certainly, losing their pursuers.

Finally, Brown held up a hand. "There. They won't find us. Unless they get really lucky."

"Us?"

The man sighed. "Yeah. It looks like I'm stuck with you for the moment."

"Why?"

"Because the place I need to go is close to the coast. And that's the same place you need to go." He spat onto the jungle mulch. "And it's on the other side of those fucking morons with the guns."

***

Julio César Guzmán was a patient man. Years among the trees, scratching a living from a tiny patch of poor soil which he'd burned out of the jungle years before, had taught him that rash actions and hurried thought led nowhere. He watched rains and sun equally placidly, and faced both hunger and plenty with equanimity.

But now he was angry. All he asked from the world was for it to respect his isolation and what little he had. His kingdom consisted of a small shack of corrugated metal driven into the soft side of a hill and insulated with leaves and grass from the forest, a pair of fields that could have been covered by a pocket handkerchief and his enclosure of animals. His rule was that if nothing interfered with that, he saw no reason to interact with the rest of the world. It was a formula that had worked well for him for nearly thirty years, ever since he'd decided that a life alone in the forest was better than to be worn away by the grim grind of a Bogotá shantytown.

Armed groups had come and gone. In the eighties, they were unashamedly funded by the unlimited wealth of the cartels. Then, still fueled by drug income, but marching under ideological banners, they had taken a slightly more hypocritical edge. But the people who made up the groups were always the same: poor Colombian peasants, sometimes coerced into the groups but more often there because it was better than the flat-line of a life that never changed. The leaders of the modern groups were no longer drug enforcers but university-trained ideologues. Julio César preferred the enforcers. Those men were honest, at least.

Preferences aside, he'd never had trouble with any of them, on the rare occasions when they encroached on what he thought of as his territory, they'd been polite, even respectful. Even though he knew they were sometimes underfed, they'd never taken his meager vegetables or scrawny animals.

His nearest neighbor was a strange Frenchman with more food than he could ever eat. He would never have robbed Julio.

And yet, someone had.

The chicken wire he used to hold his tiny flock had been patched too many times to count, but it was still proof against even the largest of the forest's creatures. But something had unwrapped the wire from around its support pole.

That didn't just take intelligence. That took fingers.

The anger he felt now seemed to fit in, the perfect complement to his fatalistic sense that his life was preordained, that *qué será, será*.

In his mind, it was fate, not his own free will, that gripped the worn machete handle. Fate that followed the clumsy track of someone who wasn't used to the jungle. Fate that brought the sounds of breaking foliage to his ears.

The sound stopped and Julio knew that whoever was in front of him had heard him coming. He raised the machete and hacked aside the final concealing curtain of green. There would be one less *cabrón* in the jungle shortly.

"*Madre de Dios*," he said. He nearly dropped his machete.

The monster staring back at him was a thing of nightmares. Drugged, feverish nightmares. Shaped like a man, it had enormous round eyes set off to the side of its face, like a fish. And scales. Iridescent black scales which turned to green at it shoulders and head.

A beautiful abomination.

The creature stood there, staring at him and breathing heavily, as if the short trek through woods had been too much for it. The chest was massively muscled—it looked as if it had the strength of ten men.

Julio's chicken dangled from a clawed, froglike hand, and the dull, bovine anger welled up again like a dying ember. At least a human would have waited to reach his destination before killing the chicken. That would have given Julio a chance to get it back. Now, he would have to eat it immediately.

If he could take it from the monster.

He advanced, machete held high. The creature stared impassively, unafraid but also unthreatening, as if curious to see what Julio would do next.

"Give me back my chicken," the farmer said, holding out a hand.

The monster's eyes went from Julio's face to the outstretched arm. It took a step forward, arm held out as well. Julio stepped back instinctively. Not only was it built like a gorilla, but it was also taller than he was. Muscles rippled under the shiny scales.

"No. The other hand. My bird."

He gestured towards the dead chicken. The thing followed his gesture and pulled the dead fowl back, hiding it behind its bulk like a three-year-old with a stolen trinket.

Julio reached for the chicken and the thing screeched.

It wasn't a human scream. It wasn't even the scream of an animal. It sounded like the dying cry of some enormous bird, the grinding of metal against metal.

The entire forest went silent at the sound.

Julio recovered quickly. "It's mine. Now that I know you're just a dumb creature, I don't want to hurt you, but I need that back."

He took another step and the creature backhanded him and knocked him onto his butt. Now, the anger broke over him in a wave of black fury. All the repressed emotions, the years of barely surviving, the pretense of being satisfied with his lot broke the dam he'd built to hold back those emotions and flooded him.

He bounced to his feet and balled his fists, unconcerned that he'd lost his one advantage since the machete had been knocked from his hand by the blow. All he wanted was to destroy the thing in front of him, to tear it to quivering gobbets with his bare hands.

Nothing would stop him.

He charged forward and tried to tackle the monster, but he was barely able to budge it. He bounced away, tossed aside by a negligent claw.

Julio's anger subsided, and he now realized what he'd done. Crashing into the abomination had felt like slamming into a brick wall.

He'd felt every corded fiber of tendon and rock-hard muscle. There was going to be someone torn limb from limb, but he suspected it wasn't going to be the creature.

He scuttled backwards on his ass, waiting for the thing to pounce.

But it wasn't paying him any attention. It had cocked its head, listening. Then, with an agility that belied its bulk, it sprinted off into the underbrush, leaving the carcass of the chicken behind.

Julio couldn't believe his luck. He got painfully to his feet and took stock. Nothing hurt too badly, but he was going to be bruised and sore the following day.

He bent to pick up the chicken and turned back towards his little hut.

For the second time that day, he froze.

A triangular head peered at him out of the foliage. Yellow eyes, slit vertically, studied his every movement, level with his own.

The dragon—he never doubted what it was, not for a single second—let fly a roar that made the earlier creature's screech sound puny by comparison. This, without question, was the lord of this jungle.

Then, the head snapped forward as if mounted on a spring.

The last thing Julio César saw before the powerful mandibles closed around his neck were row upon row of teeth the size of his thumb.

***

Philippe often listened to the sounds of the jungle. Its silences told him as much—if not more—than its chirping ever could.

On this day, he could tell that the creatures were nervous. A large group of men must be moving through, disturbing their rhythms.

He'd already expected that, of course. The disappearance of a number of his animals was warning enough that humans were in the area. This was a bigger disturbance than he expected, but it wouldn't last too long. Even in normal times, large groups moved on quickly from this area: there was nothing to eat once you hunted it out, no rivers to fish, no extensive fruit groves.

The knowledge that these times were anything but normal made him smile.

He'd also been tracking smaller disturbances. Those had been localized in the woods near his complex. But today, the nearest tree inhabitants were almost back to normal. That meant that his babies were finally leaving the nest to see what the wider world held.

They would learn about danger.

They would learn about pain.

His thoughts were interrupted by the triumphant roar of one of his dragons, hundreds of meters away, and he smiled.

And, yes, they would learn about food.

CHAPTER 7

Coca signaled for silence. Only one of the three men with him noticed. The other two kept yelling into the trees.

"Shut up!" he growled. Silence fell immediately. These troops were badly trained and inexpert. If left to their own devices in the jungle they'd probably get lost and end up in Belize… but they weren't dumb enough to ignore an order from Coca. From any of the others, perhaps, but not from him. They'd learned better. "We've shouted long enough. Time to see if we've spooked our prey. Be quiet and listen."

"I hear something. Over there."

Coca cocked his head. The man was right, the distant sound of rustling and shaking vegetation reached them through the trees. "All right. Silence now, they didn't get that far. We'll circle around behind them."

As they walked, Coca studied the men with dismay. They were pathetic. When he was first recruited to the Comando, he'd been part of an elite unit located closer to Medellín. Those troops had moved through the jungle like ghosts. They could take out a government command post without ever revealing their presence until it was too late. In fact, their training consisted of getting close enough to touch tents and fences before fading back into the vegetation like the wraiths they were.

The men here? They were the ones too old or too ham-fisted to fit into the good units. They fitted into teams the Comando used to carry out easy missions like capturing a bunch of scientists so distanced from reality that they probably still couldn't get their heads around the consequences of what had happened to them.

The loud snap of a branch underfoot made him grind his teeth.

His climb through the ranks had been long and painful. With a name like Pablo Escobar, half the people he met thought he was joking when he said it and the other half expected him to possess both a murderous temper and a magnificent business mind. He spent a good deal of his time in fights, proving that he might not be a murderer, but he was certainly someone to respect.

After doing well in the Medellín squadron, he'd been offered a leadership role. It was further from the center of the action and it meant switching over to Max's command, but he accepted it.

Max was a legend among the more seasoned troops, albeit not in an entirely good way. He was generally considered a border guard more than a real commander, and his unit's function was to act like a canary in a mine. The northern border was never a real threat sine the fight was obviously in the south, against the capital.

But...

But if the Americans ever decided to actually make good on their war on drugs, Panama would be the perfect place from which to stage an invasion. It wouldn't be an Iraq-style armored strike, but a strangling mission deploying jungle commandoes working their deadly way south, cleaning out any cells they encountered along the way. If Max's tam went silent, it would be the first indication of such an incursion.

Pablo had known all of that when he accepted the transfer. But in the Comando, one did as one was told, even if one was told to join the ultimate expendable unit.

He often wondered if he'd been identified as a dead-ender, or if it was just the first leadership opportunity that presented itself. He grunted. Probably the latter—he wasn't a bad soldier, and his luck ran to Murphy's Law.

Or maybe the Comando wanted to complete his indoctrination before rotating him back to a real unit. Max might be a clown as a leader, but no one doubted his commitment to the cause of socialist revolution. Most of the jokes about him centered around the fact that he was in serious denial about where the money was coming from. Most of the other leaders were much more cynical: they'd take the drug dollars and spew the ideology. But the final objective for most of them was a plush office and a ministerial title in the new régime.

Max wasn't like that. Coca suspected that the guy secretly dreamed to die with the last bullet of the last battle of this particular war, like that famous American general in the movie, and that his death be immortalized, a legend like Che Guevara.

Instead, he'd been earmarked as expendable.

Ironically, the expendable idiot had also been in just the right place at the right time when a target of opportunity blundered into the area, and now got to fire the first bullets of this stage of the rebellion. Coca wondered what the real motive behind the thrust was. Finance? A good ransom could bring a few million in, if the Americans wavered from their long-standing policy not to pay or negotiate with terrorists. Unlikely. Propaganda was a more plausible reason: this would put the Colombian resistance back on the front page of every news site on the planet.

Of course, the story would be much more effective if the assault wasn't shown to be an incompetently amateur effort, which meant that Coca needed to run down the missing hostages as quickly as possible. The operation would make Max an undeserved hero, but it would help the cause of everyone else in the team.

Coca was on point, with Old José bringing up the rear. The veteran might be too old to remain with more competent troops, but the guy was reasonably good in the forest... unlike the others.

He held up a hand and, for a miracle, everyone stopped without filling the jungle with noise. Their quarry was in a small open space right ahead, tramping through the jungle like a herd of elephants. He motioned for José to take one of the men off to the right, and led the other to the left. They'd cover them from both sides and keep the possibility of an escape attempt—which would only end in people getting shot—to a minimum.

Coca jumped into the clearing. "Put your hands up," he shouted as he pushed aside the last of the foliage.

But there was nothing there except for the carcass of white chicken, crimson with blood. He kicked at it with a toe. The blood was new, matted with dark mud where it had flowed into the dirt.

Except... there was too much blood on the ground for one chicken. Maybe someone had slaughtered a few and left this one behind. Maybe the bird had been abandoned because it was sick. He kicked it away in disgust. They must have been following the sound of one of the local subsistence farmers.

"Damn." Coca was furious, but there was no use showing that to his men. "Let's get back."

"Watch out!"

Old José was the first to recognize the danger, but his warning arrived too late to be of any use.

A huge serpentine body thundered from the underbrush and, in a lightning-quick strike, tore the arm from the man standing next to him.

Only Coca's reflexes saved him. He dove to one side just as the body was upon him.

Even so, he wasn't quite fast enough. The thing's torso, the size and shape of a tree trunk, slammed into him and his dive turned into an uncontrolled spin which ended against a tree. He tried to get up but his legs gave out under him and he fell back to the ground.

All he could do was watch the triangular head, covered in blood—he could see with incredible clarity, and realized that some of the blood was bright red, and still more had dried around its mouth, older blood—approached. He knew he was going to die.

He tried to scream his defiance, the certainty that he shouldn't have to die young, but his voice refused to answer to his call.

The clearing thundered as Old José brought his rifle to bear. Coca saw the muzzle flash, saw the dragon turn away from him and watched it move in slow motion. Whether it was searching for the sound or if the bullets had hurt it—gnats attacking a whale—he would never know. But four pillar-like legs powered it towards the old man.

José barely had time to flinch before the headbutt launched him into the air. He landed with a bone-breaking crunch, but broken bones were the least of José's worries. The creature landed on top of him just a second later, muzzle tearing at his stomach. Blood and viscera rained around the clearing.

All Coca could do was watch, mesmerized as the dragon tore his former companion to pieces and began to feed. He felt a tug on his shoulder and tore his eyes away from the spectacle.

The fourth member of their little squad was shaking his arm. "Coca, come on," the youth whispered. He was little more than a boy, maybe twenty, if that. His name? He thought it was Fernando, but he'd never really bothered to learn all their names. "We need to run now, while it's distracted."

He allowed himself to be pulled through the trees. They didn't bother to hide or even try to get their bearings, just plowed headfirst along the widest path they could locate. They ran until the panic subsided and exhaustion dictated that they could run no more. Then they leaned on each other and panted.

"What the hell was that thing?" Fernando—if that was even his name—asked. "It looked like a fucking dragon."

Coca thought back to the scaly thing they'd caught and eaten a couple of days earlier. "I think it was a dragon," he replied. "Close enough for me, at any rate."

"Dragons don't exist."

Coca thought back to the scaly thing they'd caught and eaten a couple of days earlier. "A lot of things that aren't supposed to exist might actually exist without anyone knowing about it." He had an epiphany.

"Maybe this is something the gringos created and sent into the jungle after us."

The boy looked doubtful. "You can't create something like that."

There was more to this kid than he'd suspected. First, he'd kept his head in the face of a dragon attack and now he was showing healthy skepticism in the face of obvious propaganda. Once they got back to camp, he'd talk to Max about him. Max loved to teach intelligent students. Of course, he preferred them to be female, but he would still enjoy molding this one's intelligence into a sharper revolutionary knife.

"We need to get back to camp," Coca said.

They studied the trees around them. Nothing looked familiar. They'd zigged and zagged across a dozen trails in their mad flight, and would never be able to find their way back. Not easily, at any rate. Coca hadn't thought they'd need a GPS to find their way back, so he hadn't asked Max for one of the precious units.

"This way," he said.

It was a beautiful day for a hike, not too hot, it hadn't rained in a couple of weeks, so the ground wasn't soft with mud. Coca led the kid to a dry streambed and then turned downhill.

"Where are we going?"

"We need to reach the coast. From there, we can move along the beach and try to figure out where we are."

They followed the dry streambed until Coca realized that they were following it uphill. It wasn't a stream, just a slight gully. "Damn," he said.

The kid looked around. "Now what?"

"Honestly, I don't know. I need to sit down and think."

***

The revolutionaries, if that was what they were, stank to high heaven. They were probably proud of the fact that they'd been out in the woods for however long, but as far as Gaar was concerned, they were offensive. Even in camp, he'd made it a point to wash off the grime every night, and the worst of the sweat.

Their leader was the worst of the lot. He sported a couple of weeks' beard, not enough to look like Castro, just enough to look unkempt.

He strutted up and down their camp, spewing rhetoric.

"I know you don't think of it that way, but you should really be proud to be here. You'll be famous, more famous than any of your countrymen for a while. And when our revolution succeeds, your names will be burned, inexpungible, into all the history books."

Gaar wondered how many other tinpot revolutionaries had used the same words. From what he knew of Latin American politics, even if these guys did win, their regime would only last a couple of years before the next political fad ousted them.

"You live sheltered from the real world," the guy was saying. "America. What do Americans know about anything?"

"I'm not American," Stephane said. "And Gaar was born in Brazil."

"That's even worse. You were presented with a different way to live, and you chose to be smothered by the capitalist north. If you'd been born there, I could understand, but to willingly do so…" He paused, glaring at the statistician and, for a moment, Gaar feared he would react violently. Stephane already sported a purple bruise from the initial assault.

It didn't seem to have phased him, though.

Finally, the revolutionary turned away from Stephane to look at Amber, theatrical disgust in his expression. "I guess Americans never had to question anything. But here are two examples of how seductive your lies can be. Two men from other lands overcome by the strength of your lies." He turned back to Stephane. "And where are you from if not America?"

"I'm Belgian."

"Belgian. I can see why you'd be smitten. Europe is just as bad as the Americans. Capitalism where the minimum concessions are made to the poor masses so that they won't revolt, thereby allowing the rich to live unmolested. The only difference is that the Americans are less hypocritical about it.

"Well, you may not think it now, but you'll come to understand what we're trying to do here, and unless your mind has been completely ruined, you'll appreciate the opportunity to learn what the other half sees."

He turned back to Amber again and looked her up and down. Had the man not been armed, Gaar would have said something about how inappropriate it was. But he kept talking politics, so maybe it was just Gaar's jealousy coming to the fore.

"You," he said. "You're American, right?"

"Yes." It was almost a whisper, not at all like the Amber Gaar knew, the woman who'd think nothing of climbing into some guy's tent to study his drawings, and who'd roll her eyes and just ignore any accusations of impropriety if she'd been seen.

"Now that I know the rest are foreigners seduced by the sweet visions of excess in America, you're the only one I have hopes for. Perhaps, under the imperialist veneer, there's a mind that can see. If it hasn't been destroyed, of course." He held her gaze. "I know you're afraid, but we're not monsters. The guides you hired have been released.

We gave them food and water and sent them on their way. They aren't the enemy. No person who is simply a product of their situation is really the enemy. I'm certain we can see eye to eye on this.

"That's what I'd like from our time together: to give you a greater appreciation of the cause and its objectives. Then, once you're released, you'll be able to go back to your corrupt society and spread the word about what we're doing here. It's a noble struggle."

Amber looked up. "Released? When are you planning to let us go?"

The man feigned sadness, holding out his hands, palms up. He was a terrible actor. "Unfortunately, that is out of my hands. The council will negotiate with your government and, quite possibly, with your university. They will create the timeline together. While I bear each of you nothing but goodwill, and hope you can reach enlightenment while you stay with us, my superiors must also think of the bigger picture."

He stared down at her. "And you are part of that bigger picture."

"So you won't hurt us?" Stephane said.

The would-be revolutionary answered without turning away from Amber. "You will all be well-treated. We need you alive and in good health. Let's be honest, though: you are hostages. The life of a hostage is one of continuous uncertainty. There is a reason you have been taken and a reason you will be held. If unfortunate things should come to pass... well, I will regret them."

Now he stared straight at Amber. "Of course, the more you cooperate, the more you help us to achieve our goals, the more arguments I will have to try to convince the council that you are worth more to us alive than as an example."

Gaar was certain of it now. There was a second message going through. The leader of these jumped-up schoolyard bullies was telling Amber that, if she wanted to live, she could buy immunity by giving the leader special considerations. And he was pretty sure the considerations wouldn't be political.

He was angry enough to speak. "And what about me? I'm from Brazil. I'm getting my doctorate in America before returning to my home country to work in the Amazon doing species conservation. How does that make me an enemy of the Colombian people?"

The guerilla barely glanced his way before turning back to Amber. "All great struggles have taken innocent lives. You are a symbol of the reach of American brainwashing."

"I'm nothing of the sort. I am just going to the best place in the world to learn what I need to know." It was true. UCSD was synonymous with excellence in ecology.

Now the guy looked at him for a few moments. It was an unnerving experience to be studied by a man holding a rifle that he'd already fired in a most irresponsible way. "You don't look Brazilian," the kidnapper finally said.

Gaar was about to retort, about to tell the story of his impoverished family emigrating to open a tiny little supermarket in Campinas. Of the daily struggle to keep ahead of debt. Of the day they were finally free of their creditors. Gaar, the youngest of six brothers, all Brazilian-Born, had been in high school when that happened. It was that single moment in his parents' life that had allowed him to go to college.

He never got the chance.

Distant cracking noises cut through the air and the guerilla held up a hand. Gaar bit back his retort, suddenly terrified.

The man barked questions in Spanish, a language similar enough to Portuguese that most Brazilians could understand at least the gist of what was being said. The leader was asking his troops what the hell that was. He was being answered with shrugs.

One of the women replied that it sounded like gunfire.

He cursed and turned back to the students. "I hope that wasn't your leadership team saying goodbye to it all. But if it was… well, you've just become much more important to us. Congratulations."

He stormed off to investigate and two women with dead eyes and guns stepped in to guard them. The way they glared at Amber convinced Gaar that he hadn't been imagining the leader's intentions toward her.

CHAPTER 8

"Where's Coca?" Max said when Emilio returned to the camp an hour later.

His lieutenant shrugged. "I couldn't find any trace of him or of the other men. All we found was the body of a farmer, badly mauled by something. I suppose it must have been a jaguar. There wasn't much left except for the face and the clothes."

"You're certain it wasn't one of Coca's men? Or maybe Claudio?" The disappearance of the soldier still preyed on Max's mind.

"Not unless they changed clothes. This was some peasant shit, jeans and an old shirt. It wasn't them, just some poor guy who died of something else and got scavenged."

"All right, but that doesn't solve our problem. Four of our men are gone. With Claudio, that makes five. There's something going on, and I don't like it."

Emilio said nothing, his expression unreadable. Max knew that Emilio was the only one of his lieutenants he could trust absolutely. Coca was an asset—violent and capable—but not a man who believed in the cause. And the girls… he was convinced that women could never be truly loyal. They only cared about the power dynamic, and there was always someone more powerful around the corner.

But Emilio could be trusted to speak the truth. "What do you think?" Max asked.

"I don't like it either. I don't trust Coca. He thinks he's better than everyone else. I wouldn't be surprised if he's planning to ambush us tonight and take over the mission. After all, it's a success. He probably wants to take credit for it."

"It would be more of a success if we could find the rest of the Americans."

Emilio's eyes fell. "I wasn't able to find them either." He raised them to look into Max's. "So what do we do now?"

"We need to get out of here before nightfall. Coca might be dangerous, but he can't track worth a damn. Tell the troops to break camp."

"What about the missing Americans?"

"We can't afford to keep looking. They're probably halfway to Panama City by now."

***

The day wasn't developing how John Vincent expected. First, the unexpected attack on the camp and their flight through the forest in the company of a strange man with a gun.

Now this. He hadn't climbed a tree since he was ten.

"Are you sure this is necessary?" he asked Brown, who was on a thick branch a few feet away. Cora sat in a different tree, an amused expression on her face.

"I think so, yes."

"Why?"

"I can't tell you."

"Then why should I trust you?"

"Because I have a gun."

That pretty much summed up the entire situation. John hadn't seen the revolutionaries who overran the camp, he'd just taken Brown's word for it. It was true that the subsequent sound of gunfire appeared to support his claims... but any number of other explanations fit the evidence equally well.

The main argument, other than the fact that Brown did, indeed, have a gun, seemed to be Occam's Razor. This was a tool that scholars often used to maintain their discipline and avoid disappearing up their own theoretical asshole. Essentially, it postulated that of many explanations for a possible phenomenon, the simplest, the one that assumes the fewest things, was usually correct.

By that logic, Brown had to be telling the truth. Every other explanation was too fantastic to take seriously... except for one: if Brown himself wanted to kidnap them, a gun and a good story would be a much easier way to do it than tying them up and trying to drag them through the jungle single-handedly.

As for why he'd suddenly decided they needed to climb up a tree... John had no clue, not even one that failed the test miserably.

Maybe Brown had spent too much time in the sun.

"Don't move around so much," Brown said. "Listen."

Something was coming through the underbrush. It approached from behind, along the path that they'd just left, headed in the same direction they'd been moving. Whatever it was, it was bigger than a rodent, and it sounded like there was more than one of them. In this jungle, that could really mean only one thing: people. Maybe Brown's revolutionaries had found them at last.

Or not. Several figures approached along the path, but if they were revolutionaries, they were oddly-dressed ones. In the distance—John was short-sighted without his glasses, which he'd safely stored in his thigh pocket in the hope that they'd survive the trek through the jungle—it looked like two men dressed in frog suits, complete with single-cylinder SCUBA tanks.

Then they got close enough to see clearly. Not diving gear. Skin. Scaled skin. Hunched backs that made up the "tanks". Elongated skulls with thick necks that gave the illusion that their heads sprouted out of their torsos.

Costumes? That was the only possible explanation, but who would dress up as a fish-man hybrid in the middle of the forest? The locals were utterly unlikely to hold a costume ball where the dress code was 'Creature from the Black Lagoon'. It made no sense whatsoever.

Then, just as one of them passed underneath, a flap of skin opened up to expose dark pink tissue underneath, and John suddenly felt certain that those weren't costumes.

He removed his pith helmet and wiped the sweat from his brow. He wanted nothing more than to discuss what he'd just seen with another biologist—but Cora was too far away to whisper to. He turned to Brown.

Instead of marveling at the mystery below them, Brown had pulled his weapon out and was pointing it at the specimens. Only when they waddled out of sight without looking up did he return the pistol to its holster.

"You can't shoot them," John said.

"Knowing where they came from, I can assure you that, if they'd seen us, we would have had two choices: shoot them or get killed."

"Pfft," John said, before he realized what he was doing. It was his standard reaction to a grad student saying something stupid. You couldn't do it with undergrads, of course, lest one of them become offended and lodge a complaint. Fortunately, most stupid undergrads disappeared off campus reasonably quickly, getting their base-level degree and setting out to annoy the job market. "Even granting the hypothesis that those things aren't just guys in monster suits, we wouldn't have been in any danger. Those claws on their flippers really didn't look capable of climbing trees. They looked designed to live in water. And I'm pretty sure they had gills." He stopped and thought. "And obviously lungs as well, or they wouldn't be able to walk around in the air like that, but even so, they couldn't be efficient in the air. Definitely not tree climbers."

Brown was looking at him the same way the last few women he'd gone out with had. Like he was some kind of freak.

"Are you some kind of freak?" Brown asked.

John chuckled. "No. But I get that a lot. I'm a biologist. This kind of stuff fascinates me."

The other man rolled his eyes. "Those things are monsters. Not safely caged specimens for you to study. They've been bred for one thing and one thing only: to defend a dangerous madman."

"That's stupid. They'd be useless as guards in this kind of terrain. If you can breed monsters to your heart's content, you'd select genetic material from…" he stopped talking when he saw Brown's expression. "I'm doing it again, aren't I?"

Brown nodded.

"All right. Can I ask you a question?"

"Depends on the question."

"Is there a mad scientist here in Panama who breeds enormous monsters?"

"He doesn't usually breed enormous monsters. He usually breeds exotic pets for billionaires."

"So why the fish-lizard-monster-things?"

Brown thought about that for a long time. Then he grunted.

"He must know I'm coming."

***

Coca growled. "What the hell is this place?" he said.

Outwardly, it looked like a couple of huts and a fenced garden, better maintained than most of the farms in the area and with an enormous corrugated-metal-roofed animal shed off to one side, but otherwise pretty much standard.

But Coca had been trained to identify underground bunkers. No matter how well they were hidden, certain signs gave them away. The easiest was ventilation. People underground needed air, and they needed exhaust pipes to remove heat and unwanted air.

The complex hidden in the side of a wooded hill was big, and no one had made a huge effort to hide it. Metal pipes dotted the hillside, the little roofed air vents typical of the breed. The forest hid it from observation from above, but anyone on the ground would spot it immediately.

That, then, was the key. Whoever had built this wasn't hiding from the locals, and he wasn't hiding from anyone who might be wandering around in the forest. That meant they had to be on good terms with the Panamanians, the Colombians and any drug armies in the region.

It also meant that he and Fernando could knock on the door and expect a cordial, if perhaps not enthusiastic, welcome.

Of course, he could be completely wrong about that last bit, and the reason the people in there were not bothering to hide effectively was that they were unconcerned with who might stumble over them. In that case, anything could happen, from the door staying obstinately shut to an elite DEA strike force swarming out to arrest them.

Unfortunately, their choices were limited to two: knock on the door and ask for help or keep wandering in the forest with no real chance of finding the rest of their troop. He wished he had a radio, but they'd been ordered to maintain silence by the simplest of methods: they weren't given radios. Cell phones didn't work in the Darién Gap... and the team's single satellite phone was for Max's exclusive use.

"We're going in there."

Fernando didn't argue. He just nodded and followed Coca down the well-worn path to the door. The kid would work out well enough: a soldier who not only knew when to act on his own initiative but also knew when to follow orders in silence was an asset to any army.

Up close, the illusion of innocence was more convincing. One of the buildings, clearly a storage hut, was a typical forest shack of rough, unpainted boards nailed together. Next to it was a house made of logs. It had large openings to let the gentle breezes in, well covered with mosquito netting, and a tin roof painted green, as if to lose itself among the trees. This one was a bit too shiny and well-built to be able to pass as the abode of a poor farmer, but it could easily be the woodland retreat of some well-to-do eccentric.

Except you had to be well past eccentric to set up housekeeping in the Darién Gap. You would have had to be stark, raving mad.

The people who'd built this weren't mad. They'd known exactly what they were doing.

The fence around the house and the shed was a simple latch-secured affair, so he popped it open and walked up to the house, shouting "Hello," as they went. The rule was to make it obvious that they weren't trying to sneak up on anyone.

He banged on the door and waited. A couple of minutes later, he banged again.

"Maybe nobody's home," Fernando said.

Coca signaled for the soldier to be silent. Of course there was someone home, and most likely watching from a hidden camera nearby, deciding whether they would be allowed to enter or not.

Just as Coca was about to conclude that no, their host wouldn't be letting them in, the door opened to reveal a young woman with dark skin and shoulder-length black hair. Her skin was pockmarked with the scars of some childhood disease.

"Hello. My master says you are welcome to enter, but to please leave your weapons outside." She spoke Spanish with a Colombian accent, the sound of the slums around Bogotá, and Coca was transported back to his youth. A sudden sense of homesickness gnawed at him, even though, as a middle-class member of society, he should never have had any contact with a girl like this: not even the shops would have hired her to work behind a counter. Of course, that didn't take into account the vagaries of economic life in South America: by the time he was twenty, this kind of speech was the kind that surrounded him everywhere he went.

He shrugged and removed the AK-47 from his shoulder, motioning for Fernando to do the same.

"The knives too, please."

Evidently they had some kind of scanner that detected metals. He remembered flying to the U.S. with his parents when he was a teenager, and having to stand with his hands above his head in a scanner. They must have something similar here, albeit better hidden.

Coca didn't like to think of those days. They were before his father had lost everything in the economic crisis and they'd been reduced to living in borrowed houses and, eventually, after his father's suicide, in the slums.

He pulled the knife out of its scabbard on his calf and Fernando pulled a wicked-looking machete from a sling on his back. Once they were deposited safely onto the floor, the woman motioned for them to enter.

Inside, the house was a little more luxurious than it had seemed from the path. The floors were polished and waxed hardwood, and it had a roof fan which, in turn, meant electric lights. None of the farmers in the wilderness had electric lights. Even a small generator was worth more cash money than they would see in a couple of years, and wiring a house yourself was a good way to die in a fire.

The house itself consisted of a bedroom, a small living room containing an assortment of wicker furniture and a short hallway between them which led to a wooden door, presumably the back entrance. There was no sign of the house's owner.

"Please wait here," the girl said, pointing to the living room chairs. "The master will be with you in a moment."

They sat and she walked away, closing the door behind her with a soft click.

"Now what?" Fernando asked after their wait had extended about five minutes.

"We wait. In silence," Coca replied.

The boy understood the message. Their hosts had already demonstrated that they didn't need to be physically present to eavesdrop on them. After the scanner at the door, a bugged room would be child's play.

He wondered who they'd dropped in on, the feeling that it had been a terrible mistake growing stronger in his gut.

The door clicked softly open and a man walked in. He had greying hair, pale white skin and a pronounced limp. Without any introductory remarks, he sat on the wicker chair in front of them.

Coca hardly saw him. His eyes were immediately drawn by the creature that skittered into the room behind him. About the size of a small poodle, it gave the impression of scales and fur. Then it hid under the man's chair.

"My name is Philippe," the man said in heavily accented Spanish. "How can I help you?"

"We…" Coca nearly mentioned that they'd been attacked by a huge dragon-like creature, but he supposed this man probably knew more about that than he did. He settled for: "We got turned around in the woods and we can't find the rest of our group."

"You don't look like tourists," Philippe said.

"We're not."

"Ah. You work for Bolillo?"

Bolillo was the nickname of the current head of the Cali cartel. It wasn't a name to throw around lightly with people you'd never met before.

"Not directly," Coca said. "We're part of the Comando Republicano Democrático. We want Colombia returned to the Colombian people."

Philippe's lips turned upward in the ghost of a smile. "Not directly," he repeated. "You mix honesty with your propaganda. I like that. How can I help you out?"

"Do you have a phone?"

"Perhaps. Who are you going to call?"

"My superior officer."

"Does he have a phone?"

"A satellite phone."

"And do you know the number?"

Coca's heart sank. The number was safe in a notebook, in his backpack... in the American scholars' campground. "No. I need to call Bogotá to get it."

"Ah. That complicates things. I could have allowed a single call, but more than one... you never know who might be listening in. I'd rather not risk it." He studied them for a moment, then sighed. "But how about if we have some dinner? I know it's still a bit early for that, but some food and water might do you good. Night will fall soon, and that isn't the best time to be out in the woods. Especially not now."

Coca's stomach growled. "Dinner sounds wonderful."

"Good. I think the staff can probably get dinner ready in an hour or so. You can have the guest room across the hall to freshen up. You'll find it has a functioning shower." He smiled. "Has it been very long since your last shower?"

Coca smiled.

***

The shower felt wonderful. The last time he'd had a decent shower in a decent bathroom was longer in his past than the few weeks or months that Philippe probably meant. Ever since they lost their last loaned house, Coca's mother had lived in a one-room cinderblock shack with a small toilet. To take a shower, you had to go to one of the communal bathrooms in the red-light district.

This place was heaven. Cream-colored tiles, truly hot water and incredible pressure. He stood under the warm shower for half an hour before Fernando knocked and asked if everything was all right.

Coca emerged wrapped in a soft towel. Philippe had apologized for not having any clothes he could lend them, but it made little difference. While Fernando took his turn, Coca enjoyed the breeze caressing his skin. He studied the mosquito netting on the window and realized it was thicker than normal, not something you could cut through with a knife.

On a hunch, he left the room and checked the door they'd entered through. It was locked and, from the inside, Coca could tell it was fortified. He wouldn't be knocking it over anytime soon.

They were at their host's mercy.

He realized he didn't care. Let the man keep them for as long as he wanted, as long as he let them take a shower in that bathroom every once in a while.

CHAPTER 9

Dust hung in the air as they plodded along the path. Gaar glared into the back of the Colombian terrorist ahead of him, daydreaming with each step about how he could run off into the jungle, taking Amber with him.

As each foot fell, however, he just picked it up again to follow the man in front of him. Just the thought of actually putting his plans into action made his stomach turn cold and his legs go wobbly.

He cursed himself silently. It wasn't as if the Colombians expected anything. He was reasonably sure they wouldn't react quickly enough to shoot him before he got into the jungle, and after that, it was a question of trying to see if he could stay out of their reach until they gave him up as a bad cause.

His odds weren't, he thought, terrible.

But he wouldn't do it. He was too much of a coward.

They moved through the forest at a decent clip. What he'd heard before the leader of the guerillas decided to pull up stakes and move camp had led him to believe that they'd be there a while. No one outside the camp itself knew of the abduction, so interference from relevant authorities would only come once the group decided to announce the hostage situation.

So the revolutionaries were discussing things like—as far as he could tell with his rudimentary Spanish—how nice it would be to sleep in new tents, and how good the Americans' food would taste after months in the jungle.

But then, a few gunshots had changed everything. The lassitude had become urgent, focused action. Gaar had expected the men to grumble, but they'd been surprisingly pliant. All they'd really done was to speed up their quest to ransack everything in sight for their own use. They'd been able to pack quite a few supplies, all the tents—including the ones formerly owned by their guides—and had left the tattered, well-worn equipment they'd been using in its place.

Then they'd set off into the jungle, and it hit Gaar that this wasn't just going to be a question of waiting in their comfortable little camp while negotiations progressed. This would be the hell of precarious conditions piled atop the already uncertain outcome of their captivity.

He began to hyperventilate, a panic attack on its way.

"Stop," he told the guerilla behind him. "I need to catch my breath."

The only response was a rifle butt to his back and something barked in Spanish. He didn't know most of the words, and supposed they were particularly vile local slang.

He wanted to protest that he was being mistreated, to explain that he really needed to stop. Couldn't they see he was uncomfortable?

But he said nothing, because as soon as he opened his mouth to protest, the guerilla hit him again, harder, and shoved him forward along the path. This time, he caught the word *maricón*, which he knew. It was a derogatory word for a homosexual, used to denote someone who is soft, a lack of toughness.

This was just one of the foot soldiers, a man who wouldn't dare to really hurt him. But clearly, the man had a very different concept of what 'hurt' would mean than Gaar did. The two blows were going to raise bruises, and the guy hadn't even blinked. He laughed ruefully, remembering his life in California; he wondered what they would do if he requested non-dairy milk.

The panic attack passed even before it truly had a chance to get started. The sheer shock of having his debilitating episode not only dismissed but actually getting physically attacked for it had replaced anxiety with anger… tinged with the kind of terror that made you do what they told you to, not the kind that caused panic attacks. And now he was able to tell the difference.

He stopped fantasizing about escape. There might be people who would risk getting shot for a chance to run, but he admitted he wasn't one of them.

One foot would go in front of the other until they told him to stop.

Ironically, the command to rest came down the line just as he finished the thought. Everyone just dropped into a seating position— obviously well-practiced—and a young woman with a baby strapped to her back came down the line with a canteen, offering a drink to each of the prisoners.

A short time—much too short—later, they set off again. Gaar marveled at the path in the forest. Who'd made these? They weren't game trails, certainly... the number of large animals was too small. Were the trails created by runoff during the wet season? As a biologist, he knew he should know the answer... but he was only interested in the environment insomuch as it affected the species he was studying, not as something worthy of study in and of itself.

Ants, of course, didn't use forest trails.

The only exception to that rule was the Amazon River and the surrounding jungle. But that ecosystem was so different, so much richer than this one, that the lessons learned there were pretty much irrelevant here.

Lost in thought, Gaar stared at his feet, only noticing that they came to an open space in the woods because the light got brighter at intervals and then dimmed again.

Another bright interlude arrived. He didn't bother to look up.

Gunfire erupted behind him, and Gaar swore he heard bullets zip past his ears. He screamed and dove to the ground.

That saved him.

An enormous body flew past him on short, thick legs, a triangular head mounted on a long neck above. The head had obviously been poised for a killing blow, an attempt to tear his head from his shoulders, foiled by the fact that he'd dropped to the ground.

Now the gunfire deafened him. Bullets were fired from three different places as the revolutionaries reacted to the unexpected threat.

Curiosity beat out terror and Gaar lifted his head to see what was happening.

They were being attacked by a dragon.

He shook his head, certain he couldn't be right.

They were still being attacked by a dragon. He hadn't been imagining things.

The column had halted in a sunken clearing in the forest, and formed a ring around the huge creature. The bloody body of a man sat in the middle of the clearing, grotesquely twisted. He could see his two companions, each still held by one of the revolutionaries. Amber in the hands of the leader—no surprise there, if Gaar was any judge of character, he wasn't going to let her out of his sight—and Stephane held by a man who barely reached his shoulder. Stephane's jailer was one of the men pouring bullets into the dragon. Another man stood beside him, firing as well.

The other gun firing was to Gaar's left, one of the women—not the young girl who'd brought the water, but another—was firing into the thing's back.

The dragon roared in fury and turned to the group surrounding Stephane. A swipe of its tail, unexpected, ferocious, lightning-fast, tossed one of the men into the forest and nearly knocked down the guy holding Stephane. That man, however, kept firing.

Then, for a single instant, the clearing went silent. The guy who'd been firing looked down at his gun in nearly comic dismay, evidently wondering what had happened. By the time he reached for another clip, it was too late. One of the trunk-like legs landed on them, pinning both the revolutionary and the statistician to the ground. Then the dragon lunged with its head.

The sickening sound of flesh being ripped as bones snapped into splinters signaled the end of both the revolutionary and of Stephane.

Driven mad by the blood—and possibly by the bullet wounds peppered into its side—the dragon tore into the bodies with gusto.

Gaar turned away just in time to see the revolutionary woman, the one who'd been firing earlier, pull a rifle out of one man's unresisting grip and jump onto the dragon's tail. Then, she ran up its smooth back and stopped right behind its head.

Then, she emptied the clip into the dragon's ear.

The creature buckled and screamed. With each roar, Gaar was certain that he would never recover his hearing. The sound made his head ache, tried to push his eardrums deep into his brain. It was somehow a bass rumble and the highest-pitched screech he could imagine.

The woman tried to ride it out, but it was no use. The second buck threw her high into the air, to land beside the revolutionary leader.

To Gaar's amazement, she got back up, standing woozily to look back at the monster, her enemy. She even raised the rifle defiantly.

But it was an unnecessary bit of bravado. The magnificent, monstrous creature was done for. All that was moving was its head, and that was sinking to the ground. It finally landed with a soft thump in the wrecked carnage of what had once been Stephane's chest.

A moment of shocked silence greeted the victory, and then the revolutionaries cheered as one man. A chant began: "Liliana! Liliana!"

The woman held her arms up and strutted like a peacock. Max, the leader of the revolutionaries, stepped forward and tried to kiss her, but she pushed him away, which brought a collection of cheers and catcalls from the audience.

Max took it well, however. He smiled and raised her hand like a victorious boxer and led her in a victory march around the clearing. Then he stood back and watched as she put her foot on the head of her vanquished foe.

But she didn't seem to care about the dragon. Instead, she looked around the circle until she found the one revolutionary who wasn't cheering: another woman, again, not the youngest one. Liliana took two steps toward her and raised the rifle.

The other woman squeaked, dropped her own rifle, and fled into the woods, and the group, already primed for blood, laughed.

The vanquishing Amazon then pointed her weapon to the skies and, with a primal scream straight out of a Tarzan novel, fired a burst into the air.

***

A couple of miles from the camp, Serena sat, humiliated tears flowing down her cheeks. She knew she was worth ten of that skank Liliana. The woman was a barely literate piece of shit, a slut of the highest order who had warmed Max's bed because he was the leader, the alpha male of their little pack.

But she would have done the same for any of the fat, bearded bastards who ran a jungle unit. And she wasn't even smart enough to know why that was wrong. To her, the difference between the pawn of a drug cartel, a man who was there for the money and violence, and a true leader like Max was something she would never be able to comprehend.

Max was a true believer, but more than that, he'd seen the light in a way that made him the perfect teacher. Patient when necessary, gentle even, he could suddenly become the harshest of taskmasters when a student turned recalcitrant or—much worse in his eyes—when she argued a point of doctrine. Anger, true anger, would only come if a student refused to leave aside conventional visions of the world. Being stuck in the ultimate rut, the vision that the imperialist powers had chosen for the world back in the 19th century… that was the ultimate crime anyone who had been taught of something better could commit.

He was real in a way that so many others in the revolution weren't. He was what she'd imagined when she attended the rallies. He was what she was thinking about when, fueled by the rage within, the injustice of a world which turned half of its population invisible, she'd left behind her comfortable middle-class life as the daughter of two academics, to join the cause.

And now, he would be left with nothing but a semi-literate excuse for a jungle bride. Whatever. It's not like loyalty was one of Max's strong suits.

But what choice did she have? She couldn't go back. Liliana might have the IQ of a falling brick, but that lack of imagination had served her well in the fight against the dragon. She was the current hero, the flavor of the month, and if Serena walked back into that camp, the other woman would kill her.

She had no doubts about that whatsoever. And she would do it with the complicity of every man in the group and, probably, of that poor girl Esmeralda, who didn't know that getting into bed with Max had put her onto Liliana's shit list just as squarely as Serena was. And now that her real rival was out of the picture, Liliana would be able to torture the peasant girl at her leisure.

Well, screw them all. Her problem was to get back to civilization without running afoul of any of the dangers of the jungle, most notably hunger.

While you could usually find water somewhere—and, dry season or not, it would rain soon—food was a different thing altogether, and she'd been in camps where the hunting had been so bad that a juicy tarantula had been hailed with cheers.

She certainly didn't want that.

While she was at it, she wished she hadn't dropped the rifle. Yes, firing it was risky, but it also made the likelihood of killing game much higher. Sneaking up on them to use her knife was a very different proposition.

A loud rustle in the underbrush caught her attention: could she actually be lucky enough to find food at the very outset of her trek? She knew she had a few days ahead of her, still, and stocking up on meat was a good idea.

She pulled her knife from her pack—most of her fellows wore theirs in ankle sheaths or scabbards, but she didn't go in for any of that posturing Rambo shit—and headed off the path as quietly as she could.

About ten yards from the path, she heard the bubbling of a stream and smiled. Animals congregated around water, so this was an important find. In fact, she could see a form through the foliage.

Serena jumped through the final bush and brought her knife down on whatever animal was drinking. Her knife struck true but instead of the sense of the blade plunging into yielding fur and flesh, she felt it slip against something hard and scaly.

The momentum from her lunge took her past her target and Serena rolled into the underbrush. She turned back to see what she'd attacked, expecting a crocodile.

But that was no croc.

The figure she'd seen in silhouette had been low and rounded. Now it stood straight, and she realized that it was something human-shaped that had been bent over to drink water. Up to its full height, it was taller than she was and built like a truck.

It was also angry, inspecting a shallow gash in one arm—inflicted by her knife—and hissing furiously.

Serena didn't waste any more time studying it. She fled.

At first, she thought the thing had been too surprised to come after her, but as she crashed through the forest, she began to hear sounds that were out of place. A keening whistle here, an answering hoot there. Those weren't the sounds of this jungle. In fact, other than those noises, the jungle had gone completely silent—which was natural since she was making enough noise to scare every animal into hiding.

Her lungs burned with exertion. She felt her legs begin to burn, but she forced herself to keep moving: her pursuers were not losing ground.

She thought about what she'd seen. The creature chasing her—apparently there was more than one—looked a bit like a fish, a bit like a reptile and a bit like a gorilla. Neither fish nor crocodiles could climb trees.

Serena rushed through, looking for a likely candidate, a tree she could scramble up without slowing down.

There! It wasn't too thick, but it should hold her weight well enough, and the lowest branch was about chest-high, which meant she could just grab onto it as she passed. At the last moment, she veered off the path and climbed.

She misjudged the speed and scraped herself badly against the bark, but she managed to get a hold. Then she began to haul herself up, exhaustion—which tried to break her grip—warring with the terror that gave her strength. She nearly fell several times, nearly gave up, but in the end, she ended up about fifteen feet above the ground, praying that the tree wouldn't break under her weight.

It bent. But it held.

A hoot below her announced the arrival of her pursuer. She looked down in disgust as the fish-gorillas stared up at her with big, glassy eyes.

"Man," she said, "you are an ugly bastard."

It cocked its head at her and clawed the tree, but didn't seem to understand what it was, or why she was suddenly out of reach.

Serena spat down onto it, satisfied to see that, despite her agitation, her aim was still true. It moved its arm to wipe spittle off its face.

And she froze. The mark from her knife wasn't there. Had the creature healed so quickly?

No.

Another creature stepped into sight beneath the tree. This was the one she had scarred. It also looked up at her, uncomprehending.

A third arrived, and then a fourth.

It was the fifth who changed the dynamic. Slightly smaller than the others but equally fish-like, this one looked at the tree and tried to pull itself up by the branch. Serena's blood froze, but the creature heaved and gave up. Apparently, its arms simply didn't bend the way it needed to climb.

"Next time, chase things that can't climb trees," she called down.

This seemed to enrage the creature. It slammed an arm into the tree, causing it to shake and sway.

It froze for an instant, and then did it again.

Then it looked up at her, and she swore she could feel its evil intent.

The smaller creature approached one of the bigger ones reverently, and gripped it by the arm. It pulled it to the trunk and hit it again.

The bigger one imitated the movement and hooted.

They began to hit the tree. Each thump made Serena sway up in her perch. She looked around to see if she could swing over to another tree, maybe one with a thicker trunk, but she didn't think any of the outer limbs would hold her weight.

She calmed down when she realized that the blows, though shaking her, were doing no real damage to the tree.

Until one of the creatures below, bored or frustrated with the exercise, pushed instead of striking.

The tree moved. A lot.

Worse still, it made a soft splintering sound before it righted itself.

As if understanding the significance, all the creatures began to push at once and the tree bent to an alarming angle before, with a final sickening tear, collapsing in slow motion onto the forest floor.

Serena was ready for it. As her branch approached the ground, she timed a jump and rolled along the floor, stopping with a gasp against a small dusty bank. A second later, she was on her feet, trying to get her bearings.

She spotted an opening in the vegetation, a path between the trees and darted towards it. Ahead, the way seemed to be clear of obstacles, and hope surged. If they were all together behind her, and she could get a good sprint going, she should be able to stay ahead of them long enough to find a thicker tree… and then she could wait them out.

Serena applied a burst of speed.

She never saw the clawed hand that struck out from beside her and tore deep into her stomach. All she knew was that, one moment, she was moving full speed, and the next she was spinning out of control, barely managing to keep on her feet.

Serena didn't fall, only bent over, holding a hand out onto a tree to steady herself. Her other hand pressed onto her stomach and tried to push the pulsing red ruin back into her body, not understanding at first what had happened. But the wound was both deep and wide, and the gushing blood was sufficient explanation, even in her confused state. She swayed as blood turned the dirt at her feet into thick mud.

With a scream of pain, she straightened to see where her pursuers were.

One of them stood a foot away. Her eyes dropped to its arm, where the gash she'd made in its scales was crusted with blood.

That was the arm that reached up. The hand, webbed like a flipper, closed around her neck and squeezed.

But Serena didn't asphyxiate. The long claws at the end of each finger tore through the skin of her neck and severed every artery. Even as she died, she felt the vertebrae in her neck separating, the head lolling to one side, no longer supported.

Then, the mercy of death.

CHAPTER 10

No one expected the second dragon, certainly not Max. One minute his troops stood in a circle, flushed with victory and patting each other on the back to celebrate their triumph over the infernal creature that they'd shot down and the next, a second beast, nearly indistinguishable from the first, was in their midst.

There was no chance to mount a defense. No time to move. Three soldiers fell as they gawked. Two more ran for the woods.

Only one man reacted the way a seasoned combatant should: Emilio. He took Max by the arm, and pulled him to where the hostages stood. He took the woman by the hair and, disregarding the chain of command, ordered: "Max, grab the guy," before setting off after the two troops that had disappeared into the woods. Esmeralda, with her baby on a sling, had been standing beside them and she slotted behind.

From the safety of the trees, Max heard the sound of men dying behind them.

The two fleeing soldiers had left a trail a blind man could follow, and they soon found them cowering up trees a few hundred yards from the clearing. When they saw Max, they climbed sheepishly down and joined the group.

After an hour, Max called a halt and took stock. His glorious troop was reduced to three soldiers, Emilio and a baby. Some leader he turned out to be. All the jokes about him, all the humiliation... he'd always thought he'd prove them wrong one day. Instead, he ended up proving them completely and utterly correct.

He was a failure.

Except... Except he still had his hostages. Two of them, anyway. Real, live, American prisoners they could show off on the internet and parade around. They could force them to chant slogans and explain how sorry they were for the wrongs of capitalism. He could still come out of here smelling like roses. The higher-ups might not exactly applaud the loss of a dozen troops and several officers, but he knew the way they ultimately thought: soldiers were cheap. They could be found in any village or idling on any street corner in Cali. Hostages were worth their weight in gold, both for the difficulty in getting them and the value they held as political tools.

American hostages were worth even more.

His duty now was clear: to get back to Colombian territory before the Panamanians—or the Colombian army itself—got wind of what had happened and sent troops into the forest to investigate. Once that happened, things would become much more complicated... and they were already quite complicated enough for his taste.

He regretted his decision to liberate the guides immediately. Unlike the two senior academics he hadn't been able to find, the guides would not wander around, lost in the woods. They'd make a beeline for the nearest outpost of civilization and report what had happened.

Also, the sooner they got away from the cursed coast the better. They hadn't seen any strange creatures until they approached the Pacific, which made him suspect that dragons roamed here only. The further they left the area behind, the safer he'd feel.

Unfortunately, the only real way to get their bearing was to hug the coast. Without the compass and equipment he'd left behind in the clearing, there was no way to navigate the jungle except by walking along the ocean front.

He looked up at the sun and checked his watch. "That way," he said. "We'll circle around to avoid the creatures and then head for the coast."

His troops nodded dumbly. The hostages seemed shell-shocked, unable to process anything or even to remember where they were. Unfortunately, he knew the state wouldn't last. Prisoners who were off-balance were easier to manage, but they wouldn't stay that way; it was his job to keep them from recovering.

They started to trudge into the trees again when a voice behind them froze his blood. "Leaving without me?"

Liliana stood along the path through which they'd entered the grassy open space. Flushed with her earlier victory and with the run that had allowed her to catch up, she looked more desirable than anything he'd ever seen.

But the memory of how she'd brushed him off, refusing to validate him during her moment of triumph, stood jagged in his memory. With that single action, she had declared her independence of his leadership.

No. Not independence. She'd declared herself a rival for his crown. She wanted to lead the troop.

But this wasn't the moment to confront her. He had more important things on his mind.

"The rest of them?" he asked Liliana.

"Dead."

"How?"

"I don't want to talk about it. They're dead. If you wanted to see it, you would have stayed to watch."

Max didn't reprimand her. The acid test came now. She would either follow his orders or be shot.

"We're marching towards the coast," he said.

Liliana nodded.

He didn't know whether to be relieved or disappointed. Shooting her would have allowed him to vent some of his frustration, but having her obey orders without question was a much easier path than the alternative.

They marched again. It sometimes felt like he'd spent his entire life walking through the jungle, instead of just the past seven years. If the world suddenly turned any color other than green, he didn't know if he'd believe his eyes. He was beginning to think that this was all that existed.

As a younger man, he'd felt the same once before, but not in a jungle. A steppe in central Asia had taught him that the world was a thin slice of life sandwiched between the grey rock below and the cerise sky above. Enemies could not approach unseen... but the counter-point of that was that you could not approach anyone unseen except during the bitter night.

He'd only been there one year, but the North Korean in charge of the unit had taught him much in his broken English and sent him back to his homeland with the highest of recommendations.

Apparently, being a revolutionary meant you spent a lot of time in monotonous geographies. He laughed inwardly at himself.

The day wore on as they approached the coast. They hadn't made good progress—they'd be lucky if they covered a kilometer—but there was no choice other than to find a good spot to make whatever camp they could with what they had. The tents were a distant memory... but a real freedom fighter didn't need a tent.

Emilio returned from the point. "You're going to want to see this."

"Is it somewhere we can camp?" Max replied wearily.

"It might be even better."

They hiked up the side of an incline and into another open space in the jungle, much bigger than any they'd seen so far that day. A house stood at one end of the clearing, its rear against the hill behind it. An enormous animal shed with a vaulted roof had been erected beside it.

"Obviously a farm," Max said.

"A pretty big one," Emilio observed.

"Still, a farm. He can probably sell us supplies."

"A witness. And we have quite a bit for him to witness."

Max smiled. "You are a good man, Emilio, but farmers in these parts know how to keep their mouths shut. You can relax."

His friend didn't look convinced, so Max continued in a quiet voice. "Besides, I have something much more important for you to focus on." He looked around, trying to make certain they weren't being overheard. "Liliana wants to take command of our unit. She thinks that, because she killed that beast back there, she can do whatever she pleases. I... I'm afraid she might try to kill us when we aren't paying attention."

"That would be crazy."

"Women do crazy things, my friend."

"And you get involved with all of them."

Max laughed. "We each have our passions, my friend."

"Women are more than a passion with you, they are an obsession."

"You say that about everyone who spends more than one night with the same girl."

"I'm right about everyone."

"Suit yourself. Can you help me keep an eye on Liliana?"

"Yes." His eyes told Max that he could trust Emilio implicitly.

"Thank you. Now, I'm going to go knock on this door." He lifted the catch on the gate and walked up to the house. The neatly maintained wood met with his approval, as did the place's solid construction. He knocked.

Moments later, the door opened. A woman dressed in the uniform of a maid stood there. His sense that all was right in the world disappeared. Maids were not something one expected in the jungle. Worse in his eyes was the fact that a maid existed at all; the class system which forced some members of society into what amounted to indentured servitude—with livery designed to make the situation clear to all and sundry—was abhorrent to his sensibilities.

At least she spoke Spanish with a Colombian accent. "How can I help you?" she said.

"We'd like to speak to the owner of the house," Max replied.

"You must leave your weapons outside."

"That is out of the question."

"Then, I'm afraid I can't let you in."

Max toyed with the idea of letting himself in. The woman wouldn't represent much of an obstacle.

But that would break the codes of this place. While it was true that the farmers often helped the revolutionaries only out of fear, it was also true that the conventions were to be upheld. As long as no one spoke out of turn, it wasn't obligatory to help the cause. That was the unspoken contract between the farmers and the soldiers. As frustrating as it might feel, it was actually better for everyone in the long run. Silence was more valuable than supplies.

And silence was not purchased by massacring the people you wanted to keep quiet.

"Give me a few moments," Max said. When the woman nodded, he retreated to the gate and conferred with Emilio. They agreed that if Max wasn't out in ten minutes, that Liliana would go in after him.

Emilio and the final man would guard the prisoners.

It wasn't the ideal solution, but he didn't trust Liliana not to run off with the hostages as soon as Emilio's back was turned. The woman was clearly unbalanced. She wouldn't care if night fell while she ran. He handed Emilio his rifle.

At the door, the woman asked him to remove his knife as well, and he shrugged and dropped it beside the door.

As soon as he crossed the threshold, he came in for a major shock.

"Hello Max. Am I ever glad to see you."

"Coca? I thought you'd run off into the forest and abandoned us."

Pablo Escobar was dressed in nothing but a yellow towel and looked like he was a single step removed from Nirvana. "No. Unfortunately, though, you're never going to believe me when I tell you what actually happened to us."

"At this point I'm willing to believe anything."

"Even a story about a dragon?"

"Yes. In fact, we ran into one ourselves. Killed most of the men before we managed to take it down."

"Impressive. We shot at it, but I don't think it made any difference. How many of us are left?"

"Just me, Lili, Emilio and three soldiers. Oh, and we managed to save a couple of hostages."

"I think you should probably bring everyone inside. I wouldn't want to be out there at night."

"Why not?"

"Because I'm afraid there might be more things out there, and they might be coming this way."

Max wondered why Coca would assume that, but he didn't ask. Asking a subordinate's opinion was a sign of weakness. "You're probably right. We encountered a second dragon after we killed the first. In fact, that was the one that did most of the damage."

"I think there are other things out there as well."

"Like what?"

"I don't know. And I prefer not to imagine them. Just call them inside."

Max looked around. "It's a pretty small farmhouse for eight people and a baby."

"Nine. Fernando survived, too." Coca looked around, probably to see if the woman was listening to them, then shrugged. "I think we'll find that it's a lot bigger than it looks. Also... this isn't a farmhouse."

***

John Vincent watched the people in front of the farmhouse.

"Give me your gun," he told Brown.

"Absolutely not," the man replied. "What do you want with it, anyway?"

"I'm going to shoot that bastard and free Amber and Gaar. He's the leader, isn't he?"

"Yeah, it looks that way. But I'm not letting some hopped up teacher give our position away to a bunch of guys with AK-47s. That isn't healthy, and in my line of work, one tends to avoid unhealthy activities, or one tends to die."

"I'm an expert marksman. They'll be dead before they even figure out where we are."

Brown chuckled. "I almost believe you."

"I never lie."

"That's pretty stupid of you. Now shut up and let me watch. I need to see how this plays out."

John remained in silence, studying the scene in front of them. The first thing he felt, apart from anger, was relief. Brown wasn't a psycho using a weird story to kidnap them: the situation, apparently, was exactly as he'd described it.

The other thing was gnawing worry. He couldn't see Stephane among the people beside the gate. And Gaar and Amber appeared to be pressing close to the men who'd kidnapped them, as if seeking protection. Could Stockholm syndrome be closing in so soon, or was something else going on, something even more serious than a hostage situation?

The man who'd gone to the door returned and conferred with two other revolutionaries, a man and a woman, slightly apart from the group. They seemed to disagree on something. The woman waved her rifle around.

In the end, the man who'd gone up to the door stamped his foot in a gesture that would have been comical if the situation had been different, and led them towards the buildings. All except the woman, who shouted invective after them.

At the door, the revolutionaries did something unexpected. They dropped their rifles and then assorted knives to the ground before filing in, one after the other, with the hostages between them.

With a frustrated shout, the woman who'd stayed behind joined them at the last moment and also entered the house.

"Interesting," Brown said.

"What is?"

"They actually left their weapons outside. I didn't think he'd be able to convince them."

"Who? What the hell are you even talking about?"

Brown pointed at the door they'd disappeared into. "That complex is owned—or at least occupied—by a French geneticist named Philippe. His job is to create impossible hybrid creatures, things that never existed before... and he makes a huge amount of money selling them as pets or curiosities to rich people around the world. Things like the creatures we saw earlier, although most of them are smaller."

"That's not true," Cora cut in. She'd been observing in silence, clenching and unclenching her fists as she watched her students being led inside the house by the revolutionaries. "I'm one of the top biologists in the world. I run a bleeding-edge department at one of the world's top biology-oriented universities. What you described just isn't happening anywhere."

"Sorry to be the one to tell you this, lady, but neither you nor anyone else at a university is anywhere near the bleeding edge. Not until you get the kind of funding that the Koreans and the Cubans give the labs. Those guys are working on human genetics, but they pop out an animal hybrid every once in a while, just to keep their hand in."

"And the Frenchman?"

"A rogue. His specialty used to be mixing human and animal genes. He was working in Paris but the government came after him. He barely made it out in time and spent a year or so in West Africa until something went really wrong there. I don't know what it was, but it's rumored to have been heavy shit. He disappeared and the French only heard about him again a month or so ago."

"You seem to know a lot about him."

Brown held her eyes. "I'm the one the French sent after him."

"An assassin?"

"As I already told your friend here, I'm not going to hurt anyone. I'm a computer expert who happened to have the necessary field training to do a jungle operation in hostile territory and be able to deal with anything that came up. I'm here to arrest him, but more importantly, I'm here to impound his files without damaging them."

"Look," John said. "Over there."

A pair of men approached the house from the side and picked up the guns the troops had dropped. Then they disappeared back into the trees along the hill behind the house.

"It doesn't look like our quarry lives alone," John said.

Brown glared at the building like it was personally responsible for everything. "No. And I don't like it. He was supposed to be here by himself. And I've counted at least three servants: the woman who answered the door and the guys who picked up the guns... and if they weren't armed before, they certainly are now."

"I think they were already armed," John said. "Apparently, we were the only ones dumb enough to come to this place without weapons."

Cora chuckled. "Thanks for making me look like a complete imbecile, John. Appreciate it."

He suddenly felt himself blushing. "That's... I mean... no..." He stammered and, despite a lifetime of answering awkward questions at budget meetings, was completely unable to get the words out.

Then he caught Cora's eye. She didn't look reproachful. Mischievous, but her look was also tinged with regret. "Sorry. I couldn't resist. But you're right. I was a complete idiot. Everyone and his brother told me that I should be careful in the Gap, but I'd done all the right research, checked every website from the CIA data site to the United Nations'. Hell, I even spoke to a bunch of people in the Panamanian government. Everyone said the same thing: inhospitable, but no longer lethal. They recommended taking a good guide, so I hired the best three I could find." She slapped a tree branch with her open palm. "And I smiled smugly at everyone and told them we'd be fine, that there was no cause for concern, that we were taking all the necessary precautions. Hah. They were all correct in the first place." She turned to Brown. "I want my students back. I owe then that much. What's our next move? Will you be doing a James Bond and ringing the doorbell of the evil madman's lair? Did you bring a tuxedo?"

"No. We get in by stealth and we secure the information first. Other considerations come second, even your students. But at least you can take comfort in one thing: the thugs in there don't have their weapons any more. Your students might still be prisoners, but if they are, it's Philippe who's holding them, not the Colombians."

"If you meant that to reassure me, I'm not sure you know what you're doing."

"Just stating the facts. Philippe isn't a violent man. He's perfectly nice, in fact. Except he's stark, raving mad."

"Do you know him?"

"Read so many files on the man that I'm starting to feel like I know him better than I know myself. Anyhow, I'm sure there's a secondary entrance somewhere. Those guys who grabbed the rifles didn't just appear out of…"

His voice trailed off. Five fish men just like the ones they'd seen walking through the forest earlier appeared on the trail leading to the enclosure behind the house. They lumbered sluggishly, claws stained with what looked like blood.

Suddenly, unexpectedly, a huge form flew out from beneath the trees and darted into their midst. The fish-men scattered, all except one unfortunate who hung from the maw of the dragon and was dragged back under the trees.

The group sat in stunned silence, hardly daring to breathe.

Finally, Brown shook himself and stood. "All right, people, change of plans. You're going to ring the doorbell."

"Us? What about you?"

"I'm going to find another way inside, but I can't do it if I have to keep you two alive. And, trust me, there's no way I'm going to be able to defend us from a thing that size. Now go. And try not to tell Philippe I'm out here, would you?"

"What…"

But Brown was already halfway up the tree. He turned. "I'm not going to argue with you. I'll cover you from here if you go in, but I'm leaving in two minutes. I suggest you get inside."

He disappeared into the upper branches.

CHAPTER 11

Cora cried in Gaar's arms as the Brazilian looked around, unsure of what, if anything, he could do. John felt like he'd been punched in the gut, even to the point of having trouble breathing.

Stephane dead. He couldn't quite wrap his head around the enormity of it. He'd spent a couple of days with the statistician and had immediately grown fond of the man: a quick, dry, slightly pessimistic wit that made everyone laugh with him at the foibles of the rest of humanity. Even better, the guy could also laugh at himself. Belgium, Stephane had explained, was a country of pessimists who made the French look positively sunny by comparison. When asked why, he'd simply replied: "Because we're smarter than everyone else, of course."

And now this beautiful human being was dead. On their watch. It was hard for John to bear. Of course Cora was sobbing: she'd selected him herself, after interviewing a dozen interested candidates. Had she given him a miss, he would be alive now, probably sitting in a bar complaining about the quality of American beer.

The scene when they entered had been surreal. The house had two rooms, a living room and a bedroom. A short hall ran between them and ended at a wooden door. It was open to reveal a second door beyond it.

The second door had no business in a jungle cottage.

It was a polished door of brushed metal, a couple of inches thick with a black lock in the center upon which blinked an array of lights: green, red, amber.

The woman who opened the front door led them to this one and placed her thumb on the reader while keying in a four-digit code. John noticed she used her body to conceal her hand so no one could see the numbers. More sophisticated than he expected from a jungle maid.

The door led into a smooth-walled tunnel painted a light greyish-blue. On one side a glass door led into some kind of lab. John tried to see what might be inside, but other than some pretty big equipment, he could make out little. The woman kept moving down the carpeted hall which sloped downward, giving John the sense that they were diving deep underground. Their footsteps, muffled by the deep pile still managed to echo in the long passageway.

The lights ended at a wide doorway on the right. The corridor extended further, but it was lost in blackness—and the woman was gesturing towards the door, anyway.

They entered a large dining room with a dark wood table in the center. John got the impression that the room had been built around the table, because it was too big to have fit through any of the doors they'd passed

Nine people sat around the table. Seven were dressed in the olive-green uniforms that every dodgy country in the world seemed to prefer for both their standing military and any insurrections they might currently be enjoying. Sitting as far from them as possible were Amber and Gaar.

John and Cora rushed over to greet them.

That's when they heard about Stephane.

At first, Cora thought the revolutionaries had killed her student. John had to physically restrain her from walking over and attacking them. Amber and Gaar soon explained the situation and assured her that, aside from frightening them, they'd never been in danger from the Colombians.

The truth affected her badly. Unable to take action, to go after the parties responsible, Cora broke down.

The revolutionaries themselves didn't look much better. Ragged, bleeding from a hundred scratches and dirty, they even smelled defeated. John could catch the acrid scent of scared sweat mingled with the body odor of a half dozen people who'd been out in the jungle much too long.

One of the women held a baby. He walked over to her and all the revolutionaries flinched. They really weren't much to look at without the guns, just thin, dark-haired and too young. None of them tried to protect the young mother.

"Can I see him?" John asked.

The woman handed the baby over. It was clear she didn't want to, equally clear she was too scared of the big, clean gringo to resist.

John quickly put the child on the table and pulled off the soiled cloth diaper. He inspected him, looking for sores, parasites, signs of malnutrition. The kind of once-over that, as an assistant zoo-keeper, he'd given to countless newly acquired primate cubs.

To his relief, the baby looked well-fed, clean and in robust health. As if to underline the point, he let out a loud, full-throated cry.

"Doctor?" the woman asked in a trembling voice. She said it in the Spanish way, with the accent on the second syllable. She looked too young to be a mother, but that was the American in him speaking. In rural South America—especially in the jungle—things were very different.

"No. I'm…" he had no idea how to say it in Spanish. He looked up at the other revolutionaries. "Do any of you know English?"

One of them, the one he'd identified as the leader, spoke. "I do."

"Tell her that I'm not a doctor, but I've had training, and that I want to congratulate her on the way she's cared for the baby. He's healthy and, from the looks of it, happy. Well, not right now, but you know…. Just make sure to get him bathed and to find clean swaddling." He knew that the nearest disposable diapers were probably in Panama City.

The other man nodded and, John supposed, translated.

The girl beamed, and the smile brightened even further when he turned to the woman who'd let them in and said, "Can you bring me a tub of warm water and some towels?"

The woman just shrugged, so he turned to the revolutionary who spoke English. "Could you translate for me?"

The man apparently did so, for the woman listened to him and disappeared into the hall.

She returned with a large plastic tub in which about three inches of water sloshed in the bottom and a number of spotless soft white towels.

Seeing what John intended, the young woman pushed him gently aside and proceeded to bathe the baby, singing s soft, sweet tune the entire time.

John smiled to himself, sense that life went on restored, at least to a certain degree. He knew that nothing could bring Stephane back, but at least he had done *something*.

Cora had stopped sobbing and was wiping her eyes. Gaar appeared relieved that she wasn't hugging him any longer.

She looked at the baby and nodded approvingly. Amber still seemed a bit shell-shocked, though, so he approached her.

"You going to be okay?"

She nodded. "Yeah." Then she looked out over the table at the men who'd kidnapped her. "Just not for a long time."

John patted her shoulder. "I can only imagine," he said.

A man entered the room. He was tanned and thin and dressed in tropical whites. He walked with a pronounced limp, but that didn't affect his smile as he sat at the head of the table to be greeted by deep silence. The two men John had seen picking up the discarded weapons earlier positioned themselves on either side of the door. John was certain they were armed, though he couldn't see any evidence of it beyond the confidence they exuded as they stood there.

"Welcome, everyone," he said in accented English. "My name is Philippe. Pardon me that I must choose a language to address you in, but perhaps one of you can translate for the others? English is easier for me than Spanish." He paused and waited for a nod from the English-speaking revolutionary. "I would say that I'm glad you've joined me for dinner, but that would be a lie. The truth is that I'm sorry you were forced inside, and I'm especially sorry to hear that you've had such a hard time of things."

He beamed at the two very separate groups of people around the table.

"I find it strange that we have three groups arriving, yet two groups who seem to belong together."

The leader of the revolutionaries spoke now. "These four are prisoners of the Comando Republicano Democtático," he said. "Naturally, they stick together."

Philippe considered this. "Your Comando… that is a Colombian group, isn't it?"

"Yes."

"So you really have no business being in Panama, and no right to take prisoners here. Am I correct?"

"Technically…"

"No one is a prisoner."

"You can't—"

"I said no one is a prisoner, and I mean it." Philippe's face had hardened. "And don't think of threatening me. I have an understanding with everyone who matters in this jungle, and they will be annoyed if you break their word."

The revolutionary glared, but nodded. Once, curtly.

"Good. Now that any possible misunderstandings are out of the way, let's eat." He clapped twice and the woman who'd let them in entered the room pushing a large, heavily-laden cart. With the aid of one of the guards, she quickly set out dishes and cutlery. A soup was served from a porcelain tureen.

It was clear that the movements were well-practiced and that this wasn't the first time a dinner party had taken place in this room. John wondered who might come out to visit their strange host, especially who might bring enough people to justify a table that could comfortably seat twenty.

The soup was excellent, a dark, peaty green, and everyone ate in silence for some moments. Though the atmosphere was tense, the hunger was real. No one wanted to stop.

Finally, the soup consumed, John let his spoon fall to table and looked over at his host who, unlike the guests, had been eating at a measured rate. "So, what brings you here?"

Philippe studied him for a moment. "I suppose you'd say I wanted to get away from it all. I had a stressful job and, one day, in the middle of the night, I realized that a move to more tropical places, places where the daily rhythm was different from France was exactly what I needed." He smiled. "I guess you could say I felt like France was trying to lock me up."

"Sounds awful. What business were you in?"

"I was in the livestock trade. You wouldn't believe how cut-throat that can be."

"I can only imagine. I'm a scientist myself. A professor of biology, in fact."

"A teacher?"

John nodded.

"But that isn't really a scientist, is it? Do you do research?"

"Not at present."

"But you have?"

"A long time ago."

"That makes no difference. I respect any man who has added to the sum of human knowledge. What could be more important?"

"Then I'm delighted to introduce you to Dr. Cora Gomez, one of the leading researchers in both climate science and entomology."

Philippe frowned. "Not specialties that are closely related, one would think."

"They…" Cora cleared her throat, trying to clear the last vestiges of her grief. "They're much closer than you might imagine. Insects, by their movements and populations, can serve as a barometer for the way climate patterns are being modified across the world."

"Interesting. I had never thought of it that way."

"Are you a scientist yourself?"

Philippe smiled wistfully. "Perhaps once. But then I became much more of an engineer, applying well-understood thesis to production technology."

"And you're retired now?"

"Yes. I dabble in things, but not in a formal way. What I do now is more a hobby than an occupation."

John looked around. "Well, you certainly don't seem to need any more money. This place must not have been cheap to build."

"Oh, most of this place was already here." He nodded towards where the revolutionaries still ate in silence, only their leader paying any real attention to the conversation. "One of their countrymen needed an underground complex to store certain chemicals which are... how shall I put it... best kept out of the light. Unfortunately, he had a falling out with some of his business partners, and the authorities never found all of him. I just bought the place for the cost of the surrounding jungle from the Panamanian authorities, who wanted to get rid of it. I also promised to do some free consulting, but they haven't asked for that, yet. Removing a potential source of embarrassment was apparently more urgent than actually using their consulting hours."

The main course arrived, slices of some kind of meat smothered in wine sauce, a strangely European dish completely out of place in the tropics. It would have been impossible to reconcile were it not for the fact that the room had grown steadily chillier as the meal progressed. Whichever drug lord had built the place hadn't skimped on the air conditioning.

He tried to identify the meat. It didn't seem to be beef. Also not chicken or lamb. John finally settled on pork, even though it tasted very different from any pork he'd ever tried. He attributed that to the sauce.

The Colombian who knew English spoke up. "Mister Philippe, I must ask you to reconsider. My superiors will be extremely disappointed if we don't return with the prisoners. They are key to our aspirations, key to what is coming for the Colombian people."

Philippe said nothing, just stared in his direction. The man interpreted the silence as interest, because he kept talking. "You said you have an understanding with our superiors. I have no reason to doubt you, but there are things you don't know. The revolution is beginning again and these people," he gestured absently towards the group on the other side of the table as if they were just so many objects, making John seethe, "are critical to those plans. We can't simply let them go. It might mean the end of all hope for the Colombian poor."

Philippe's expression didn't change. "You know as well as I do that the identity of the hostages makes no difference. You can use these, or simply grab a few tourists off the streets of the red-light district in Bogotá. In fact, once you don't report in, I suppose that's exactly what the Comando is going to do. Am I wrong?"

"The symbolism of capturing an entire expedition..."

"Makes no difference to me. I will not discuss this again."

The man returned to his meal, sullenly.

Cora spoke. "Thank you. Our university will be most grateful for your intervention. I'm sure they'll offer you a large reward, and probably all sorts of honors."

This evoked a thin smile. "None of that will be necessary," he replied. "But I thank you all the same. I have everything I need right here." He tapped the side of his head.

Something slinked into the room when the dessert cart rolled around. Dessert consisted of strawberries in whipped cream and some kind of crème brûlée, but John didn't really even see what was on the menu. His eyes were glued to the tiny animal, apparently half dog, half monkey, that sidled up to their host's side.

Philippe scratched it behind the ears and then shooed it away.

"What's that?" Cora asked.

"That? Just something that wandered in out of the jungle. I'm not really an expert on the wildlife around here."

"Do you mind if we study it?" She couldn't hide her excitement. She sounded as surprised as John felt. Gaar, too, was staring at the animal that had just left. Even Amber seemed to have woken from her trance to watch it leave the room.

"Only if you're very careful. I've grown quite fond of little Chapeau, so there's no question of you dissecting him or anything. But I'd be more than happy to let you have a look."

"Can you bring him back?"

"Oh, no. That's out of the question. We're having dinner now, after all. And then, I'm sure you'll be very tired. Tomorrow will be soon enough."

So they had dessert and then the coffee came in. Once everyone was served, their host sniffed his cup and sighed contentedly. "Most of my food comes from a long way off. But the one thing I don't need to worry about is the coffee. I buy it directly from the processors in Colombia in bags." He drank deeply. "I'm certain there's no better coffee being drunk anywhere outside the Arab world."

John tasted it and was inclined to agree. The stuff was excellent: strong without being bitter, not the washed-down stuff they served in the university cafeteria. Not even the stuff they served you at Peet's. Something about this brew made him very certain that it was the real deal.

He did, however, take exception to their host's love for the Arab brew. That stuff, thick and black, was so bitter it puckered your face for days.

"And now, it's time to go to sleep. I'm afraid I don't have enough rooms for all of you, but if you can sleep two to a room, you'll be comfortable enough. Come with us."

Philippe led them down the hall, with the two men who worked for him bringing up the rear. The area that had been illuminated when they came in was now dark, and the other side was lit.

Doors opened to either side, and into these, he herded the group in pairs. First two of the male revolutionaries, then the two women and the baby and another two men. The Colombian leader got a room to himself.

Gaar and John were next, and they found themselves in a reasonably sized, carpeted enclosure with two single beds. The walls were painted in a pastel blue of a lighter shade than the hall. It held a bathroom and no windows.

"I could kill for a shower," Gaar said.

But John's mind was elsewhere. He crossed the room and tried the doorknob.

The door was locked, and he fell onto the nearest bed, suddenly worried, and wondering where Brown had gotten himself off to.

CHAPTER 12

Brown was up a tree, as far as he could get. He'd decided to climb after watching what looked like a Chinese dragon from a parade—except very much alive and looking like it could kill him with a single swipe of its scared tail—march past. He'd chosen a perch that allowed him to watch the side of the house and the animal enclosure.

The shed seemed to be full of animals, but Brown couldn't quite see far enough into its interior to see whether the dragons were there or not. All he could do was watch the movements of the people, what there was of it, anyway.

The staff outside appeared to consist exclusively of the two men they'd already seen removing the revolutionaries' guns from beside the door to the house. Every few minutes he would catch a glimpse of one or another of them. He timed the appearances to see if he could spot a pattern, but they seemed to be random. That was consistent with what he saw: the guys seemed to be doing routine tasks and maintenance work.

On the animal front, it appeared that the creatures had returned to the shed for the night.

He hoped.

The only other explanation was that the diurnal creatures preferred to be inside to avoid whatever horrors haunted the night. It wasn't a comforting thought; darkness fell as he waited.

Whatever the case, Brown had a job to do. He skinned down the tree and approached the compound, keeping to the underbrush. It was a calculated risk: the path would have been a lot quieter, but he was sure that Philippe had a camera system at the very least—probably equipped with night scopes.

Ingress looked challenging. There didn't seem to be any entrances into the actual house other than the front door.

That presented a conundrum. Brown had watched two separate group of people—the revolutionaries and their hostages and the two academics that had been with him earlier—enter through that door, but there was no way the house would hold them all comfortably for more than a few minutes.

That meant there had to be another way out of the house, and that meant either a subterranean tunnel or a back door into the hill behind. The hillside appeared to be a more likely candidate, so Brown hoped that the animal shed, also pressed right against the same small mount, might conceal an entrance.

He took a deep breath and let it out with the intention of calming himself. The rank smell of animals that reached him on the wind created the opposite effect. He suddenly felt like Daniel about to enter the den of the lion. Deadly wildlife was not something he'd trained for.

And yet, he still had a job to do.

The shed opened onto the jungle through a hangar door big enough to get large pieces of equipment through. The far corner of the entrance abutted against the trees. This allowed Brown to creep almost as far as the door and peer inside without leaving the relative safety of the foliage.

The shed was dimly lit and cavernous. Cage-like enclosures filled every nook and cranny, but the ones near him contained nothing but some small weird-looking animals that were most likely herbivores, at least judging by the food on the floor of their cages. The enclosures were constructed of steel bars thick enough to make him nervous.

He steeled himself and entered. As soon as he moved through the hangar door in front—also reinforced, he now realized, albeit open wide—a new kind of silence fell. The whirring of insects and the sound of the breeze through the trees stopped dead. The only noise was the faint scuffing of his shoes against the surface of the floor. The creatures in the cages were all playing dead.

Sliding into a nook between two enclosures just inside the entrance, Brown bent to feel the ground. He was surprised to realize that someone had decided that polished concrete, well-waxed by the feel of it, would be a suitable material for a floor in the middle of the jungle.

What had this been before Philippe got his hands on it?

An airplane hangar, most likely. Thirty years had passed since it had been used by the drug cartels, so the jungle had probably reclaimed any nearby runways. And use had been light enough that it could still be polished to a high shine—all Philippe would have to do was add the cages, and the place would be ideal to house any monstrous creations he'd cooked up, from tiny stuff no larger than a mouse all the way up to the huge dragons he'd seen a little while earlier.

He just hoped Philippe had the things locked up for the night. He probably would: the cages nearby had automated closing and locking mechanisms on them, ideal to contain any stray creatures returning to their lairs. And, by no coincidence, to protect Philippe's investment. After all, the night could be tricky in this jungle.

Brown hadn't gone there to look at animals, though. He was there to try to get into Philippe's stronghold and capture the man... preferably without having to shoot anyone on the way in.

Unfortunately, the presence of at least two guards who'd already confiscated a number of assault rifles if they weren't already armed to begin with, made that scenario unlikely.

Still, he would use stealth as long as feasible, resorting to violence only once he was spotted. It wasn't a question of if, but of when.

The west wall was the one against the hillside, so if he was right about the complex being hidden behind the house, that was where he'd find the ingress to any hidden chambers.

He proceeded cautiously in that direction, not using a light, and hoping any cameras or motion sensors wouldn't be good enough in the dark to be able to tell him from one of the fish men who'd already filed in. With so many guests, perhaps Philippe would be distracted.

But it wasn't a good idea to bet on that. The Frenchman had come by his paranoia the hard way. He'd been betrayed more than once and even had his house hit by a midnight commando operation which had narrowly missed putting him behind bars forever. He was probably watching his monitor for Brown even now.

So Brown would pretend to be unarmed, hoping to keep at least a tiny element of surprise working for him. But this operation had gone to hell much faster than he'd expected.

To make things worse, the French hadn't called. He'd told them to give him another twenty-four hours, and was now regretting that decision. Backup, in the form of big guys with heavy weaponry, was looking more and more attractive every minute.

The smell of animals, rank, oppressive and nearby, haunted his every move. It looked like none of the animals resided in this sector, and that even if something were here, it could do little more than make noise from within its cage... but even that noise would mean he had to run back into the woods and try to hide out for the rest of the night. Retreat and regroup.

He walked cautiously, trying to avoid making any sound and studying the far wall without using a light, which would be a dead giveaway, as well as making him effectively blind in the darkness if he had to turn it off quickly to avoid detection. So he went slowly, ignoring the rising sense of urgency and his thumping heart.

There. The door set into the wall couldn't lead anywhere but the hillside. He approached it and breathed a sigh of relief. A good physical security system would have been one obstacle too much. Fortunately, Philippe had probably feared that the French—when they came after him—would resort to brute force measures, so he'd installed a reinforced concrete door. Luckily, he'd made the mistake of adding a keypad to the door.

Most jarheads would have had to try to blow either the pad—which would likely lock the entrance—or the door itself to smithereens.

Philippe's first miscalculation was that he hadn't expected the French to send Brown.

The door, unlike the guerillas and the dragons, was exactly the kind of thing that he'd come prepared for. These locks were usually electronic, and there were only so many designs on the market. So unless Philippe had gotten something custom made for his back entrance, Brown should be able to identify the kind of lock and break in.

Sadly, industrial-grade electronic locks were not like in the movies. Yes, all of them had exploits, but it wasn't as simple as connecting a couple of wires to a little device and then waiting for the right combination to pop up and magically open the door.

If you tried that, the result would invariably be a lot of alarms in a lot of places. That wasn't what you were going for.

So the first thing to do was to identify the lock.

Like almost everything in life, that was easier said than done. The thing was buried behind an anonymous black panel which looked like it could take a bazooka attack and not flinch. Even the keypad was robust as hell.

Brown opened his pack and pulled a small black square from its depths. Unlike the movies, this wouldn't open the lock, but it would tell him what kind of lock he was dealing with.

He then opened his laptop, plugged the square into the computer and pressed it against the side of the lock beneath the keypad and along the edges of the door.

An image appeared on the screen, automatically cleaned up by sophisticated algorithms stolen from the medical profession.

His little black box was a handheld sonic scanner, with enough of a power boost to be able to see through metal—at least to a limited degree—and the capacity to create images from reflected vibrations. Using it was a risk because some of the newer bespoke locks were set up to trigger an alarm if the mechanism was probed in this way. But if Philippe was using that kind of tech, then Brown was already screwed. It meant that the man was expecting a hacker and not paratroops. And that, in turn, meant that the information in his systems would be set up in such a way as to prevent being secured with the kind of stuff Brown had brought with him. If that turned out to be the case, the mission was already over, and France could just send in the heavies with the sloping foreheads and big rifles, because they weren't going to get the information.

Meanwhile the laptop was matching the image to its database of electronic locks.

"Bingo," Brown whispered as a match between a commercial lock and the stuff he was scanning appeared onscreen. "Magnetto 3.17."

The first thing he needed to understand was how the lock worked. The electronics were embedded in a cubbyhole on the inside of the concrete wall, so he wouldn't be able to reach them manually until the door was open. That wasn't a problem. What was a problem was that this kind of lock was designed to sound an alarm after three failed login attempts, so that he would need to set the system to reset after every two attempts.

But that only mattered if he tried to break the code the way the hackers in the movies were always doing. For this particular lock, there was a better way.

He pulled out two electromagnets and, using the computer image to place them precisely, he moved them in a circular pattern.

Somewhere deep inside the lock's cables, this motion would, if he did it right, send a tiny electric charge hurtling through a sensor which would interpret it as the command to open the door.

Of course, there was about a thirty-percent possibility of it interpreting the charge as exactly what it was: an attempt to bypass the lock and set off all the alarms.

But the door clicked open and Brown sighed in relief.

He was in.

***

This was the time for men of action, Max decided. His host might mean well—in fact, he might even have been telling the truth about his relationship with the region's major power brokers—but Max needed to understand what was going on for himself.

He tried the doorknob and smirked. It was unlocked. The Frenchman's trust was misplaced, and he could go reconnoiter.

First things first. He needed to get in touch with Emilio. His friend had been billeted with Coca, which wasn't ideal, but might be turned into an advantage: it would be a good opportunity to see if Pablo Escobar was still loyal to Max. The explanations for his presence here had been rushed. It was a plausible explanation, but Max wanted to look into it further. He smiled. It wasn't going to be a pleasant interview for Coca.

The door to their room was directly to his left, so he tried the knob. Locked.

Damn it. Were they scared of a couple of guys who were obviously little more than servants? He couldn't believe it. Not from Coca and Emilio.

He knocked softly.

"Who is it?" Coca's voice was querulous, angry.

"It's me," Max replied in a whisper he hoped would carry through the door. "Max. Open up."

"We can't. It's locked."

"You didn't lock it?"

"No. It was our hosts. Didn't they lock you in, too?"

"No."

So it hadn't been trust on Philippe's part, but oversight. Max nodded to himself, knowingly. He'd been right about the servants; they weren't good for much of anything. But far from being alarmed by the turn of events, it was a comfort. He understood his host, now. A predictable man was one you could stay a step ahead of.

Better still, the man would be confident in the knowledge that his prisoners were safely locked in their rooms. Hell, he might even have gone to sleep.

He tried all the doors, ignoring the calls of "Who's there?" and "Let us out," that reached him from within. If any had opened, the people in the room would have been recruited into his exploration of the tunnels… but none did.

Too bad. He would have liked to have a few words with Liliana, to get things straight with her while she was cut off from any possible source of support from the other troops. He knew that Esmeralda would have his back—he'd seen the look of worship on her face when they'd lain together—so Liliana would find no support from that quarter if she tried to disobey him.

The train of thought made him wonder about Serena. It was the first time he'd thought of her since Liliana had chased her into the forest. Evidently she hadn't meant much to him other than a palliative for the loneliness of command and the rigors of the jungle. It was strange how clearly one could view a relationship once it was over.

Where was she now? Knowing her, probably halfway back to Bogotá. She'd signed up because she truly believed the slogans, and didn't have the intelligence to understand the sacrifices that might be involved in turning the words into reality. Serena was probably delighted with how this had turned out. She wasn't the kind who'd enjoy real action, and now she could always claim to have been pushed out of the Comando at gunpoint. It would be perfectly true, and would increase her reputation among the political wannabes in the university.

Well, at least someone's day was going better than his.

Max explored alone. He penetrated deeper into the corridor they'd brought him down. About ten meters from his door, the carpeting ended and the dust began. Clearly, this area was used less than the others.

He kept going until the light became too dim to see by, and then walked a little further in the dark. His fingers found a door, and he kept feeling around until he found the handle. Then he opened it.

The space beyond the door was just as dark as the hall he'd been in earlier, but it felt larger somehow. Maybe it was the way the air moved against his face as he opened the door.

He put his hand in and felt around for a switch. To his surprise, he found one, one of the old-style long-levered switches that worked vertically. On flicking it up, a dim bulb lit up, casting its orange glow over a mess of dust-covered cars.

Max whistled. The vehicles were from the eighties, and they'd been really hot stuff back then. The nearest was a Range Rover, ideal for the terrain, while the next two were Mercedes-Benz Gelandewagens. He had a feeling those would be worth a fortune today.

The last car was just ridiculous, the bulbous, hump-backed shape of a 1980s Porsche 911. How the hell had they even gotten that in through the jungle?

For a second, he wondered what it must have been like to be a part of the movement when the drug money was really flowing. It took a special kind of idiot to park a Porsche in the middle of a jungle, but it also took a special confidence, a feeling that one was not just beyond reach of the law but actually above the law.

That didn't come alone. In those days, the drug lords had ruled this forest with an iron fist. Neither the Colombian military nor the Panamanians dared to come in force lest their own weakness become apparent. A serious defeat would tell the people of both countries who really ran the countries—although, to be fair, there was little doubt about Noriega before he was ousted.

And yet, despite all the power, all the money, all the political connections, the cartels had suffered defeat after defeat. The FARC revolutionaries—drug armies looking to recapture some of their lost glory—that came next had fared little better... and now the Comando, returning to action after months of cease-fire, was failing in its first mission.

He ground his teeth. No. The Comando wasn't going to fail. He would recapture the academics even if he had to do it with nothing more than a steak knife.

The fact that he was free was the sign he'd been waiting for. It was one thing that the supercilious Frenchman wouldn't be expecting.

He looked around the hidden garage. Cars were only part of what was stored there. Off in the distance, there were piles of stuff under dust sheets. Crates, equipment, tools.

Max smiled. There was stuff here he could use.

CHAPTER 13

Brown cursed. Another dead end. The corridors in the hillside had obviously been designed to aid whoever knew where the exit was and to hinder pursuit.

In a different situation, the thoroughness of the planning would have been admirable. After all, in a raid, you wanted a quick getaway that would confuse whoever had found you as much as possible. A dark underground maze—likely with exits that emerged far from the complex—was an admirable way to pull that off.

But he was much too frustrated to analyze elegant problem solving by long-incarcerated drug lords. He needed to get to the center of the complex quickly. The night was already well advanced, and it wasn't getting any younger.

Unfortunately, there was little he could do to speed up his search other than painstakingly double-check each intersection to ensure that he hadn't been there before and that he wasn't just doubling back endlessly.

Despite all the precautions, Brown wasn't entirely sure he wasn't walking around in circles.

Finally, he rested. Taking action while tired and angry was a good way to screw up, and screwing up could mean being captured—or worse.

He took a long pull from his water bottle and ate the last of the cereal bars he'd brought with him from Panama City.

The place wasn't entirely dark. A soft reddish glow illuminated the corridors from emergency lighting which ran along the bottom of certain walls. Unfortunately, it only served to confuse him more. He found himself doubting everything, even his sense of direction.

A sound in the distance made him lift his head. Someone was approaching, so he eased his way to the next intersection and flattened himself against the corner. Then he peered back around the wall, trying to remain as invisible as possible.

The sound of footsteps was clear. They weren't the confident strides of a servant getting from one place to another but the hesitant paces of someone lost in a maze. He'd probably sounded exactly the same himself, only moments before.

The owner of the footfalls entered the corridor where Brown had been resting. He caught a quick glimpse and pulled back out of sight.

Impossible, he thought to himself, not believing what he thought he'd seen. *You'll need to take another look.*

But the footsteps kept advancing and made it impossible for Brown to expose his head for another look. Doing so would eliminate the one advantage he had: the element of surprise.

So he held his breath and waited, trying to time his movements just right. He'd already unholstered his pistol, and held it by the barrel, ready to use the butt as a club. He breathed in slowly, breathed out, counting the steps.

Now that he wasn't alone anymore, the darkness seemed darker, much closer. He felt the weight of the inky, humid air pressing on his shoulders.

Even though his pounding heart and trembling muscles screamed for action, he forced himself to wait a little longer. It wasn't time yet. Listen. Just a little more. And another breath.

Now.

Brown jumped around the corner and brought the butt of the gun crashing down with concussive force on the head of the figure that materialized in front of him. To Brown's relief, it crumpled to the ground without a sound. He didn't think the sucker had even registered his presence before he went down.

His eyes hadn't deceived him: the man he'd incapacitated was none other than the leader of the guerillas. Eyes weren't actually necessary to identify his quarry; his nose was more than enough. The man stank of stale sweat and unwashed clothing.

Grimly, Brown checked his prisoner's breathing. The guy was still alive and appeared to be breathing normally—which was probably a good sign. If he'd cracked the man's skull, he guessed the breathing would be anything but normal. Then, holding his breath, Brown searched for weapons. Nothing. Not even a knife.

That, at least, told Brown something. If the guerillas were allied with Philippe, there would have been no need to disarm them this thoroughly. Of course, if they were allies, the guerillas wouldn't feel any need to have their weapons with them at all times while inside the complex.

On balance, Brown decided that they weren't working together. The kind of people who joined one of these Mickey Mouse revolutions wouldn't go anywhere without their weapons, not even on friendly ground. They'd carry something, even if it was just a knife in an ankle holster. His captive was wearing an empty scabbard. That was completely out of character.

Now Brown was faced with a choice. He could wait until the man regained consciousness and see what he knew, or he could continue to search for a way out of the warren.

The second choice meant leaving a live enemy behind him. In the dark.

Damn. He sat beside the prone guerilla, already regretting the ambush. Far from getting used to the revolutionary's smell, the reek seemed to intensify with every second. And every second was one less moment the night would last.

***

John woke with a start, the unfamiliar surroundings and deep silence bringing him to his senses instantly. In the moments before he remembered the events of the past few days, he was a child again, listening to the creaks of a darkened room for the sounds of an approaching monster or prowler… or, he prayed, a parent. His hands twitched with the desire to pull the blankets over his head.

The feeling subsided and he simply got up and went to the bathroom. Strange how the rooms in the complex each had their own bathroom, not at all like a house but more like a hotel, as if everyone who might come would need their own room and privacy.

He wondered what kind of a man Philippe might be to desire such a place. Quite apart from what Brown had told them, he would have liked to know what lurked in the guy's soul. He seemed perfectly pleasant, but somehow off, as if the world as it was didn't quite agree with him, that he was slanted a few degrees from the axis of normality.

John took a long shower, long enough to wash away the drowsiness and to leave his skin bright pink. Then he dressed again, wishing he could clean his clothes as effectively as he did his body. He flirted with the idea of washing at least his socks and his underwear, but decided against it. His watch told him it was nearly eight o'clock, and he suspected that their hosts would be around to gather them all up for breakfast at any moment. The Frenchman might be a sociopath, but he seemed like a stickler for politeness and protocol. It was funny how much you could learn about a person in a single dinner, he reflected.

As if on cue, a soft knock sounded at the door and it opened to show the features of the woman from the night before. One of the men—almost certainly a guard—hovered behind her impassively.

They walked through several corridors and up a long flight of steps before emerging onto a terrace on the hill. The space had once had a large flagstone pavement, but this had long since been attacked by the jungle. The stones, though still visible through clearing efforts, were cracked and stained, with grass growing between them.

Their host had set up a long wooden table complete with beach umbrellas and folding director's chairs. It looked more like an eco-resort than a hidden hideaway in a remote jungle.

The view was amazing. Though hidden from casual observation by trees on three sides, the terrace overlooked a thin cutting down the side of the hill—which appeared natural from below, but was obviously artificial seen from their current vantage point—and gave them an unparalleled view of the forest, including the house and the animal shed. Better still, they were high enough that John could actually see the shape of the ground around them, the hilly terrain and lush valleys.

It was a relief. When you were actually inside the blanket of vegetation, you could barely identify what was twenty feet away, much less the lay of the land.

Another thing they hadn't seen when they approached the complex was that a tendril of black water—a finger of swamp, most likely—abutted against the back of the animal complex. The druglords who'd built the place had probably valued that, as it made approach from the rear much more difficult, but he didn't like the ripples on the water. They felt sinister.

"You OK?" Gaar asked him.

"Yeah. Just wondering why the hell I decided to become a biologist. I hate jungles."

Gaar chuckled, obviously happy to be out of the clutches of the revolutionaries. "And yet, you wear pith so well."

John removed the hat and laid it on the table before sitting in one of the chairs. The rest of the party from the previous night's dinner were delivered in pairs. Esmeralda smiled shyly at him, while the other woman, whose name he hadn't caught, glared menacingly.

Next to arrive were Amber and Cora. Like John himself, they looked rested and that made him wonder whether they weren't relaxing just a little too much. After all, no one had any real idea of what their host intended to do with them.

Four more guerrillas—all male—completed the group, but there was no sign of the man who'd led them.

A wheeled tray of coffee, juice and toast appeared and everyone dug in.

"I'm glad your appetite seems to have survived your various ordeals," a voice said.

John turned to see their host, attired in a white tropical-weight suit with no tie, step onto the flagstones. He limped to their table and sat at the head. "Please don't stop eating on my account," he said. Then Philippe turned to the guerrillas and spoke to them in Spanish, before speaking to the Americans again. "I'm sorry for the necessity of speaking a language you can't understand but, sadly, the leader of our other group of guests has wandered away somewhere."

All of John's inner peace suddenly vanished. "That's terrible. He'll come back with another set of heavies to capture us again. Now that he knows you won't allow it, he'll shoot first and ask questions later."

Philippe shook his head, an amused smile on his thin lips. "Nonsense. In the first place, there isn't another guerilla group for a hundred kilometers in any direction. It would take him weeks to bring anyone back." Then he turned more serious. "And besides, once the doors of the complex are closed for the night, you can't just walk out. Every single lock requires a code or a key… and there are no broken windows. I'm afraid he just got turned around in the tunnel system downstairs and we'll find him sleeping in a deserted hallway. He'll turn up."

John didn't feel comforted by the man's words.

"What happens to us, then?" Cora said.

John smiled. Cora was always Cora. She had little patience and less diplomacy when she thought she was being mistreated. Evidently, being held against her will at a complex in the Darién Gap counted as mistreatment.

"You can go as soon as you like."

"But…" Cora prompted.

The Frenchman smiled. "No buts. You can walk away right now and no one will try to stop you. The guerillas will remain here a couple more days so you can get clear of them. I have no desire to imprison you or to allow you to remain imprisoned."

"Then why did you hold us last night?"

"For your own safety."

"And you expect us to believe that?"

"Ask your friends who saw the dragons in action."

Amber and Gaar paled and looked down.

"We know the creatures are yours," Cora said.

"I've never denied that."

"You'll let us walk away even though we know what you've done?" Cora seemed genuinely interested. If it had been up to John, he would simply have grabbed some bread and a bit of water and put the Frenchman's promise of a free pass to immediate test.

Philippe looked sad. "I'm not a murderer. My life has been a series of moves from one place to the next, hounded by a government that decided, without truly understanding it, that my research was unethical. They spend billions on weapons research, but genetic engineering on the bleeding edge of human knowledge is unethical." Philippe shook his head and chuckled ruefully, a desolate sound.

"You built the dragons. The dragons killed people." She seemed to be about to choke up.

"Yes. An excess. I... I was angry and not thinking. Too many of my babies were being butchered, and I wanted to make something that could take care of itself. Perhaps I succeeded too well."

"That is no excuse."

"Then I cannot prevail upon you to stay quiet about my whereabouts?"

Cora set her jaw. "Out of the question."

Philippe nodded curtly. "So be it. I shall have to move."

"You're actually going to let us go?"

"Of course. I've given you my word. I am good for it."

Cora stood. Philippe held up a hand. "Perhaps, however, you'd prefer to see the animals before you leave. They should be getting up shortly. And from this distance, we will be safe."

John gazed down the hill. Sure enough, a long, lizard-like form was emerging cautiously into the sunlight. It reared up on its two sets of back legs and his blood froze for a moment; the front half had to be at least twice as tall as a man.

Other forms, smaller and quadrupedal darted into the forest before the dragon could react and snatch at them with its jaws. Bigger forms, dark green bipeds, rushed out behind when its back was turned, soon leaving it alone.

They watched the dragon in awed silence until it, too, disappeared into the trees.

"Now's the time for the babies. Another couple of new dragons to replace my losses."

Two pale gray shapes, looking more like earthworms than the fearsome beasts that John had seen the day before, emerged clumsily from the enclosure. They tried their legs and stumbled back to the ground.

John realized the struggling worms reminded him of something, and he watched the impossible creatures, fascinated, for some minutes before he managed to put his finger on what it was. A foal trying to find its feet for the first time, standing and slipping before, after a titanic struggle, managing to remain upright.

That was what the dragons were doing. The big ears, tightly wrapped against the skull when they first emerged, had also begun to unfurl. And they were less grey now. The scales beginning to darken and take color. Could that simply be a consequence of circulation reaching them more effectively? Or was there something else?

"Beautiful, aren't they?"

Philippe's question was aimed at Cora, who was watching the creatures with a fascinated expression. "Amazing. How did you do this?"

The Frenchman laughed. "I thought you were in a hurry to get away from here. I even had my people fill backpacks with food and water for you." He nodded towards three green rucksacks one of his servants had brought in.

"Yes, of course... but I'd like to come back under more favorable conditions to—"

This time, their host cut her off with an exasperated wave of his hand. "I can't stay here. The French will come and put me in jail as soon as your report goes out."

"We won't..." but her protest died away. They both knew he couldn't trust the American academics to keep a secret of this type. Not with so much at stake.

Philippe studied her for a moment in silence. "Do you really want to see how this is done?"

"Of course. I've spent my entire adult life studying animals and their ecosystems. You've obviously developed a technique no one else can duplicate, one that allows you to combine genes basically at will regardless of where they originally came from." She looked out at the young wyrms taking their first steps. "If someone had told me about this while I was sitting at my desk in San Diego, I would have said that you were a dangerous lunatic and should be jailed." She stared in silence for a minute as one of the dragons stumbled and regained its footing. "But I challenge anyone in the field to look at that and not want to know how to do it."

"I'm hardly the only one who can do this."

"But you're the only one I know. And I suspect you're the only one not working for a rogue state."

John felt his insides freeze. That was information given to her by Brown. He didn't know what Philippe would do if he learned about Brown, but he didn't think the man would be at all pleased.

His fears seemed unfounded, though. The Frenchman was lapping up Cora's flattery like a sponge. He nodded. "Yes. But I've paid the price for my vision." Now it was the Frenchman's turn to pause. John could have killed them both, especially Cora. He understood her fascination, but there were more urgent issues at hand: they needed to get the hell out of there before the crazy person holding them prisoner changed his mind. No interesting research could possibly come before that. Nevertheless, he held his peace and let their host continue. "Perhaps. Yes. Perhaps I can look for you once this is all over. Do you promise me to keep my secret if I call for you later?"

Cora nodded her head solemnly. "Yes." John knew her word, once given, was better than gold.

"Good. Then we will meet again," Philippe said. "But for now, I'm afraid it must be farewell. The clock is ticking. I have but a few days to get out of this forest before my time runs out. So you need to leave now. I'm sorry we didn't get more time to discuss things. Perhaps you are finally the one who can understand. Yes, I will look for you once this is over."

John didn't wait for further instructions. He hefted one of the bags, shook Philippe's hand and started towards the forest behind them. That direction had the enormous merit that it took them away from the dragons.

That was what saved them.

John turned back to see what was keeping Cora, Gaar and Amber. At that moment, he was the only member of their group looking down the hill while everyone else, even the guerillas who probably didn't understand a single word of anything that had happened over the past half an hour, was looking up the hill at John.

The largest of the dragons suddenly lunged out of the trees, heading straight for the table.

"Look out!" John shouted.

Everyone turned to see where he was pointing, and they scattered as the monster hit the table and sent the umbrella and several chairs flying through the sky. The dragon used its front claws to pin two unfortunate guerillas to the ground and hit two more with its tail, sending them sprawling towards the tree line...

Out of which a group of fish men emerged and fell upon them. One of the dazed guerillas tried to fight back with his bare hands, but the creature nearest simply grabbed the man's fist in its claws and twisted. The gunshot-like report of breaking bones reached John an instant before the man's scream of agony.

Philippe had reached the armored door that led into the hill. "Come on, this way!" he cried.

Everyone who could piled inside. John, bringing up the rear, realized that the guerilla girl and her baby were caught on the wrong side of one of the creatures.

"Wait for us!" he shouted, and sprinted in that direction.

The fish-man saw him coming without turning its head. *Could they see to the sides like real fish?* he wondered before pushing the thought aside as something to contemplate later. If there was a later.

Not getting too close to the creature—the only one that wasn't already gorging on the dead men—he picked up a stone the size of his fist and threw it at the thing's head. His aim was off and it pelted harmlessly against a scaled chest.

But now the creature's entire attention was on him. It advanced, grunting inarticulately and opening and closing its claws. John knew he'd be having nightmares about those claws for weeks... if he lived.

The girl sprinted for the door and John ran as fast as he could away from the fish-thing. It lumbered after him, surprisingly fast for something so obviously water-based, but not quickly enough to catch up. After a long circle, John dove through the open entrance.

Philippe slammed it shut behind him and they sat panting in the dark landing at the top of the stairs.

Finally, Cora broke the silence. "What was that?" she asked.

It was a rhetorical question. They'd all seen what it was: the dragons and the fish-creatures working together symbiotically to catch as much food as possible.

To John's surprise, though, Philippe answered.

"Betrayal," the Frenchman said. "Always betrayal."

And then the pounding started. Something enormous was trying to break through the door.

CHAPTER 14

"There's a garage," the revolutionary stuttered. "Full of old cars and machine tools."

"Where?" Brown asked, pressing the tip of his knife into the man's neck. He watched a small bead of blood bubble up around the blade and grinned to himself. The tough guy was already breaking down. What would the feel of his own blood running down his throat make him promise?

"Just down that hall, around the corner. There's a door that opens into the middle of the corridor."

"Show me." Brown hauled the man to his feet and pushed him ahead. The guerilla wobbled, but he managed to take a few steps under his own power. "If you try anything stupid, I'll blow the back of your head off. The nice part is that I doubt anyone will even hear it, all the way down here."

The door was exactly where Max had said it would be, and Brown cursed himself and the brilliant design. It swung open with little pressure, but if you didn't know it was there, you would never have been able to find it in the dim light. Only a couple of cracks to either side of the entrance gave it away—apart from that, it looked like any other segment of the wall.

The garage, too, was precisely as described. Cavernous and full of dusty old cars, probably from the eighties, by the looks of them... but Brown had never really cared much for cars. They were a good way of getting from one place to another, but he'd never really understood the kind of men who obsessed over them and had to have the very latest, had to be different from his peers or faster than everyone else.

Cars were fine in their way, but they made no difference in the real world. A good computer, on the other hand… well, you could do a lot of things with a good computer, and some of them would allow you to buy as many cars as anyone could ever want. Apparently 1980s drug lords never understood that simple truth. If they had, many of them might still be alive.

"How do we get into the main area?" Brown said.

"There's a door behind that row of cars. It leads into a long hallway with bedrooms and a dining room."

Brown hesitated. He needed to understand where the guerilla stood.

"Why were you in the corridors?" he said.

Max studied his face, but Brown kept it impassive, not willing to give anything away. Finally the guerilla looked away. "I was trying to find things I could use against the Frenchman."

"Good. You've found one."

He looked back up. "You'd let me keep my hostages?"

"Before we can even begin to discuss that, we've got to get control of this place. How many guards does he have?"

"I've only seen two."

Brown nodded. That gelled with what he'd seen; the men who did the odd jobs probably doubled as guards. "And weapons?"

"I don't know what they had before we arrived, but now they've got several AK-47s." Then, the revolutionary smiled. Ruefully and unexpectedly. "They don't have much ammunition, though."

"Two slugs are enough to kill us both," Brown replied.

"There are certain things, my American friend, that you don't have to explain to a man who has dedicated his life to the cause of revolution. That is one of them," the Colombian said. He seemed to be regaining a measure of his confidence. "So, what now?"

Brown sighed. "I guess I have to trust you. We're going through that door."

"And then?"

"I won't know until I see what's on the other side… but one thing is certain: try anything stupid and I'll shoot you in the liver." If the man knew as much about guns as he boasted, he would know that being shot in the liver was a slow, unpleasant death.

"Fair enough. I suppose I'm going first, right?"

"Excellent guess."

Brown watched as Max pulled the door open and then followed him into a long, blue-painted hallway.

They searched the dining room, opened each of the bedrooms, walked all the way up the corridor.

There was no one around.

"They must have gone outside," Max said finally.

"Not the way I came in," Brown replied. "I didn't see anyone, and I've been down there all night."

The guerilla shrugged. "They must have left through the house."

"Lead the way," Brown said.

***

If you knew what to look for, the little house was obviously more than it appeared to be on the outside. Brown knew exactly what to look for.

For starters, the walls were much thicker than they should be, which meant they were probably armored.

Additionally, evidence of electronic security measures lay everywhere. A thick bundle of cables ran alongside one corner of the hallway roof. Had this been a real jungle cottage, you could probably have fed its entire electrical requirements with a single wire no thicker than Brown's pinkie finger.

Finally, he knelt beside the bedroom window. "Have a look," he told the Colombian.

"What?"

"See this little shield down here?"

The guerilla knelt to peer at the corner of the glass. "I think it says BCE."

"Exactly. That's armored glass. They use it for government buildings, and I really doubt that the original owners of this house had it installed."

"Why does the Frenchman need so much security?"

"He's afraid of his government. They've been out to get him for years."

Max laughed. "I know the feeling," he said.

Brown wondered why a man would do what this one was doing. He would have had to be completely out of touch with reality to believe that the cause he was fighting for was anywhere near pure. After all, everyone knew that the leftist ideals of the current crop of 'revolutionaries' was nothing but a front that the drug cartels used to keep control of Colombia's back country by the simple expedient of making it disputed territory, and turning a simple criminal enterprise into a human rights question that would have the support of the international left.

And yet, people flocked to the cause. Not just peasants who wouldn't have known any better, but men like this one, leaders who evidently knew the score, but didn't seem to be in it for the drug money.

Brown almost asked, but thought better of it. They needed to get out as soon as possible, and dawdling with philosophical matters would be of little use.

He holstered the gun. Max wasn't a fool. They both knew that Brown was his best chance to get what he wanted—even though he probably suspected that Brown had no intention of letting him take his captives again. So the Colombian would bide his time until an opportunity presented itself. Only then would he double-cross his captor.

But now wasn't the right time. They walked out of the room and towards the front door.

"Someone's been naughty," Max said, pointing to the key still in the lock.

"It will probably still set off every alarm in the complex."

"It doesn't matter. We'll be caught on the scanners as we leave anyway."

Brown sighed. He hated the thought of leaving traces, but something was wrong here—even if you ignored the fact that a madman was breeding dragons—and normal procedures simply didn't apply. Finding Philippe was his only mission, and the man clearly wasn't inside. "All right. Run on my count."

They pushed the door open and sprinted for the trees and stopped only once the undergrowth hid them from the clearing. Then they each climbed into the branches of a different tree, choosing a good vantage point to see any activity around the complex below.

No movement was visible, but animal noises came from a certain distance away. Brown guessed they were coming from beyond the animal shed, and halfway up the hill.

He checked his watch. 9 AM. It had been more than twenty-eight hours since he last slept, but he couldn't drop his guard now. At minimum, he needed to lose the guerilla before he could rest. Brown had no illusions about how long that particular alliance of convenience would last if he dozed off. The Colombian would waste no time at all before braining him with a rock to steal his gun even if it wasn't the best time—and possibly to add him to the hostage list.

He'd half-expected Max to run for the hills as soon as they got out but the man obviously had other ideas. He'd evidently decided that the best place to be for now was right where he was: next to Brown, waiting for the action to start.

The action, however, didn't seem to be in any hurry. They could see nothing. No animals. None of the people in either group—Colombians or hostages. Even the two servants seemed to be resting, not doing their usual rounds that morning.

He chuckled. If Max had wanted to be near the center of the action, he'd chosen the wrong guy to follow.

The man was probably furious.

***

Lounging on a branch several meters away, Max was not furious. He'd learned patience the hard way. Since joining the Comando in the field, his existence had been anything but eventful. The old saying that army life consisted of years of mind-numbing boredom punctuated by minutes of sheer terror held true for them.

Or at least the first part did. Living in a jungle under a cease-fire with the government was like watching paint dry. Your days blended into each other. Even the nights which, when he first came into the forest, had been magical, noisy, alive and fragrant, had become routine. Emilio criticized him privately—and often openly—for being too fond of the women assigned to their troop, but Emilio was a true fanatic. He would never feel the emptiness that came from the sense that one's life was ticking away, second after second, and that all you were achieving was to grow old.

And terror? Well, he'd certainly felt terror when the dragons attacked them, but it was the first time in a decade of being a freedom fighter that it had happened to him.

At least it had been real panic and not some lesser substitute.

Max watched the American while the American watched the clearing. The man's expression gave nothing away. He'd claimed to have been up all night, but there were no signs of fatigue in his movements. He was like a robot, one of those American Special Forces troops you whispered about in the night. The ones you hoped wouldn't suddenly appear out of nowhere and kill your entire team.

He didn't look like a dangerous man, however. He was pale-skinned, as if he spent most of his time in an office. But it went deeper than that: this was not a lithe, muscular killing machine. He had pudgy cheeks and, though he wasn't by any means fat, he wasn't thin, either. Max could see the slight curve of his belly, the slight sag of his butt.

But he moved through the trees like one born to it.

"Where did you learn the jungle?" Max whispered.

Brown didn't turn to look. "Asia."

It didn't take a genius to know that no more information was forthcoming on that topic. "Where do you think everyone is?"

Brown shrugged. "No clue. But there's something wrong somewhere. If we don't find out what's happening in an hour, I will move. You're free to go if you like. You kept your part of our agreement, so I have no further reason to keep you prisoner."

Apparently, the man didn't know the value of hostages.

Or maybe he did, but wanted to work alone. That was the more likely explanation.

Max determined to stick with him.

The hour passed and Brown descended. They made their way to the edge of the clearing and assessed the situation. The door to the house stood ajar, just as they left it when they'd run away. The only thing that moved in the clearing was the tips of the blades of grass, swaying in the wind.

"Look," Brown said. He pointed towards the animal sheds. At first, Max couldn't see what he was supposed to be looking at but soon several of the fish-men came into view. They advanced in a group and huddled around the house. One of them pushed experimentally on the door, and they all jumped backward when it swung open. Their caution lasted only a few moments, however, and soon the creatures crowded around the entrance, looking like a pack of monkeys studying an interesting banana. Then, one of them took three steps into the house and ran back out.

This sent them into a flurry of movement. They looked almost human as they jumped around and pointed at the opening. Finally, they calmed down and, as one body, ran inside.

"That won't make Philippe happy," Brown said with a chuckle.

"You don't like Philippe very much, do you? Are you here to kill him?"

Brown breathed deeply. "I've never seen Philippe in my life. Not in the flesh, anyway. So I have no reason to like him or to dislike him. But having that bunch of monsters inside will sow confusion... and a confused quarry is not an effective opponent. It's probably the first thing that's gone right since I landed here."

Max noticed that the American had avoided the second part of the question. He knew better than to insist, however.

"So where are we going now?"

"That's a good question. I was hoping to spot someone and follow them. Hopefully, they would lead us to the rest of them. But we could be here all day, and I don't have all day. We should probably make a big circle around the clearing, just inside the tree line, and see if we can find anything that we might have missed from the trees." He didn't sound particularly hopeful as he finished climbing down the tree to stand beside Max.

Suddenly, a shrill beeping sound tore through the forest. It seemed to be coming from the depths of Brown's pack. "Crap. Of all the…" He tore at the flap and ferreted around inside the backpack until he found what he was looking for. When he pulled it out, Max was disappointed to see that it was just a black plastic oblong. A phone.

"Yes," Brown said tersely. "I was expecting you to call yesterday."

He waited for a couple of moments.

"Yes, I can get inside without problems. But there are some complications." Another pause. "No, the computers should be fine, but we need to move in as soon as possible." Pause. "Yes. Send them in now. And be sure they're well-armed."

This time, whoever was on the other end took a long time to formulate his question.

"No," Brown responded finally. "Wildlife. But not native wildlife." Pause. "Yes, exactly."

Brown cut off the communication and sat against the trunk of a tree.

"Now what?" Max said.

"Now we wait," the American replied. "Although you should probably make yourself scarce. The guys who are about to drop in aren't known for their well-developed sense of humor, and they might find your presence in the middle of their operation annoying. You don't want to annoy them."

Max felt the anger returning. Yet another player, or some shadowy group, was interfering to take his hostages away. Was everyone out to get him? "How long will they take to get here?"

"Not long. Less than an hour. You should get moving." There was no malice in the man as he condemned Max's entire life, his complete career, to the most final and ignoble of deaths. Because everything in political life was forgivable except failure.

For a second he flirted with the idea of jumping the American and trying to take the man's weapon.

But that died within him. He felt his stomach curdle at the mere thought of risking his life. He shook his head. Some revolutionary he'd turned out to be.

A rustle in the woods behind them made them snap around. Something was coming. They jumped to their feet in time to see a sapling snap and fall to the ground in two about ten meters away.

"I think our plans just got made for us," Brown said.

Max looked at him in bewilderment. "What…"

"Run!" the American replied. He gave the example and took flight, heading straight back towards the house.

Max didn't need to be told twice. He sprinted after the American, not daring to look back at the thing following them.

He couldn't see it, but he could certainly hear it. The thundering tattoo of bass drums that heralded the lumbering gait of one of the dragons shook the ground behind him. Max redoubled his pace.

He was certain he wouldn't make it, was sure the jaws would close around him at any moment. He was convinced he could feel the creature's hot breath on his back. Five meters out from the house, he dived into the entrance and rolled to a painful stop in the corridor.

The building shook with the force of a tremendous impact.

Max looked up to see the dragon's jaws an arms-length away from his face and he crawled back into the depths of the room.

But again, death failed to arrive. The dragon couldn't get its shoulders through the narrow opening of the door. The creature was just too wide.

That didn't stop it from trying. It roared and twitched, all the while trying to bite Max's head off.

Max moved back through the hallway, across the inner door to where Brown waited.

"Close one," the American said.

"Too close."

"We're not safe yet. Remember that the frog things came in here a while ago."

"Thanks for reminding me," Max said sourly. "I wish something would just kill me and get it over with."

Brown looked at him quizzically. "Are you giving up already?"

Already? Max thought. *This uncultured barbarian has no idea what I've been through. How can he, living off the fat of the oppressed of the world?*

"Come on," Max replied, shouldering past.

They walked down the hall until the noise of breaking cutlery brought them up short. They peered through a doorway to see a large kitchen. The refrigerator door stood open and the fish creatures were gorging themselves on the remains of the previous night's dinner. Something that looked vaguely human lay on the ground beside the fridge, but they didn't stick around to see what it was. The fish-things were too busy eating to notice them.

Max and Brown walked quietly past the open doorway and headed down the hall.

Suddenly, a shape appeared ahead; one of the creatures. It stood ahead, staring at them in human-looking confusion. Then it took a step towards them.

The second step was accompanied by a roar. It put its arms up, claws extended.

Brown's own arm mirrored the gesture, but his hand held a pistol. A single explosion thundered in the enclosed space and the thing fell to the floor.

Even before it hit the ground, Brown was running down the hall.

Max wanted to follow, but his feet had deserted him. He stared down at the dead creature.

CHAPTER 15

Betrayed.

It was the same every time. You could trust no one. No one.

Philippe clutched his chest and breathed deeply, counting to ten. Pandemonium reigned around him as the silly Americans and Colombians climbed over each other to get down the stairs, but he ignored it all. His entire being concentrated on the pounding at the door, the tangible evidence that his hopes and dreams were ever destined to come crashing down around him.

He'd spent his entire career ignoring the naysayers, the small-minded people who couldn't see past what had always been done.

But on his dark days, he wondered whether the most dimwitted of them all, the ones that brayed that 'those who played in God's garden would suffer his wrath' might not be right after all. How else could one explain the chain of betrayal and persecution that dogged his every step?

First, there was… he still didn't know who had betrayed him in Paris. One moment, he was the head of a dedicated team creating unorthodox creatures, getting ever closer to the holy grail of transplanting human intelligence into an infinitely adaptable series of bodies, and the next, he was a fugitive, running for his life in the night, pursued by hard men more used to killing terrorists than arresting scientists.

He'd only been saved by Poupée, one of his creations. She'd adored him, looked to him as a God and called him 'Phlip' because she couldn't pronounce his name correctly. She was a human-level intelligence in a tiny monkey's body, a misshapen doll from the time when Philippe couldn't design things to look perfect.

But that night, she wasn't a deformed imp, she was a shining, majestic angel. Mere minutes before the raid designed to capture him, she'd pulled his hair, woken him in the darkest depths of the night, shouting "Phlip, Phlip" in her squeaky little voice. "Mans," she'd said, pointing out the window, towards the dark terrace.

Philippe had understood immediately, and he'd never questioned her loyalty or her intelligence. He knew that the little doll-like entity had more loyalty in one of her tiny fingers than his entire staff—one of whom had obviously bleated to the authorities.

He'd acted without hesitation. If there were men on his terrace, they meant him no good, so he did what they wouldn't expect and, pausing only long enough to dress and allow Poupée to climb into a sack, he left through the servant's entrance, down the eight flights of stairs to ground level and out the side door of the apartment building. He silently thanked the universe for the fact that Parisians of the nineteenth century were organized along strict class lines and would never dream of sharing an entrance with their domestic help.

Fortunately, the men who broke into his apartment moments later, confident of catching him asleep, hadn't thought to cover all the exits.

He wandered the chilly streets of Paris, hobo-like, until dawn became a suggestion in the distance and the clock struck 5:30, the opening hour for the Metro. He sat in a train and in a daze. Eventually, he got off and found himself in the Gare de Lyon. He was surprised by how busy it was at that hour of morning. His student days, when he moved around the city using public transportation, were far behind him, as were the memories of the sacrifices they'd brought. He was a wealthy member of the French scientific aristocracy, and didn't like to dwell on hardships like elbowing his way through station crowds at dawn.

Now, he barely paid them any attention, his mind more occupied with practical matters. Philippe knew he needed to leave the country, but he had no idea how to go about it.

He stared up at the departure boards for the TGV trains, not really seeing the information they imparted, but just reading them to calm his racing heart.

One word suddenly flashed into his consciousness: *Marseille*.

That was the place he needed to go. Whenever a man needed to enter or leave France illegally, he did it through the largest of her Mediterranean ports. Everyone took it as a given that the entire dockside was run by thieves, smugglers and members of the Corsican Mafia. It had been a staple of French detective television for decades, and of novels for much longer.

That was where he had to go.

As he operated the ticket machine, however, he realized that he couldn't take the TGV. The police would be watching.

So he pocketed his ticket, left the station and took a bus to Melun. There, he stopped for breakfast before boarding another bus to Sens.

In this way, Philippe hopped anonymously down nearly the entire north-to-south length of France, and before he knew it, he was in Marseilles, in a rundown area of town whose name he didn't know, searching for a place where he could get a cheap private room. He had to pay with the cash he had on hand… attempting to use a card would see him arrested in minutes. Fortunately, he had several hundred Euros on his person; enough for a month in the flophouse he chose.

That night, he slept fitfully but when sunlight woke him, Philippe was grateful for the flea bites and the itching. They symbolized his freedom.

Then, in that tiny room with stained walls, doubts hit.

He was a fool to think that the docks worked like in the movies. Nothing in life worked like in the movies. There would be controls, policemen, cameras. He wouldn't be able to go anywhere near the boats.

Depressed, he had breakfast at a bar with a wooden counter and four chairs. The man at the bar had nodded in his direction. "Bad night?"

Philippe nodded glumly.

"Want to talk about it?"

"Not really."

Miraculously, the man's next words were: "At least you don't have to run from the country. My brother had to move to Tunis. They were after him for stealing cars."

Three weeks later, he walked down the gangplank of an Estonian container ship rusted to within an inch of its existence. His first impressions of the docks of Libreville, Gabon were exceedingly positive. No chain-link fences greeted him and the guards at the docks simply smiled and waved him through when they saw him. He later learned that most white people were treated the same way, unless they were actually trying to drive an uninspected container past a checkpoint.

He breathed again for the first time in twenty days. His passport, after all, was locked in his nightstand in Paris… if the police hadn't taken it with them.

Now it didn't matter. He let Poupée out of her confinement—she'd had the run of the ship at night, of course, but this was the first time he dared let her out in the daytime—and she scuttled into a tree. He knew she wouldn't let him out of her sight.

Finances were easy. Every Frenchman—those who mattered, in any case—had anonymous money stashed overseas, out of the clutches of the overzealous tax men. His own was in Seychelles and, as soon as he convinced the manager of the main branch of the BICIG bank of this fact, they became the best of friends, and he became the *honorable monsieur Philippe* whenever he came in to do business. All of that for a few million Euros. He wondered what they would have done if he'd been truly rich.

But he wasn't there for the social life. He was there for the mangrove swamps. He built a little shack and, with a few pieces of equipment bought through a chain of false fronts, he also built Harold.

Harold.

The name made him wince. At once his greatest triumph and his most bitter disappointment. A dragon adapted to water—bigger and stronger than the ones he'd designed for the Panamanian jungle—but with the mental faculties of a human being.

Philippe should have been their God, he should have been their idol.

But he hadn't taken jealousy into account.

Poupée, his first creation, had been his undoing. Now that he had a magnificent beast like Harold to enjoy, she was certain that he would toss her aside like an outgrown toy.

Her whispers had poisoned Harold against Philippe, culminating on that terrible night they'd turned on him. He'd run, but the dragon had been faster.

Whatever remnant of the love the creature had once had for him saved his life. The monster could have eaten him, crushed him, torn him in two. But it didn't; it merely hit him hard enough to kill him and turned away, leaving him for dead.

He wasn't dead.

It had taken Philippe four days to get out of that deserted jungle, burning with fever and fearing for his limbs, and another six months to walk again. Only the cheerful efficiency of the doctor and the male nurse who'd received him when the ambulance dropped him at the tiny clinic in Iguela had saved his life. Wounds had been scrubbed, antibiotics procured—never a trivial act in equatorial Africa—and administered and, finally, he'd been stitched back together and dropped in a bed to recover.

On the first day of every month, that doctor and that nurse received a hundred US dollars from an anonymous benefactor about whom they knew nothing other than that he had money in the Seychelles.

Panama, the Darién Gap, had been his chance to start over. He even had investors this time, and he wasn't going to make the same mistake again. He would never work with human intelligence, never hire underlings who might be jealous of his research. He would create pets. Nothing more than pets.

Animals were loyal, if not to him, then to the people who fed them. You could trust them. Hell, now that he thought about it, he'd been unconsciously gravitating to dog genes in everything he'd been building. For the loyalty.

Of course, when his animals started disappearing, hunted for food by bastards like these guerillas, he'd forgotten all he'd learned, overcome by his anger. Then, it had been reptile genes and large animals. Aurochs and mammoths, experimental stuff.

He'd wanted to hurt someone.

Of course those creatures had turned against him. It was fated from the moment of their conception.

"Are you all right? Philippe?"

He returned to the present. A dimly lit stairwell. The concerned face of one of the American scientists, the man with the ridiculous hat. Pith helmets were for India, not Panama. Panama Hats were for Panama.

"Yes. I'm all right."

"What do we do now?"

Philippe tried to force a superior smile, the natural expression of upper-class Frenchmen. It was harder than he ever remembered it being. "We sit tight and drink wine until nightfall," he replied.

"What? Those things are after us!"

Every set of eyes was upon them now. Smiling became easier with an audience. "Nonsense. They are aggressive animals who decided we'd make a tasty snack. But don't forget that this place is an armored bunker buried underground. They can't get in." He paused for dramatic effect. "And tonight, they will do what they do every night: return to the food and safety of their cages."

"So? We still can't go out."

"The cages are programmed to shut behind them, and the bars are much too thick for them to break. Not even the dragons can budge them. By tonight, we can roam the jungle in complete safety. In the meantime, let's get back to the more civilized parts of the complex. Unless, of course, you'd prefer to take your chances outside? My offer still stands. You can leave whenever you want. There are several secret exits—you're welcome to choose any of them."

At those words, his audience drew away. "No thanks," John said. "I'd rather wait until your critters are safely caged."

"That is wise of you."

***

They had selected the dining room as their unofficial headquarters. People came and went to and from their rooms but mostly huddled around the table and drank champagne.

Cora watched their host carefully. Other than to give orders to the servants—who acted like nothing was amiss—he'd been silent since they came back inside. Now his gaze was lost in the distance and she wondered what he was thinking about. If he was a real scientist, he would be analyzing the cause for what happened today and tweaking DNA strings in his head.

Was that even possible? She didn't know, and she desperately wanted to ask.

But this didn't seem like the time, so she watched everyone else: the guerillas—the two that were left—stayed near each other. Far from being members of a fearsome group that could take hostages, the surviving man and woman looked frightened, as if they knew that, of everyone present, they were the least able to deal with the situation.

The young girl—Cora no longer thought of her as one of the revolutionaries—had latched onto John and, between them, they were making faces at the baby to keep it from crying. Cora smiled at that, wondering just what kind of primate John imagined it might be.

Amber and Gaar sat together at one end of the table. Cora wondered if Amber saw the way the guy looked at her. If she didn't, she was denser than lead. If she did, she shouldn't have been leading him on. Gaar was many things—among them a brilliant potential scientist—but he just wasn't in Amber's league.

They were all completely uninteresting to her. All except the brooding Frenchman. He was fascinating in so many ways. He obviously marched to his own drummer and had a nearly sociopathic disdain for what human society expected of its normal members while, at the same time, clearly being a genius of enormous proportions. Worst of all, though in his middle fifties, as far as she could tell, he was also handsome in a tropical French way. She'd never have been able to describe what tropical French was, but now she knew. Was there a villain in Casablanca who looked and dressed like he did? She couldn't remember. There was definitely one in some old movie they always showed on TCM.

Screw it. He could brood some other time. She stood and walked over to where he was sitting.

Philippe looked up at her and frowned.

"Mind if I sit here?"

He raised an eyebrow but indicated the empty seat beside him, as if granting permission.

"Look, I really want to see what you're doing here," she whispered. She couldn't bring herself to speak out loud: the fear that John would hear and think she was being disloyal was too strong.

Philippe smiled. "You wouldn't get to see much. Just a man packing the things he can't bear to leave behind." He said it with sadness that seemed too strong to bear.

"Surely you have time for a small demonstration. Then I'll go back to San Diego and wait for your call. But I can't bear the suspense."

"There's not much you wouldn't have seen. I work with the same tools as the people working on gene-specific therapies do. I even use a CRISPR machine."

"But the theory, the combinations.... You're years ahead of the gene therapy crowd."

"Not really. I just went down a different path."

"A path I find more interesting."

He shook his head. "You'll have to be patient."

Suddenly, a loud crack sounded from the corridor and footsteps pounded past the door to the dining room. Philippe looked up sharply. He stood and spoke to his two servants in Spanish. Then he headed for the door.

Without thinking about it, driven by curiosity, she followed.

One of the servants, stationed at the door, tried to stop her, but Philippe spoke to him and he let her through. The second man was in the corridor, an evil-looking pistol in his hand.

It was a surreal feeling, like playing the lead in a horror film. It checked all the boxes: a dark corridor, a guy with a gun, and a cautious walk into unknown danger. She looked behind her to see that the second of Philippe's guards had pulled his own gun out of concealment and was standing over the rest of the group, all pretense of mere hospitality gone.

They walked stealthily down the hallway. Up ahead, the figure of a man, standing dead-still and looking down at something on the floor, could be seen. In the dim light, Cora recognized Max, the leader of the former guerillas. Their guard approached cautiously until he reached him, then beckoned for Philippe and Cora to approach.

On the floor at the man's feet, one of the fish-men lay, obviously dead of a gunshot wound to the upper chest. Black blood oozed onto the carpet, a viscous goo that didn't run down the slope of the tunnel as one would expect, but pooled around the creature's head.

If there was any doubt about what creatures had gone into its creation, the smell dispelled them. The thing reeked like an unwashed fishing boat. But there was more. The general shape of the body reminded her of a gorilla, but a little taller and slimmer. The shape of the cranium… perhaps a chimp, perhaps that of a smaller monkey, but scaled up.

But she was disturbed by the whole. The combination shouted 'human' to her… Had the Frenchman used human genes for this or had he combined other traits, suitably modified, to give the *impression* of humanity? If he had, and anyone got wind of it, a firestorm would ensue. Even if he hadn't, everyone would assume he had… just looking at the thing gave her the willies.

In fact, she had the same sensation she'd gotten recently when faced with a humanoid robot that looked too much like a real person for her comfort. Uncanny Valley is what the designers had called it.

She shuddered and turned her attention back to Max. He was unarmed, which made the tableau much more mysterious. How had this creature died? Had one of Max's guerillas shot it? If so, where was he now?

"What happened here?" Philippe said.

"Brown," Max replied in a daze and Cora jumped at the name. "Brown shot the creature."

"Who is Brown? One of your men?"

"No. Not one of my men. An American." His eyes focused on Philippe and he suddenly grinned, the grin of a man barely holding to sanity. "He doesn't like you at all."

"I don't care whether he likes me or not. Why did you bring this thing inside?"

Now Max let out the madness in a single, overly-intense burst of laughter. When he stopped, he seemed to have calmed down. "We didn't bring it inside. They were already inside."

Two doors down, another of the fish creatures appeared in the hall. In its mouth was something that looked like a human forearm. Cora suddenly wondered where the female servant was, the one who'd been responsible for bringing them lunch.

She hadn't seen her for a long time.

CHAPTER 16

Jean Fernand Gounon ordered the helicopter to hover. He knew nothing about another black helicopter that had hovered over the same clearing only a few months before. All he knew was that he was hanging from a black NH90 in the middle of the Panamanian rainforest, just a few hundred meters from the coast, and that if anyone saw them, there would be a nice little international incident to write a report on.

He hated writing reports.

"Hurry, you misbegotten bastards. You don't get paid by the hour, so there's no need to take your time like union mechanics."

His men paid no attention to his words. They were used to being gently cajoled through their daily routines. And they all knew Gounon hadn't shot anyone for being too slow. Not yet, anyway.

Listening or not, they moved quickly, efficiently, and he watched them with pride. He'd trained them up from millennials who could barely survive a few insults or random undeserved punishments without crying and asking for a safe space into men their families could be proud of. Hard men who would follow orders and mete out death when the occasion called for it. Yes, he'd done a good job with this batch.

As soon as they hit the scraggly undergrowth of the jungle clearing, they scattered into the forest. Gounon counted. When the fifth man was down, it was his turn.

Just like a drill. The rope felt like part of his hand, and he landed softly. Even before he'd taken his first step towards the trees, the cord was already being hoisted up so the helicopter could fly back to the converted freighter it had taken off from and pretend it had never been anywhere near the soil of a sovereign country it wasn't supposed to be flying over.

But that was no longer his problem.

He gathered his troops together, counted heads and surveyed the landscape. Nothing seemed amiss. In fact, the clearing was emptier than he'd expected. Maybe the inhabitants had hidden when they heard the chopper.

Or maybe not. He could see a house and a large shed from where he stood. The house was small and abutted against a decent-sized hill, while the shed was big enough to store vehicles or a small plane or two.

In other words, it was exactly what the satellite imagery had said they would find.

"Claude, take Victor and Marc and investigate the big shed over there. Be careful and report back to me every fifteen minutes."

"What if we run into something?"

"Then call me immediately. We're not under radio silence here."

"Firing protocol?"

"Anyone who has a weapon and looks like they want to use it is fair game. Anyone else, take down and tie up." They had enough cable ties with them to wrap up a regiment, although, from the looks of things, there was almost nobody around.

Claude nodded and took his troops off through the jungle in the direction of the shed. They would only cross the open ground when they were ready to enter the structure.

He supposed that would make very little difference. Anyone monitoring the clearing would not have missed a largish helicopter disgorging half a dozen guys in black.

"All right, listen up," he told the two men with him. "We're taking the house. I chose to lead you in there myself because the door is open. I absolutely hate the fact that the door is open. People with secrets keep their doors shut, and an open door means that something is either very wrong or their security is sloppy." He looked at the grim faces listening to his every word. "If their security is sloppy, that means that things will be easy for us, and we'll be back on board in time for our afternoon tea."

The men remained silent. They knew he wasn't done. "Things are *never* easy for us. They don't deploy us for the easy ones. We won't be back on board for tea. We'll probably be dead, killed by something we weren't briefed on. That's the way it always is. I've been killed every single time I've had to deploy, so don't go dreaming about surviving this one."

This time, they smiled a bit.

"I see you don't believe me," he sighed dramatically. "All right, have it your own way, but don't come crying to me when you get killed." He paused and nodded. "Follow me and be careful."

They quickly crossed the open space and studied the door. No tripwires, no pressure plates as far as he could see. Just an open door leading into a surprisingly modern interior with a couple of doors leading off the hall and another one at the end.

That one was also open.

He motioned the man behind him to advance and check the room to the right, and the other soldier to check the door to the left. Those rooms were immediately reported clear, and they covered him—one on each side—as he advanced to the open door at the end of the hall, carefully checking this one for traps as well. If he'd been defending this place against an assault, this is where he would have set any traps, hoping that the invaders, failing to find anything deadly in the first two rooms, would become complacent.

But this one was also clear, and it led into a dimly-lit hall.

A dimly-lit hall with light blue carpeting.

This was not at all what he expected. Dank tunnels dug into the ground? Certainly. But a long, carpeted corridor that reminded him of the Novotel in Lyon? No way.

This was getting surreal.

"What the hell?"

He wasn't sure which of his men said it, but it echoed his own thoughts so precisely that he had to smile.

"This way, guys. It's always better to be killed in comfort, don't you think?"

They pressed forward.

***

The wall of screens showed every nook and cranny of the complex. Even with twenty-four screens working at once, they still had to rotate the image every few seconds to cope with the feed from the numberless cameras. Hallways, empty rooms, the outside of the complex, bedrooms, even bathrooms were being monitored. The camera in the dining room showed the servant they'd just parted ways with escorting Max into the room and closing the door behind them.

Cora watched Philippe's face as their host watched the screens. He observed grimly, white knuckles wrapped tightly around his cane, as men in black military garb came down the rope and disappeared into the trees.

"So that's how it is," he said. "They'll find that I'm not such an easy target this time."

"Are you going to run?" she asked.

Philippe turned to her, startled like a man who had forgotten he wasn't alone. He got hold of himself quickly. "No." Then he smiled. "Well, yes, in the end I'll have to run. It's inevitable. But not yet. Would you do me the favor of pressing that switch over there, the one that says *porte de laboratoire*?"

She was suddenly afraid. "Why, what does it do?"

He smiled. "Nothing very spectacular, I'm afraid. It simply brings a foot of concrete and steel down over the door to this section of the complex. It won't stop them forever, but they'll have to bring in a demolition expert to get through."

"Oh," she replied, suddenly feeling silly. "I'm sorry about that." She toggled the switch and was immediately rewarded with a soft whine ending in a heavy clump as, she assumed, the door locked into place. "What about us? Can we get out?"

"Of course. There's an escape tunnel… sadly not very comfortable, but serviceable enough, that leads to a hidden exit nearly four hundred meters away."

Cora wondered at that. The complex was a maze of doors and passages. Even this place, the security center, had been behind two hidden doors and one glass door with a combination keypad for access. Just finding the corridors was a puzzle if you didn't know where they were.

Philippe looked her up and down. "You have two choices, and I want you to think about it carefully before answering me. The first choice is that I can show you where the escape tunnel is, and you can make a run for it. The second is for you to accompany me into the lab and help me create something the world has never seen before."

"Something…"

"A new combination of genes. Something that can take care of the dragons outside…" he nodded contemptuously towards the screens. "And of them, too. Understand that I won't let you hinder me. If you come, you will help, and be equally responsible for what happens next."

She swallowed. Something that could *take care* of the dragons? Something bigger? Toothier? Meaner? She couldn't imagine what that might even mean. What was this madman thinking of loosing on the world?

Cora knew she should run. Four hundred meters wasn't very far. She probably wouldn't be completely safe, especially considering that the creatures she'd seen were all traversing the forest without any particular difficulty, but at least the escape corridor would remove her from the immediate epicenter of the craziness. She could try to make her way down to the coast, and then along the beach. Maybe whoever sent the guys in black would see her and save her. She assumed that anyone working against Philippe was on the side of law and order.

Hell, if Brown was to be believed—and he'd played absolutely straight with them as far as she could tell—the troops in the jungle out there were probably from the French government. Though the French had a bit of a reputation for acting superior and unpleasant, they were also a civilized nation and an ally of the United States. She could expect to be treated well.

Against that, she would become an accomplice, an accessory. To what? She didn't know, and only suspected that it would be massively destructive.

The problem was not knowing. She'd never been any good at that. The need to learn more and more every day had dominated her life ever since childhood. She literally couldn't recall a time when she'd knowingly walked away from the answer to one of life's questions.

Even though she knew it was a huge mistake, she wasn't about to start now.

"I'm in."

Philippe studied her for a long time, apparently attempting to see into her soul. Finally, he sighed. "All right. Come with me."

He stood shakily, his bad leg obviously causing him pain, and led her to another glass door. He stood before it for an instant, one hand on the transparent panel. Finally, he spoke quietly. "I'm going to miss this place. I didn't live here very long, but I feel that it will always be the place where my work matured."

When the door slid open to reveal another door, Cora understood why. Pressure-controlled chambers and a magnificently equipped lab that held a lot of things she recognized—the CRISPR facility in one corner looked identical to the one the genetics lab had fought for a year to get approved by the university board in San Diego—plus a bunch of big vat-like machines surrounded by tubes and pipes. In any normal lab, the pipes would have been labeled, marked with different colors in the case where they might be hot or cold. But here, she found herself backtracking each pipe to try to see where it came from, and what it might be carrying. It was one thing to stumble over a tube carrying water at room temperature, quite another to trip on a pipe full of liquid nitrogen.

But every tube disappeared into the warren that ran along the roof and through several holes in the wall. Only Philippe knew what was being pumped in and out.

Which made sense. If she were ever to build a lab for her own use, in which no university or institution held any stake, it would likely resemble this one in philosophy, if not necessarily in its exact configuration—she wasn't a geneticist after all. But it was the dream: a lab in which you could build exactly what you wanted, where you wanted it, without the 'helpful' input of a committee and norms and regulations be damned. Philippe obviously had the money to make that dream a reality.

The French scientist opened a cupboard on the wall and pulled out a sheaf of paper which he carefully but quickly leafed through before pulling two sheets full of drawings.

"Here we go." He passed the sheets to Cora.

She glanced down at them, not paying any particular attention, and not wanting to miss what Philippe would do next, but as soon as she looked up, some of what she'd seen registered and she looked back down.

No, she thought. *He can't be serious.*

The thing on the sheet looked like the cross between a spider and the dragons outside... except that this one had pincers like a scorpion. A human figure was drawn beside it for scale. It reached about halfway up the thing's torso.

When she looked up again, Philippe was watching her. He was smiling that half-smile that seemed permanently welded to his face. "Impressive, isn't she?"

"Sh- She?" Cora stammered.

"Oh, yes. That's the female of the species. The spider I used to design this one has a very small male." He tsk-ed and shook his head. "Not suitable at all for what we need."

Cora realized that he was completely mad.

"Of course," Philippe continued, "you can probably tell that I was not having a good day when I designed that one. I was angry and in severe pain from my leg. They broke it in three places, you know. So I designed that to deal with my own demons. I never expected it to work in a lab setting." He gestured towards the apparatus around them. "But when I went to test it, it turned out that the grafts were viable after all, with a few suitable modifications—you can see the corrections there, in red ink—so I kept the design as a curiosity." His smile broadened, creasing the skin around his eyes. "It's a good thing I did, isn't it?"

"I don't understand. How will releasing even more monsters make things better? We'll just have more of them to fight."

"Ah. I thought you'd understood. This one isn't just another monster. The outward appearance might be ferocious, but it's not a dumb beast. This one has intelligence. Real intelligence. The brain in here," he tapped the round, spider-looking head segment, "is completely human."

Cora swallowed, struck dumb by the man's audacity. Philippe appeared not to notice. He was rubbing his hands together in anticipation. "Well, you wanted to see how it was done. Now is your chance."

Cora watched. Despite years of laboratory experience, she half-expected Philippe to graft pieces of different creatures together and then scale them up using some kind of mad scientist enlarger ray, but reality, as always, was much more prosaic.

The Frenchman walked up to a terminal, hummed impatiently as it booted up and opened what looked to be a database program from the 1990s: a grey background with white boxes for text. Painstakingly, referring to his notes, Philippe began filling in information. Cora noted that once the first field was completed, the rest auto-filled. Philippe read over each of the fully created records—often deleting several items—before hitting enter.

Each record apparently corresponded to certain gene strings from different organisms, and the modifications Philippe was making would remove certain combinations from the finished product.

It took him an hour, an hour during which Cora stood beside him, watching enthralled. "Now the fun starts," he said as soon as he finished typing.

He walked to a large container-like box at one end of the room. It, like most of the equipment, was painted a creamy off-white and immediately began whirring and clicking to itself. "Look here," Philippe said.

He indicated a round porthole about eight inches in diameter set into the side of the box. Within, a small robotic arm was delicately grasping test tubes from a rotating rack at the far side of the enclosure and placing them into a small centrifuge which spun them for a few seconds before another arm opened them and deposited them into a second enclosure she couldn't see into. The operation was repeated six times.

"Now comes the delicate part."

Philippe moved to the opposite end of the enclosure and pulled out a shallow tray—the tray the robot had just filled—which he then inserted into another machine, one covered with wires.

"The DNA will be sequenced by that one and then injected into a viable egg—we'll be using an emptied out crocodile egg for this one—by that machine over there."

"Shouldn't you be using the CRISPR for that?"

"Oh, no. This needs to be done automatically and on a larger scale than CRISPR can manage. I use the regular machine for more simple grafts, or for preliminary stages."

Cora nodded. It made sense: CRISPR's limitations had been the basis of her surprise at what Philippe had been able to achieve thus far.

"All right. Now all we can do is wait."

"How long? Even reptiles have a gestation period of a couple of months."

Philippe laughed and pointed to one of the large cylindrical machines that dominated the room. "Not in the least. That is an accelerated growth apparatus... and it works surprisingly well. Although I will admit that I always prefer to let nature take its course once I've done my part."

"No. Impossible."

Philippe just chuckled and ambled back to the security room, leaving Cora watching the machine. She followed him into the dim, monitor-lit chamber.

"Look there," she said, pointing at one monitor. Flashes of light had drawn her attention to the screen showing the interior of the animal shed.

Two of the men in black uniforms were firing their assault rifles at the largest of Philippe's dragons. A third of the assailants was on the floor. He wasn't moving.

Once again, Philippe's grip tightened on his cane as he watched his creation under fire.

The dragon recoiled under the onslaught, but then it lunged forward, catching the men by surprise. It managed to knock them both down with the movement and then, to Cora's shock, stomped on the nearest one's head with all its weight.

Cora estimated that it must have weighed about as much as a bus.

The final French soldier was trying to crawl away, one leg dragging behind him, but he never really had a chance. Mercifully, the dragon blocked the camera as it bore down on the man... but it wasn't hard to imagine what those huge jaws and teeth would do to human flesh.

Cora looked away. Her gaze fell on Philippe, to whose face the mocking half-smile had returned.

"Well, that's three less of them to worry about," he said.

CHAPTER 17

Something pounded on the door and the scattered groups huddled together amongst themselves, never getting closer to the rest of the people in the room, as if everyone was a threat except for the people they'd chosen to sit next to. The beating consisted of a single deep thud followed by scratching and then another thump. No demands to open the door, no communication at all, just a mindless assault on an armored doorway.

The two guards stood in front of the entrance, guns drawn. The pretense that these were civilized house servants had been discarded, and their role had been transformed: they were the thin line between the people inside that room and the ravening, genetically modified monstrosities on the other side. They'd magically gone from jailers to protectors. Suddenly, they were the good guys.

The young Colombian woman—Esmeralda, John remembered—clung to him. She was so frightened that she'd left the infant in his care for the past few minutes without taking him back to check on him.

"It will be all right," he said to her in the most soothing voice he could muster, all the while wondering who'd elected him to position of knight in shining armor. A quick look around the room showed that there were no other candidates. Gaar and Amber were still locked in some secret world of their own, separated from everyone else in the room by dint of their generation and their shared experience. The other Colombians—only three of them remained, which didn't really cause John much in the way of sadness—sat together, but the leader seemed somehow separate from the other two. The remaining guerilla woman, older and somehow much more cynical-looking than Esmeralda, glared daggers at Max, whose mind seemed to be elsewhere.

And Cora… Cora had disappeared with their host to God knew where, leaving him and their surviving students to their fate. Surviving students. He couldn't believe he had to say that. Still, considering how the supposedly armed and dangerous guerillas were faring, he supposed they should be thankful to have had limited losses.

He stroked Esmeralda's hair and wished he spoke Spanish. Nevertheless, though it was obvious she didn't understand a word he was saying, it was equally clear that his voice was a balm. She was all the better for his presence.

He disengaged himself gently and handed the little boy back to Esmeralda. He still hadn't been able to learn the infant's name. He'd pointed at himself and said his own name, and then pointed to her and repeated hers, and then pointed to the baby. She'd just smiled and shaken her head. Perhaps the child hadn't been named yet. He tried to remember whether that was common among rural Colombians, but he had no clue. He didn't think so.

Free of Esmeralda's arms, he approached the guards. "What's the plan? What did Philippe tell you to do?"

They looked at him blankly and shook their heads.

Just then, something slammed into the door and dust fell from the ceiling. But the door didn't buckle or even vibrate too much—they might not be comfortable waiting in that dining room, but they would be safe for quite a while.

John shrugged and returned to his seat. There was nothing else he could do.

***

Max sat numbly. Emilio couldn't be dead. He was indestructible, the spirit of revolution. Immortal.

He was the student talking socialism in the Vienna café at the end of the 19th century. He was the shirtless worker leading a Bolshevik charge in 1917. He was the long-haired hippie in the crowd at Woodstock, and the equally long-haired Argentine rocker who disappeared, never to be seen again after a night playing at a bar in Buenos Aires in 1977. He was an archetype.

He was also the only friend Max had ever made in the Comando, the only man who'd ever understood him, understood the depth of his belief. Emilio forgave Max's weaknesses because, at the end of the day, they were exactly alike: both of them lived for the cause and, though both also knew, though the source of the finances that kept the Comando going was far from pure, that the ends most certainly justified the means. Like the rest of South America, Colombia suffered from an endemic case of social injustice, with the haves living lives of comfort that would have been the envy of any European or American… but the have-nots, a full seventy-five percent of the population, were left out of the rush of global progress, used by the system until they were used up and then discarded. Emilio was the only other member of his force who understood that one had to get one's hands dirty when cleaning a sewer. He'd been willing to do it.

And now he was gone.

He looked up to find Liliana's smoldering glare burning a hole in him.

"What?" he said.

"We're waiting for your leadership, o' great and noble Max Cipreyes."

He grunted. "Sometimes, you have to wait to see the cards you've been dealt. To understand the lay of the land."

She nodded and smiled. "Nah," she said, her voice dripping irony. "I don't think I'll do that. How about you go fuck yourself in a corner, and we'll forget the mistake that ever set you up as a leader of men. I'm not following you ever again."

Max looked over at Coca, but found nothing there, just a blank, expressionless stare and the hint of a shrug. *You're on your own here*, the man's body language said. *I'm just here for the popcorn.*

"That's stupid. I'm the only hope you have of ever being taken back in. If I say you deserted, they'll leave your dead body hanging from a tree in the forest for the carrion eaters."

"That's only if you ever make it back."

Max laughed. "Are you threatening me?"

She threw his laughter back in his face. "No. I'm just extrapolating from observed facts. At the rate you've managed to kill us so far, there's no way you'll survive. Once you run out of other troops to order to their deaths, you will simply make some imbecilic decision and get yourself killed. I wouldn't be surprised if you drowned in a shower."

He glared at her. "I should have known. As soon as I replaced you with Serena, you've been bitter and angry. This is just the culmination of that. Maybe the tribunal that hangs you will take it into account. I hope not, though. You were an awful person even before that. Barely good enough to pass the time until the commission sent us a better woman."

She sat back as if he'd slapped her and Coca suppressed a smirk. Max saw it, though. The man's loyalties were undecided. If Max could rout this upstart bitch, Coca would simply say that he'd been on Max's side all the time, and his silence during the exchange would argue on his behalf as well.

It wasn't the kind of loyalty he preferred. It certainly wasn't Emilio. But it would serve where none other existed.

Liliana got herself together and glared in his direction without speaking. He looked away, not wanting to allow her to think that he was concerned with anything she might be doing or thinking and held Coca's gaze.

"Pablo, I guess it's just you and me," he whispered. The Americans didn't speak Spanish, but the guards did, and he wasn't sure how they'd react if they overheard. Their master, after all, had expressly forbidden that he try to take the hostages back into custody. Twice. And then there was the matter of Esmeralda. Her case was more understandable, of course—the American was clearly good at taking care of infants, so it was natural that she'd be drawn to him in this hour of desperation—but they had to be careful about her as well. She might be stupid enough to translate what they were saying... if they let her overhear. "The important thing is to ensure that we come out of this with at least a few hostages. To do that, we'll need guns. I explored the entire complex last night." Max smirked at the way Liliana's head snapped up when he said that. "Unfortunately, I wasn't able to locate our weapons."

Coca regarded him without a readable expression. The man was still waiting, still playing the game wherein he would join the winning faction once it was obvious which one would win. He wouldn't commit himself before that.

"The other option is to jump the guards."

Liliana snorted. "You couldn't jump a blind, deaf old lady."

"Since you've already proven you can't be trusted, maybe you should stay out of the conversations of your betters. Actually, you should go join Esmeralda over there. Who knows, maybe you'll be good at taking care of babies."

Liliana didn't respond, but she didn't move either. Max supposed he would have to be content with that. He returned his attention to Coca. "I'm thinking up how we can get the guns away from those guys."

Coca broke his silence. "If we're going to pull a stunt like that, don't take all day to think about it. That door looks all right now, but if it does break at any point, I don't want to have to attack the two guys defending us."

"Good point." It always paid to compliment the troops on their perspicacity. It made them feel like they were part of the decision process. In this particular case, Coca actually was... without him, Max couldn't take the two men on by himself. It just wasn't possible.

Liliana was still watching him with undisguised contempt. She was excellent at that. Back when she'd been doing it to Serena, he hadn't cared—it had been flattering, in its way—but now, he could have killed her.

As he turned away again, a flash of light reflecting from something on the floor caught his attention. He bent down and retrieved a steak knife from the previous night's dinner.

He smiled. For the first time since the whole mess had started, things were coming together.

***

Gaar breathed out slowly, very much aware of the skin of Amber's warm shoulder against his own, and not wanting to make any sudden moves that might cause her to notice they were pressed together—and therefore to pull away.

She was still pale from their ordeal, from watching Stephane… But no, it was better not to dwell on that. The important thing was that Amber was recovering.

She'd begun to talk again, softly and slowly at first, but now more normally. At times, the challenging cadence of her husky voice returned to make his heart ache with desire.

"Well, I guess we can forget that Nobel Prize," he said, and immediately regretted his words as soon as they left his mouth. Why did he always have to say the wrong thing?

Instead of sending him to hell, though, Amber just chuckled ruefully, the first laugh of any kind he'd seen from her since the dragon attack. "Yeah," she replied. "But if we get out of this alive, we'll be much more famous than any Nobel Prize winner ever managed. Who knows, I might give up this whole science thing and run off to Hollywood."

Gaar's stomach gave a backflip at the words. Amber was already nearly out of reach for a guy like him. If she became an actress, she would be so far beyond his level that she would probably refuse to admit she even knew him. He imagined passing her on the street and stopping to say hello, only to be ignored as she brushed past with some leading man on her arm.

He shook his head. He was being ridiculous. Amber was just a woman, a human being like he was, with whom he had a ton in common. People all wanted the same thing, to be able to laugh and talk and feel the companionship of others. Sure, some were more physically attractive and some less… but that was a secondary consideration, and Amber was mature enough to know that.

"Yeah. I don't think Hollywood would want me, though." Again, why had he even said that?

But Amber laughed. "I don't know. They prefer famous people to people who can act… but if they decide they don't want us, that's their loss. We can always claim to have studied the things down here first-hand. The research schools will be all over us."

"Yeah, I guess."

"What's wrong?"

Now it was his turn to laugh, but he didn't. If he let the laughter out, he'd have to explain it… and the explanation would be something along the lines of: 'Well, we're here, in serious danger of losing our lives and getting eaten by genetically constructed monstrosities, and all I can think of is whether we'll ever see each other again when we get back.' Yeah, it wasn't the kind of thing he could tell any woman, much less Amber.

"Do you really have to ask?" he said instead.

"I guess not. That was a pretty dumb question, wasn't it?"

"No, no. That's not what I meant at all. You can ask whatever you want." And the awkwardness was back.

They sat in silence for a while. He wondered if she knew how he felt. He thought his bumbling must have made it extremely obvious… and wondered why she didn't just move away from him in disgust. He thought the pressure of her arm on his would disappear any moment, and tensed against it.

Wanting to look anywhere but at Amber, he watched the animals who'd kidnapped them. Three of them sat silently across the table from where he and Amber were. It actually gave him quite a bit of satisfaction to see these imbeciles brought low. He remembered how they'd strutted around, pretending to own the jungle. He remembered the leader's speech. It felt like a million years ago, back when the revolutionaries inspired fear and the man actually thought he could make a pass at Amber.

That made him smile in spite of everything. Right now, there was no one in the room more contemptible than Max. Without his gun, he was just a schoolyard bully who'd suddenly realized that everyone else was suddenly bigger and meaner than he was. He was nothing, nothing at all.

The woman with them stood up to stretch her legs and, as soon as her back was turned, Max leapt to his feet.

At first it looked to Gaar as if he'd punched the woman in the back. But then, when he pulled his hand away, Gaar realized it held a knife, the front half of it covered in blood.

The woman fell with a muffled whimper, a dark bloodstain already spreading on the back of her shirt.

Gaar's exclamation was much louder, an alarmed bark that emerged involuntarily from the depths of his being. It was one thing to be involved in a tragedy like the dragon attack, but something quite different to watch a man murder another person in cold blood. If he'd had any doubts about the guerillas' capacity to kill the hostages for their cause, here was proof that this man wouldn't hesitate to murder... not even when the victim was one of his own people.

Everyone turned to stare at Gaar and, from him, their eyes moved to where he was pointing: to the woman on the floor and the man with the bloodstained knife in his hand.

The guards turned as one and pointed their guns at the guerilla. The one nearest Gaar shouted something in harsh Spanish.

The revolutionary smiled and dropped the knife. He held his empty hands up for all to see.

The guards looked like they didn't know what to do next. They spoke rapidly, but made no move to apprehend the murderer or to tend to his victim.

Only John moved to the woman. With a glare for Max, he knelt beside her and turned her onto her back. He put his hand on her neck and his head on her chest. Then, with the careful movements caused by shock, he straightened and shook his head.

Then he stood and took a single step towards the guerilla. He hit the Colombian once, striking him across the jaw and snapping his head back. Max stumbled, but didn't fall, grinning at his assailant through blood-stained lips.

The guards still didn't move, but kept shouting and gesticulating with their pistols. Neither John nor Max paid them any heed. In fact, John was advancing, clearly intent on tearing the revolutionary a new one.

He never got the chance. A burst of gunfire from outside the door froze everyone in the room.

A man's voice came through the thick wood, shouting in French. No one responded.

John, however, acted again. He strode to the door and shouted in English. "We're in here! Who is this?"

"This is Jean Fernan Gounon of the French Commandos Marine. Open the door."

John tried the handle and the door swung open. It hadn't been locked, and Gaar shuddered, wondering what had been outside, unable to figure out a door on the latch.

"Thank you," a man in black clothing said. He was holding a rifle, bringing back memories of the assault when the guerillas had captured the expedition. "Now please come out with your hands visible. One by one. Monsiuer Philippe L'Espert first please."

"Philippe isn't here," John replied.

The man didn't seem pleased. "Where is he?"

"We don't know. But if you find him, I'll help you shoot him."

That got a smile as the soldier glanced down at his feet, where one of the fish-things lay immobile.

"All right. Come out now."

They filed out one by one, and the soldiers—Gaar realized there were three of them—ordered the group to stand against a wall after patting everyone down thoroughly but professionally. The two guards took one look at the unwavering black rifles trained on them and surrendered their guns without protest.

"All right," the leader said. "Who can tell me what the hell is going on here?" The man's English was excellent, with barely any accent.

Only John seemed capable of speech. "Your countryman's creations are loose. Luckily, they aren't good at doors."

"There's a big thing out there, too. We saw it as we came inside."

"Yes. More than one."

As if to prove his words, a sudden sound of thunder blasted down the hall, followed by one of the baby dragons, the ones that had gone outside for the first time that day, in the breakfast display that had ended so badly.

Gaar tensed, ready to die, but the creature simply rushed through the soldiers like a bowling ball, scattering people all over the place before continuing on its way.

The leader of the commandos picked himself off the ground and said something to his men in French. Once they convinced him they were all right, he turned to the rest of them.

"Is everyone okay?"

"Yeah," John replied, his head cocked. "But there's another one coming."

CHAPTER 18

John got to his feet slowly, shaking his head to clear the effects of the blow. As the first dragon passed, his first instinct had been to cover the girl and her baby with his body, pressing both tightly against the wall. The only thing that stuck out was his back, and that was what the creature had run into as it passed, because there wasn't enough room for everything in the hall. It had knocked him ass over appetite, about six yards down the carpeted tunnel.

He would ache in several places in the morning, but he was essentially all right, so he looked up to see Esmeralda.

She was right where he'd left her, still flat against the wall, clutching the softly mewling bundle that was her child. Both were untouched, and he breathed a sigh of relief.

As others ran deeper into the tunnel and called for him to join them, to get out of the next creature's way, John ignored them and went back to the young guerilla.

"I hope this works again," he said.

Wide eyes stared back at him uncomprehendingly, but she let him press her against the wall once more and braced himself for another bone-jarring impact, gritting his teeth against the pain he expected.

The impact never came. The dragon went through at full tilt, but he only felt the breath of air as it went past.

He silently thanked his lucky stars and, pulling away from the woman he'd been protecting, took her hand as he contemplated what they should do next. They couldn't continue down the hall. That was where the dragons had gone.

They could go back into the dining room. That was probably the safest option, but the thought of being locked in there, trapped without any way to move if the situation deteriorated, made him want to scream.

"Come on," he whispered, "this way."

They headed up the hall, in the direction they'd entered the house from. At one point, John almost panicked and ran: behind him, the thundering, train-like sound of the rushing monster had stopped. He could see its immobile bulk in the corridor.

It was trying to turn around. Obviously, its juvenile brain had finally realized that those things it had been knocking over like ninepins were edible... and now it would come back for them.

But the corridor's close confines proved a little too close for the monster and it roared in frustration before setting off the same way it had been moving once more. Good, let the soldiers and the guards deal with it. They were much better prepared for it.

The rank smell of rotting fish heralded the next discovery: one of the fish men on the floor, trampled in a pool of its own blood. They stepped gingerly around it.

A few meters further ahead, John saw the door to the kitchen. The smell of fish was so strong there that he was certain it had to be filled to overflowing with creatures, but when he looked around the open door, he saw none.

The kitchen was a war zone. Cupboards had been smashed open, drawers lay strewn on the ground alongside what had once been their contents.

The body of the woman who'd been serving them their meals for the past two days lay discarded and gnawed among the detritus. Esmeralda gasped when she saw the corpse, but said nothing. She simply hugged her baby tighter and watched John for more instructions.

John had no instructions to give. He was looking for anything he could use as a weapon. He studied the detritus on the floor before finally settling on a solid-looking meat cleaver and a long knife. Then they emerged from the kitchen and, after assuring themselves that the coast was clear, they continued their trek up the hall. About twenty meters away, a rectangle of light heralded the presence of a door to the outside world.

He thought about the bigger dragons that lurked out there and shuddered. But being inside was worse. At least out there, you could run; run for your life like the devil himself was behind you. You'd most likely die, but at least you wouldn't be caught in this rat's warren.

Besides, it looked like there were more of the creatures down here than out there. He'd take his chances with the dragons.

But when they reached the outer building, the little house that had seemed so out of character for the jungle setting when they'd first entered, and which now seemed so normal by comparison with the rest of the complex, he reconsidered. If he'd been alone, there would have been no doubt in his mind: the jungle beckoned, and he would die with his boots on, if it came to that.

But he wasn't alone. Far from it. He was responsible for a girl who couldn't have been more than seventeen or eighteen years old and, perhaps even more importantly, a helpless, innocent baby. He didn't know much about the ways of babies—he'd never married, and the occasional women he'd dated seemed to intuit from the first that he never would—and had successfully avoided his relatives until they were old enough to walk, so he wasn't certain how old this one might be. Since he couldn't ask its mother due to the language barrier, he decided on six months. It was too big and healthy to be a newborn, he thought.

Instead of rushing out the door like his body screamed to do, he stopped and led her into the bedroom. Esmeralda immediately sat on the bed, bared a breast and began to feed the child.

John felt the flush creep up his face and began to let himself out of the room, but the woman's voice stopped him. He turned to see her looking at him with a plaintive look on her face, and she repeated the word, followed by one of the few phrases in Spanish he knew from ordering food in San Diego: por favor. *Please.*

She was begging him to stay, not to leave her alone even for the sake of privacy.

So John remained in the room. He fiddled with the curtains until he found the mechanism for pulling them open and then he turned to look out.

A large eye with a vertical pupil stared back at him.

He nearly voided his bladder as he realized that the dragon was looking into the room. The big one. He desperately backpedaled towards the door as the monster slammed into the window with a huge crash.

The window held.

Confused, John looked around. The glass should have exploded inward with the massive impact, showering the interior with shrapnel, but it hadn't even cracked. Hell, the wall should have collapsed on them, but the house hadn't even shaken all that much.

The dragon appeared to be just as puzzled as he was. It experimentally bashed its head against the wall a couple more times—with the same result—before growling in frustration and walking off.

"The entire place must be armored," John explained out loud, more to hear himself say it than in any expectation of being understood. But even bulletproof windows should have broken under that kind of a hit. Or at least the frames... but apparently, whoever had built this place was afraid of getting nuked from orbit.

Esmeralda had looked up from feeding her baby with the first of the impacts, an expression of alarm on her face, but, seeing that John appeared to be calm, she returned to her son.

John sighed and sat on the bed an arm's length away from her, too shocked to worry about the impropriety of doing so. His heart beat as he thought about the eye, balefully looking in through the reinforced glass.

He would never laugh at the image of the Eye of Sauron from the *Lord of the Rings* ever again.

***

The first dragon knocked Max down. He saw people flying all over the place around him in the dim hall like some scene from a carpeted version of Dante's Inferno. But while the others groaned on the floor and gathered themselves back up, he pulled himself together more quickly.

The soldier who'd taken the guards' pistols happened to be standing right beside him when the creature charged through them and had taken a serious blow. He was groaning and trying to right himself, paying little attention to the gun he dropped.

Max grabbed it and hid it inside his shirt.

Then someone shouted that another one was coming, and the group, even the dazed soldier, took off down the hall. Max grabbed Coca as he passed and pulled them both into the dining room whose door was still open beside them. The second dragon ran harmlessly past.

"What are you doing?" Pablo Escobar asked him.

"I'm regaining the element of surprise," Max replied.

"You just separated us from the people with the guns," Coca retorted furiously. "Now we're going to become monster food."

Max felt the old anger flare in him. He wondered if this bastard had been sleeping with Liliana, if that was why he seemed to question everything his commander said. Was he secretly looking to avenge her execution, well-earned and legitimate as it was?

He took a couple of deep breaths and got hold of himself. He was jumping at shadows: Coca was just scared out of his wits. As the leader, it fell on Max to bring him back in line.

"Actually," he said, pulling the stolen pistol from the depths of his shirt, "we're the ones with the gun. And no one expects us to have one."

The shadow of a smile crossed Coca's face and he nodded. "I'm sorry. You're right."

"We'll come up behind them, let them get destroyed by the dragons and the other things in the complex... and then we'll rescue our hostages. If we play this right, and inform everyone about what happened here, we'll come out of this as heroes. The Comando will be on the front pages not only because we have a few hostages, but because we'll have been the ones to expose this sinister plot by the Americans and the Colombian government to fill the forest with dragons in order to drive us out. Can you imagine the outcry that will create?"

Coca looked dubious but held his peace.

"Trust me. World opinion is already against the Imperialists. This will be one of the final nails in the coffin."

"Whatever you say, Comrade." He turned towards the door, and then bent over to tie his shoelace. "I suppose we'd better get started before they get too far away."

Coca never called anyone 'comrade'. He felt it was for idiots who thought they were still living in the twentieth century and, furthermore, had never been shy to say it to everyone who would listen. It had obviously been said in mockery of his commanding officer and Max's finger itched on the trigger.

It would be so easy: the man had his back turned as he bent to see to the shoe. All Max would have to do was to raise the gun and put a slug into his head. Hopefully, the exit wound would tear away most of the little bastard's face.

But no. There was a time and a place for that kind of thing, and the time was when the person you were going to execute had outlived his usefulness. The place? Wherever there were witnesses to understand what could happen when one turned away from the chain of command and the beauty of socialist ideals.

"Let me go first," he told Coca. "I'll try to hold anything we find off. If they knock me over, run for the exit as fast as you can. At least we don't have anything behind us."

Coca nodded, surprised. Had the man expected to be sent forward, used as cannon fodder? He should know that a true leader's place was in front.

They made their way down the now-deserted hall. The good thing about pursuing a group through a tunnel was that there was no easy way to lose them.

It would be a different story once they entered the maze-like area behind the garage, though. Then, the terrain would work against them.

Of course, a couple of men would always be much quieter than a large group or a dragon. They wouldn't make as much noise, wouldn't need the corridors to be quite as ample.

That was how Brown had ambushed him in the first place: through stealth and treachery. Well, he would take a page from the American's book.

And then he found himself wondering where Brown might be… and whether, as the first person who'd run down this very hall, he had any idea of everything that was coming up behind him.

***

Brown was waiting in ambush, expecting the French to appear. They'd been a short helicopter ride away, after all.

When the first steps had echoed towards his hiding place behind one of the cars in the garage, he'd almost shown himself.

That would have been a bad, possibly even fatal, mistake. Six of the fish-men walked into view.

He wondered what Cora and John would have made of these things. They were shaped like humans, but the way they acted reminded John of a pack of dogs. They circled around anything interesting, and watched each other for cues on how they had to act. Strangely, though, there was no indication in the way they were built that dogs might have figured in their composition… but perhaps it was just the mind that held canine genetics.

Brown shuddered. Philippe's activities here had sounded cold and clinical during the briefings, but the reality was almost comically visceral.

They couldn't see him, and he hoped they didn't have an overly developed sense of smell. Shooting them all would make a lot of noise, and he preferred to avoid giving his position away—he would talk to the French, of course, but he didn't know if they were in the complex yet.

Muffled sounds reached him from elsewhere in the underground building. They arrived stripped of their identity, like ghostly echoes of great events. Was that a shout? It was hard to tell. That was probably a gunshot… but whose? The information he was receiving was too diffuse to decide upon.

The fish creatures moved past him and clustered around something that looked like an industrial drill. They pulled the cloth cover off it and began to shake it. The base clearly wasn't fixed to the floor, and the tall tool soon began to rock from one side to the other.

In the dim, reddish glow, it looked like a satanic ritual performed by demons. They danced as the totem swayed.

But they weren't dancing. They were just pulling mindlessly on something in much the way an animal will worry at a stuffed dog, just to see what would happen.

What happened was that they finally managed to overbalance the drill and it fell to the concrete floor with a deafening metallic clatter that echoed in the cavernous room for a long time.

With anguished howls, the interlopers fled from the garage through the door that led into the maze of hallways where Brown had spent his long night.

The next thing to enter the room looked like a scaled-down version of the dragon that had nearly killed Max and Brown when they left the house. It bowled through the door, skittered on the polished concrete and slammed into a sports car of some sort, leaving a serious dent in the vehicle's side. Then, without stopping to explore, it followed the fish-men through the second exit. This one, he saw, was small enough to be able to squeeze its shoulders through the frame.

A juvenile? Or had Philippe engineered a smaller and lighter breed suitable for hunting people down inside buildings? It seemed a little cold-blooded, out of sync with what he'd read about the man, but… sometimes, briefings were out of date. And sometimes they were just plain wrong.

Either way, he breathed a sigh of relief when it was gone. It was unlikely that the pistol would have had the stopping power to deal with something that big unless he got very lucky and hit it in both eyes.

Next, a gaggle of people rushed in. The two students who'd been hostages led the charge, followed by three soldiers in black uniforms— French commandos, no doubt—and Philippe's two male servants.

The soldiers gave the garage only a cursory glance as they too ran through. It almost looked as if they were running away from something— even as they were running towards a number of unfriendly creatures.

He decided not to show himself: a stressed and confused commando with an assault rifle was not a commando you wanted to reveal yourself to suddenly in a darkened room. That was a good way to obtain additional orifices.

The last man in line, the dark, small servant, stopped at the door and turned back. He hid behind one of the cars, a large truck-like thing.

Apparently, he knew what he was doing. Moments later, a second small dragon rushed through.

Brown wondered where everyone was going. Hard experience had taught him that the maze beyond that door only led to a gaggle of corridors and another door—locked with a code—that led outside. Not the best place to run from a dragon.

A few minutes passed with no further interruptions and Brown decided that, for the nonce, the excitement had passed.

Going quietly and keeping well out of sight, he crept towards the car where the servant had taken cover.

When the man came into view, he was watching the doors as if trying to decide which one led to safety.

He never got the chance. Brown placed the barrel of his pistol on the back of the man's head and whispered. "Don't move."

The man raised his hands and Brown frisked him, quickly, expertly. Surprisingly, he was unarmed.

With a hand on one shoulder, Brown guided his prisoner back into the deeper shadows where he'd been hiding.

When they were well-concealed, he turned the man around and placed the gun under his chin.

"Take me to Philippe," Brown said.

"No entiendo."

Brown pressed the gun harder and moved his face closer to the other man's, close enough to smell the stale sweat and to see the veins in his white, nervous eyes.

"Philippe," he insisted.

The other man got the message. He nodded frantically and said, "Sí, sí."

Brown smiled. "Good." He pushed him ahead, towards the door. "After you."

CHAPTER 19

Gaar stumbled and stopped. Amber, still grasping his arm, stopped with him.

"We're going around in circles," he said.

"How can you tell?"

"I have an excellent sense of direction."

She looked into his face in the soft light and simply nodded. No doubt, no challenge, just the trust that he was right.

"So what do we do about it?" she said.

Gaar, buoyed by the confidence she showed in his judgement, walked to the nearest of the troops. "We're going in circles," he said.

The man sighed. "You might be right. Our GPS is no use this deep."

"You don't have gyroscope navigation?"

That earned him a blank look.

"Listen," Gaar continued, "I've always had a great sense of direction. I can help us to go straight, or at least not to backtrack."

"Jean Fernand," the guy said. Another of the soldiers approached. They conversed in French and the second soldier turned to Gaar.

"You can lead us?"

"I can avoid going around in circles. I don't know where any of these passages lead, but we'll be going in a different direction."

"You don't know where Philippe is?"

"No, but I won't get lost."

"That's good enough for me. Come on."

They walked forward. "Now let's turn right. If we go straight, we'll be back in the corridor we already saw."

They walked a few meters. "What now?"

"Left."

They turned and a dragon charged at them.

Gaar tried to protect Amber, to help her find cover, but she was already moving. She ducked back around the corner into the corridor they'd come from, and sprinted towards the next intersection, dragging Gaar along for the ride.

"Thanks," he whispered.

"Shh," Amber replied. She stuck her head out for a quick visual check. "There's nothing coming. Maybe it just ran across. What do you think, should we go have a look?"

"What?"

"Not for the dragon, silly, for the guys with the guns. I feel a lot safer with some firepower on our side."

Gaar nodded. He wasn't completely certain what she was proposing that they do, but still let himself be guided by the tug of her arm on his. They returned to the intersection only to find it empty.

"Which way do you think they went?" she asked.

The raucous sound of machine-gun fire exploded to their left, just around another corner. The combatants were hidden from sight, but not so the muzzle flash from their rifles, which flashed like lightning in the dark quarters.

The dragon roared and ran back the way it came, thankfully ignoring them in the process.

Gaar saw a limp human form dangling from its jaws and his stomach turned.

Now even the babies, apparently, had gotten a taste for human meat.

The soldiers followed. "Stay where you are," the first one to reach them ordered.

Gaar and Amber watched them clear the area, establish as much of a perimeter as they could with three men, and then relax. Obviously, the dragon's victim had been Philippe's servant. The soldier's commanding officer, Jean Fernand, walked up. "Glad you're all right," he said. He rummaged inside a bag at his waist and pulled out a pistol. "Take this. It belonged to one of the guards."

"I don't know how to shoot this," Gaar replied.

"Give me that." Amber took the gun from him and did a couple of things with it which looked like stuff that people did on television, but which meant nothing to Gaar. "It's loaded."

"Of course," the soldier replied.

Amber nodded. "Thank you."

"We need as many shooters as possible." He unbuttoned the holster on his leg and turned to Gaar, proffering a second weapon. "Are you sure you can't use one?"

"No. I've never even held a gun in my life. I'd probably kill one of you if I tried to shoot it. Or me. No thanks."

"Suit yourself. Now, which way?"

The man's matter-of-factness after someone had just died on his watch shocked Gaar, but he didn't want to show any weakness in front of Amber. He tried to match the soldier's unconcerned tone. "There. The way we were going."

"That's where the dragon went."

"Then shoot it. We won't get anywhere if we keep walking through the same corridors."

"All right." He gestured to one of his men and they started walking again, much more cautiously. The man in front would look around each intersection quickly before signaling for the rest of the group to join him. The man at the back would hang back where he could actually see the entire intersection behind them and would only pull forward once the group ahead had advanced.

Gaar liked the way that worked. If something came up behind them, they would have plenty of time to prepare a response.

A few dozen meters further ahead, the man on point stopped and held up two fingers. Jean Fernand jogged up and joined him. He returned to Gaar and Amber.

"There are two of the grey ones, the ones that look like a fish, up ahead. Do we absolutely have to go that way?"

"Not necessarily. We can take the right turn on the last intersection we passed, and then hopefully go parallel. If that works, we should be able to bypass them."

They walked where Gaar had indicated and then sent the point man ahead again. The soldier looked around. "Why would anyone build this?" he said.

"To escape the police. They told us this one was built by a Colombian who sold cocaine in the 1980s. He got killed back in Colombia and this complex became the property of the Panamanian government. They maintained it just the way it was when the drug runners used it until they sold the whole thing to Philippe a couple of years go. This maze was meant to help the former occupants escape if the cops or one of their competitors came down on them in force. They knew the way through these corridors... the police wouldn't."

The soldier grunted. "It's a pain in the ass."

They walked for another thirty seconds.

The man in the rear suddenly ran up to them, silently. He exchanged information with his commander in rapid-fire French.

"They're behind us. The fish-men," Jean Fernand said. "Let's keep moving."

The passageway turned right ahead of them, and then turned left.

And ended in a brick wall, rough-hewn and looking out of place in the well-built tunnel, but no less solid for that.

The things behind them howled and charged.

***

"According to the American I saw earlier," Max told Coca, "there's an exit at the end of these corridors. That's likely where the soldiers are taking the students."

"Unfortunately, there's at least one dragon between them and us."

"Yes. But once outside, that isn't such a huge problem. Now that we know what we're up against, we just need to be certain that we select a different direction than the creatures. They live here, and sleep in the pens at night, so if we manage to get far away, we can circle back towards the coast without coming near here. Then, we can rendezvous with our people at the border."

"I've always admired your optimism."

"It's not optimism. Intelligent planning has its rewards."

Coca laughed, a short, bitter bark. "If you'd grown up where I did, you'd know that the more thoroughly and carefully you plan, the more likely it is that your newly-installed toilet will start shooting out brown water."

They moved through the maze in silence. Max, having taken to heart the lesson of the door that led into the maze, ran his hands across each wall, searching for the telltale signs that there might be a hidden passage in one of the walls. Finally, his fingers encountered a line which had no reason to be there. "Wait," he said.

They stopped, and applied pressure to the panel in several places. Though it looked like any other piece of corridor, the outline of the door was right there—once you knew it was there, it became obvious. Just when they were about to give up and conclude that it was locked from the other side, a click, loud in the dim silence, announced that the door had opened.

They pulled it towards them and found themselves facing a pitch-dark space in the wall.

"We need a light," Max said.

"What for? Is this an exit?"

"Probably not."

As their eyes grew accustomed to the deeper darkness, shapes began to reveal themselves. Piled blocks, stacked on pallets. Max felt excitement growing in his bowels. He stepped forward and tried to pull a brick off the top, but the entire thing was wrapped in cellophane. "Give me a hand with this."

Between them, they pulled the plastic off the pallet. It was hard going until Coca found a gap where he could push a finger into the plastic. It gave way with an audible pop and a cloud of dust.

After that, they managed to tear it away, covering themselves with the dirt that lay on top of it. Max suspected that the room hadn't been disturbed in decades.

They extracted a brick from the top row, an oblong about the size and shape of a regular construction brick albeit dust-colored instead of red. In slightly better light of the hall, they placed it on the floor and observed it. Like the pallet it had come from, it too, was wrapped in cellophane.

"What is it?" Coca asked after rubbing accumulated dust from the plastic wrapper to reveal that the contents were a light, probably white shade.

Max nearly laughed in his face. They were in an underground tunnel complex built by a drug lord in the 1980s, and this imbecile couldn't guess what might be wrapped in cellophane in the basement.

"Have a look." With a grunt, Max broke the brick in half and the contents, a fine white powder fell to the floor in an untidy cone.

Coca stared at the mess for a couple of seconds before he understood. "Cocaine!"

"Full points, genius."

"But… this is refined. It's not what we always see."

The jungle where they operated was full of people who produced coca leaves and coca paste, but the places where it was turned into the powder whose value—once it reached the streets of the United States—was astronomical, were hidden and secret. Max suspected that the Comando intentionally kept all but a tiny number of extremely trusted units as far away from the centers of production as possible.

He'd heard rumors, of course. They all had. That the cocaine was refined in ranches in the north. That it was processed in the mountains and then crossed Colombia overland to ship in submarines. That it was actually exported via Venezuela, whose unstable government needed to bring revenue in from anywhere it could.

The truth was that the revolutionaries saw very little of the white gold that paid for their activity, and they both stood immobile, watching untold wealth spill onto the floor.

Finally, Coca reacted. "Wait. Don't spill this. We could finance our entire war with that pallet."

Max snorted. "What makes you think it's still good? It's been stuck in here for thirty years."

"Who cares? You think the buyers will be able to tell the difference?"

Max was shocked. "You might kill them all."

"So what? The people who use this stuff are all rich Americans. I can live with a few of them on my conscience. Hell, you would probably have asked me to shoot the hostages after a few days, anyway. Would you have been surprised if I obeyed? Of course not. Those people are the enemy. And I don't think you, who'd kill one of our own over a lover's quarrel, would be too worried about doing the same for the enemy."

He was right, of course. The enormous pile of cocaine in this room was a treasure that could finance several revolutions. While their backers were stingy with funds, sending through just enough to keep the Comando operational while promising enough to ensure its obedience, this would represent the movement's independence from criminals. They could finally achieve Max's dream of being a purely political force.

They walked back into the tiny room, Max's head racing with plans for how to extricate the newfound bounty. If they'd still had their troops, splitting this load into several packs would have proved easy to do... but the men were dead, killed by stuff that was still out there, and stuff they'd have to deal with.

But the stakes had just increased for them a millionfold. It was one thing to need the hostages to drive world opinion their way... quite another to be able to ignore world opinion completely and use a windfall to gear up for an assault on Bogotá.

He bent to see just how many packages the pallet contained, in order to try to calculate the weight involved.

That movement saved his life.

A line of fire, pain as intense as anything he'd ever felt, ran up his back and he dove forward to get away from it, rolling over the pallet and landing on the other side.

He stood painfully, blood seeping into his clothes to see Coca's silhouette outlined against the slightly brighter light of the hall. In his hands, he held a knife.

Max pulled the gun out of his waistband. "What the fuck was that?" he said.

"No less than you deserved, you piece of shit." The dark shadow began to make its way around the pallet. "And this is for Liliana."

Surprise would have won the day if Coca hadn't tripped over some unseen obstacle in the darkness. He landed on the pallet with a grunt and Max reacted. He managed to tear the gun out of his waistband, pressed it to his subordinate's head and pulled the trigger.

The retort echoed in the tiny room, deafening Max. Blood sprayed everywhere: he felt it on his hands, on his arms, and on his face. Mostly, it sloshed all over the pile of drugs.

He pushed the hunk of meat that had been Coca off the pallet and tried to remove the blood with his hand. It made little difference other than to spread the stain around, so he stopped to inspect the cellophane. Satisfied that nothing would get through and damage the precious contents, he moved back out into the hallway, gun still in his hand and ears still ringing from the shot.

That was when he realized he wasn't alone. One of the dragons had just turned the corner and was eyeing him much as a mouse observes a small rodent.

Max ran.

***

The fish-men charged.

Gaar couldn't believe his eyes. Why would they attack a group of armed men? Hadn't they learned anything? There was an old saying that man was the only animal that tripped over the same stone twice, but these dudes were right up there with the dumbest of the undergrads Gaar had ever seen, the ones who populated the emergency rooms on Sunday mornings after the postgame kegger.

The commander of the French soldiers took two steps forward and dropped each of the creatures with a single bullet to the middle of the forehead. Gaar thought he remembered reading that you weren't supposed to shoot mobile enemies in the head in case you missed, and that aiming for the body was much better, but there appeared to be little chance of this man missing from that distance.

"All right," he commanded when the echoes died down. "Let's check out this wall and head back the way we came if it's as solid as it looks."

Two of the soldiers began tapping the bricks with the handles of their knives, listening for the sound of a hollow space behind and shaking their heads as each tap resulted in nothing.

So their attention was elsewhere when the dragon appeared.

It was moving so fast that Gaar didn't have time to react. He heard the sound of the Frenchman's rifle, then a roar and then the crash of a heavy body into the wall. He felt the rush of something massive through the air... and he saw nothing, because he was watching Amber.

Amber screamed. As soon as she saw the dragon, she panicked and ran back down the now-empty corridor behind it.

Gaar followed, yelling for her to stop.

At first, it seemed that it was hopeless, that Amber would outrun him in the first few yards and disappear into the maze.

But she hesitated at one intersection long enough for him to close the gap to just a few feet and then, when she stopped again, he grabbed her.

Amber screamed and went for the gun tucked into her waistband, and Gaar said: "Amber, stop. It's me. Gaar."

She kept struggling. Now all he could do was to hold her arm as she struggled to bring the weapon to bear.

"Stop, please, stop."

Amber ignored his pleas, and it soon became apparent that she was stronger than he was. The gun slipped from her waistband and came inexorably up to his face. He felt her forearm tense, about to squeeze the trigger when she blinked.

"Oh." She paused. "I'm sorry."

Her hand went limp and Gaar pulled the gun from her nerveless fingers and threw it down the hall, wanting to be as far away from that thing as humanly possible. He hugged her.

And suddenly she was crying into his chest. Great, heaving sobs that expressed all the anguish at everything that had happened to them, everything she'd seen, since they were taken hostage by the revolutionaries.

Gaar patted her on the back, unsure of what to do. He wanted to kiss her and tell her it would be all right... but he was pretty sure he'd be rebuffed. So he held her stiffly.

Finally, the sobbing stilled and Amber held her head up.

"We should try to get out of here," she whispered.

"Yeah. We haven't gone that way yet."

They walked. Once or twice, Gaar found himself turning around suddenly, certain that someone—or something—was creeping up behind them. But when he looked back, there was nothing there. He was sure he heard sounds, rustles, but again, nothing. Every time he turned it was to see an empty corridor.

"Do you hear that?" Amber said.

"What?"

"It's like heavy breathing."

"I don't hear it. Behind us?"

"No. Over there." She pointed to the corridor on their right.

"Then let's go this way," Gaar said, leading them to another hall they hadn't been around yet. The noises of gunfire and animal grunts which had followed them through the corridors when they ran from the scene of the battle had died down some minutes ago, but whether that was a good thing or bad, Gaar couldn't say. And he wasn't about to suggest going back: if the dragon had won the fight with the troops, he and Amber would be nothing more than a quick snack.

"What's that?"

It was a door, a door set into the side of the wall. A way out of the tunnels and into… well, they could think about that when they got it open. A piece of paper stuck above the keypad had four numbers written on it in blue ballpoint pen. Getting through would not be a problem.

Right now, anything was better than the endless twilight of the drug lord's dungeon.

CHAPTER 20

Brown advanced slowly, leading the former servant-cum-guard down the corridor in front of him. Being out in front would make the guy pause before giving their position away: anything that found them would eat him first.

At length, they came to a door in the hall, near the exit through the small cabin. It was one of several identical, unmarked exits. His guide paused and said something in Spanish which Brown interpreted as: "Philippe's in here."

"All right. Let's see."

What they found beyond the anonymous door was a glass partition. It took very little persuasion for the man to punch in the code that opened it up.

After that, things got interesting, but at least Brown was relatively certain that the man hadn't lied: Philippe had to be in there.

Unfortunately, 'in there' meant getting past a concrete barrier that had been lowered into his path. It was probably controlled electronically, which meant that, sooner or later, Brown would find a way in.

Unfortunately, he suspected it would be later rather than sooner, as there was no keypad to convince the guy to unlock. This door appeared to be part of the complex's security measures and it was clear that Philippe had locked them out intentionally.

Brown sighed. "You can go," he told the former servant. "But if you come back, I'll shoot you."

The man hesitated, either not understanding or reluctant to turn his back on the man with the gun. Brown gestured again. "Get out of here."

The man got the message and left through the open glass door and then the regular door beyond it. It wasn't the ideal solution, of course. The ideal solution would have been to incapacitate the man somehow. But Brown had nothing with which to tie him up and shooting him just seemed a bit too cold-blooded for his taste.

One thing was for certain, though: he would need to concentrate in order to get this door open, and having a man loyal to the guy you were trying to catch looking over your shoulder wasn't going to help him think.

Letting him wander the corridors wasn't ideal, either, but at least Brown could close the glass door behind him and, with access to the interior panel, change the access code. If the guy wanted to come back inside, he'd have to break the glass. That would give Brown a couple of seconds to defend himself.

That done, he got to work studying the concrete door.

He sighed. "This isn't going to be fun."

***

"Is that the famous Mr. Brown?" Philippe said.

Cora looked up at the monitor he was pointing at. The screen showed a man kneeling in front of what looked like a concrete door. She almost blurted out that yes, that was Brown, but then she remembered that Philippe wasn't aware she'd met that particular character in their little drama. Not wanting to risk an adverse reaction, she shrugged. "Could be. Who is this Brown, exactly?"

Philippe grunted. "I don't know. I only learned of his existence because that Max creature blurted out his name. He might have been sent by the French, although they don't seem to be working together. He might be after industrial secrets, which might explain how he got in without anyone realizing it." He paused, the light from the monitors illuminating his features. "Of course, he never would have been able to get inside unseen if we hadn't been distracted with everything that's been going on around here since yesterday."

Philippe gave the screen one last look, then shrugged and turned away. "Whoever he is, he'll regret coming here." The Frenchman walked out of the security center, back towards the vat where his creature grew.

The tranquil lab had been transformed. The floor vibrated, tubes which earlier had been slack and limp were turgid with rushing fluid. Everything was humming and sloshing and gurgling.

It was the perfect soundtrack for the creation of new life.

Cora looked around, trying to understand the complexity of the process around her.

"It's not as simple as it seems," Philippe said. The superior smile was back where it belonged, turning the corners of his mouth upwards.

"It's fantastic," she said.

"What, this?" he waved dismissively at the throbbing and pulsing pipes and tubes. "That's just machinery." Philippe laid a hand on the large cylinder beside him. "This... this is the real thing."

Cora walked around the stainless steel structure, and realized that it wasn't perfectly cylindrical but tapered on top and at the bottom to give her the feeling that she was looking at a giant egg. She smiled: it was a fitting image.

To her disappointment, there was no window in this machine. She couldn't look inside.

"How do you monitor progress?" she asked.

"Look." He tapped a couple of commands on a nearby keyboard. This one was connected to a different computer which had a large flat monitor.

Instead of the expected numbers and graphs, which she would need help to interpret, the image which came up was of... something silhouetted on a background of orange-yellow reminiscent of egg yolk. Lines swirled around it, and occasionally a nozzle, obviously mechanical came up and injected or sprayed material into a specific area.

As she watched, the central figure grew. The process advanced so slowly that, at first, she was hard pressed to know whether she wasn't imagining it. But by focusing on a single dark strand towards the bottom, she soon realized it was real.

"What's going on in there?"

"Accelerated growth."

"Of the creature? No way. I can see it happening."

"That's why I call it accelerated."

"But it's impossible. The thing in there looks more like something being made in a 3D printer than a growing organism." A sudden suspicion hit her. "This isn't a huge printer, is it? That's been tried before... it only works for tissues, not for a complete organism. It will never be alive."

He raised an eyebrow. "I'm well aware of that, thank you. No. The process you're watching isn't anything as simple as the mere accretion of organic molecules onto frames to form tissues. Any idiot can do that. What you're watching is..." He paused. "Well, I haven't named it officially yet, but I refer to it as 'fast-feeding'. Imagine what would happen if the body had access to all the nutrients it needed to grow as quickly as it wanted."

She nodded toward the screen. "That fast? I assume the mitochondria in every cell would explode… or something similarly catastrophic. The sheer energy you need to convert all of that…"

Philippe was nodding to her like she was an undergraduate who had managed to avoid saying something stupid for the first time all semester. "Very good. But you forget something: I can replace every cellular structure as fast as it wears out. Like everything else, accelerated growth is just a question of tweaking the correct genes."

Cora's mouth hung open. She closed it. "You're not kidding?"

"Of course not. This is real. In another four hours, we'll be giving birth to a creature never seen before in this world."

"I still can't believe it. What are the tubes doing if you're not printing?"

"They're bringing in the nutrients the body needs. Some of them as what you'd expect: sugar molecules, glucose and the like. Others took a little bit of work, for example the calcium slurry that allows the bone structure to be built. Other than the basic gene modifications to cause the organism to grow under these conditions, there's nothing very sexy about the process. It's just a question of engineering the complexity in order to get the timing right. In that way, it's similar to your analogy of a 3D printer: certain materials have to be delivered in precise places at specifically determined moments. In parallel and without stopping."

"Can it fail?"

"Oh, it's failed so many times I can't even count them. But you're a scientist, you must know the heartbreak of feeling that this time it will work… and then watching the results crumble."

Cora had to nod in sympathy. So many late-night tears hidden from her colleagues had followed sessions exactly as Philippe described. "God, yes."

"Well, that's how it was with the development of this technique. Worse still, with each failed attempt, I had to euthanize the results. Most of the time, it wasn't too bad, as the pain it was in would make it a mercy. But sometimes, the thing would look up at me as if begging for help. It was too young, too undeveloped for me to be able to explain that it couldn't survive without heroic action on our part… and we didn't have the facilities or the budget to save them all.

"The only time I made an exception to this rule was with Poupée. She was deformed and weak, as well as being too small, but her vital signs otherwise seemed all right and, when she looked up at me, I couldn't bear to bring the scalpel down. So she survived long enough to save me and to betray me." A faraway look entered his eyes. "I suppose, in the end, it was for the best. I wouldn't be a free man today if it wasn't for her."

Cora nodded. One day she would ask him to tell her the whole story, to let go of all that anguish. But it wasn't the right time for that. Not yet. First, he would have to learn to trust her.

She took advantage of his silence to put her hand against the cylinder as she watched the screen. Was this how it would have felt if she'd chosen to become a mother instead of pursuing her academic career to the fullest of her ability? The blood-warm metal beneath her fingers throbbed with the same energy that she imagined might come from a baby kicking its mother's hand through the skin of the womb.

She shook her head. No. How could she even imagine something like that? Could she really be comparing the machine building a monstrosity specifically designed to go out there and harm people and other monsters with the magic of human pregnancy?

Perhaps it was the wrong comparison, but the feeling in her hand was like nothing she'd ever experienced before.

"Four hours, you say?" she asked.

"Yes. But I think we won't want to be around when the incubator finally opens. The creature inside will be very confused, possibly in a certain amount of pain due to the process, and very, very angry. It will also be very big."

Cora looked around. "The lab…"

"Will be in no danger. Each incubator unit is mounted on tracks and it will disengage automatically and roll through a door in that wall over there. The creature's birth will happen in the animal pen, where it belongs."

"I thought it was human."

That earned her a piercing look. "It has a human mind, my dearest Dr. Gomez, but it most certainly isn't human."

"It won't know that."

"It won't know anything, at first. Only that it's confused and scared and surrounded by aggressive creatures. That's why I gave it armor. Lots of heavy armor." A wistful look entered his eyes. "I only wish I could be around to see it grow up, to understand its power once it subdues those brutes of dragons, and those men with little guns." Philippe shook his head. "But of course, that would be impossible. Up until now, I've lived with the hope that my creations won't betray me, that they'll show me the love and loyalty one would expect towards their creator. But not with this one. When you create a creature this powerful, you should stay well away: it will be the master, bowing to no one."

"So you're going to let something loose on the Panamanian jungle that no one will be able to stop? You're going to condemn everyone it encounters to death?"

Philippe laughed long and hard. "No. Of course not. Not me." He held her gaze, and there was steel in that look. "Us."

***

As the door opened, Gaar could have sworn something was watching them. The itch between his shoulder blades refused to go away.

Amber, on the other hand, seemed to have no such qualms. "Look. Sunlight!" she whispered excitedly. "We're finally out of that damned tunnel."

They'd entered a cavernous building with a vaulted roof that towered above them. The illumination came from a huge double hangar door in the distance. The main floor space was split into smaller enclosures, cubes of concrete with thickly barred doors.

"This is the animal pen."

"What?"

"The pen. It's where the dragons and the fish-men and the other things Philippe created sleep at night." Even if he hadn't recognized the building, the rank smell of the place would have disclosed the fact that animals were held there.

"Crap." She shrugged. "I guess it's still better than those tunnels. Besides, it's probably empty—all the animals are in the tunnels. Come on." She walked through the door.

Gaar half-expected her to be immediately eaten by something, but nothing untoward occurred, so he followed, chiding himself for being an absolute chicken all the way.

They walked among the cages, and Gaar felt like a kid again, in the Sao Paulo zoo, that enormous park an hour's drive from his uncle's place—for some reason, it was always his uncle who took him to the zoo, never his parents. Back then, they would spend an inordinate amount of time peering into animal enclosures to see if the animals were there. Everyone assured him they were around, but always ended up saying the same thing: 'they're probably asleep in the shade somewhere, out of this heat.' A distant glimpse of the Bengal tiger or some uninteresting antelope seemed hugely exciting back then.

The heat here was the same dripping, humid kind that he remembered. So much for the dry season.

And the animal pens were just as empty as the ones back home.

They reached the hangar door and stopped dead. They couldn't see any dragons outside, but they could definitely hear one. Angry roars came from the forest, occasionally punctuated by loud thumping.

"I'll go look," Gaar said, trying to make up for his earlier cowardice.

"Don't be an idiot. Stay under cover until we can see what's happening. There's no need to go out there and get eaten."

"All right."

They waited there, in the shadow of the door, for minutes that stretched into half an hour.

Every few seconds, though, Gaar would turn around and peer into the building behind them. He couldn't shake the feeling that there was someone or something stalking them. But the door was still closed behind them and the huge building appeared empty.

At one point, movement in the depths of the shadows nearly caused him to flee in panic, but when he took a closer look, it turned out to be nothing more than a plastic bag flying around in a soft breeze.

Considering how often he looked back, how obsessively he searched for signs that something might be coming up behind them, it's understandable that, when the cold muzzle of the gun was pressed against his ear, the first feeling—even before panic—was one of disappointment that the world could be so unfair.

***

Max grinned in triumph as he felt the Brazilian academic stiffen. He leaned forward and whispered in the man's ear. "Guess who?"

Gaar turned around, his eyes never leaving the gun in Max's hand. "Even with my back turned, I could identify you by the stench. I doubt there's anything else in this jungle that smells quite the way you do."

The value of this little bastard as a hostage overcame Max's desire to see his brains scattered over the jungle and he didn't pull the trigger. You could forgive a certain amount of frustration from a man just made a hostage for the second time in as many days.

The girl looked at him silently, still as beautiful as she'd been when they'd first captured the Americans, if not quite as clean and alert. She looked tired. Well, the ordeal had been hard on all of them, so he'd have to forgive that, too.

"March. Outside."

"There's a dragon out there," the girl said.

"There's a gun in here," he replied, holding it up for her to see.

He signaled for them to exit the building on the far right, where the hangar doors pressed close against the forest.

"Now go as far as that tree." He pointed to a tall trunk well inside the line of foliage, where they'd be out of sight from the clearing. He didn't know how well the dragons could smell, but he knew they could hear and see pretty well, so using the forest to mask those senses seemed like a good idea.

"Take that path. Go. Hurry."

They walked. The man sullenly, the girl defiantly. She turned back and said: "Where are you taking us?"

"The plan hasn't changed. You are my hostages. I hope you didn't get your hopes up when that Frenchman said he was letting you go. You should have known I couldn't allow you to run from me. We need you."

He thought of the pile of cocaine hidden in the maze and smiled to himself. The Comando didn't need them as much as it had before... but it would still be nice to be able to say that he had completed the mission despite the craziness they'd encountered here. There could be no doubt that the events in this jungle would make the front page worldwide—and his superiors in the movement would have to acknowledge that his success under extraordinarily difficult circumstances was exceptional.

"We're circling around to get out of the way of the dragons, and then heading for the coast. After that, it's a short walk up to Colombia, where we can find some of my comrades."

The girl's eyes smoldered. "You'll never make it. We won't let you. There's only one of you and two of us, and you'll have to sleep sometime."

"I can tie you up," he replied. "Or I can shoot one of you."

As they walked, the rhythm of the jungle returned to him, the soft springiness of the dry mulch of the paths, the occasional root snaking its way from a tree to some distant, unseen source of nutrients and water, the soft swaying of the branches in the breeze.

It was the life he'd chosen, and he waited for the peace he felt on jungle marches to descend on him as they moved forward.

But it didn't.

At first, he thought it was the constant vigilance, the need to keep the two students from running.

Gradually, however, he realized there was something more at work: the jungle didn't sound right. The normal buzz of the insects, the movement of birds among the trees was different, less vibrant, somehow. It was a subtle thing: when humans moved in the forest, the animals naturally went quiet. But this was something more.

Someone or something was following them.

CHAPTER 21

Esmeralda buttoned up her shirt while John looked steadily the other way. As a scientist, he knew that breast-feeding was natural and not in the least bit scandalous… and here he was, unable to look at a feeding mother without suffering a deep sense of embarrassment. So much for the twenty-first century.

They stood and headed towards the door. He would feel a lot more comfortable once they got a little further from the dragon, even if that meant spending more time in the damned tunnel.

A slight hint of fish, carried on the breeze was all the warning he had before coming face to face with one of the two-legged scaly creatures.

His hand, the hand with the cleaver, rose of its own accord, the razor-sharp edge raising a line of blood on the skin of the thing's chest. It was rough, like cutting through tree bark.

The monster recoiled and roared before coming back towards him. Two muscular arms topped with clawed hands reached for John's throat. He twisted away and tried to grab them, to push them off, but the creature was much too strong. It batted aside his feeble attempts at self-defense and grabbed hold of John's neck.

Time seemed to slow down. He could see the drops of dark blood running down his antagonist's scales, he heard Esmeralda's high-pitched scream drag out into eternity and the baby's lower-pitched yelping cry. He even saw individual tufts in the carpet.

The monster began to squeeze. John jerked back, forcing it to adjust its grip. It couldn't get a good hold, but still, John felt his windpipe being crushed. If it gave, he would be dead.

The cleaver.

He brought it up and hacked. It struck bone and lodged. The angle was all wrong and if he misjudged his blow, he would cut off his own face, but he didn't care. Desperation lent him strength and he pulled the blade out of the thing's wrist and hit it again and again.

The monster didn't react in any way. It was so focused on crushing his throat—or on tearing off his head—that it appeared not to realize what horrible damage the cleaver was inflicting.

John's vision blurred. His entire world revolved around the hand holding his weapon. He struck and struck and struck until he fell over backwards onto a wall. He was about to pass out, his vision inexorably narrowing to a single point. He couldn't let that happen or he would die.

Suddenly, the pressure was gone and he heard someone talking to him in Spanish. Worried tones, sobbing, nearly screaming.

Esmeralda.

He opened his eyes and raised his hand to his neck, nearly cutting himself badly in the process. He'd forgotten about the knife, and if Esmeralda hadn't gently caught his arm, he would probably have finished the job that the fish-thing started.

"Where's the monster?" he said as the world returned slowly to focus.

Esmeralda understood. She pointed out the door, and John saw a trail of dark blood—a hell of a lot of it—leading off into the trees. He must have hurt it quite badly.

John tried to take a step and his foot encountered something on the floor. He peered down to see what the impediment was, the sudden movement making him woozy again.

Two dark, greenish-grey lumps lay in a pool of blood at his feet. Clenched tight, as if still trying to crush the life out of John's throat, were the creature's two clawed hands. Disconnected from the rest of the being, they looked nearly human.

His bile rose and suddenly John needed air. He didn't even think about the risk as he headed out the open front door. The heat of the sun on his head, the wind on his face, barely registered. He breathed deeply, the pain radiating from his neck a welcome reminder that he hadn't quite been killed, close though it was. He'd have quite a bruise, but who really cared, when you lived to tell the tale?

Finally, when he felt like himself again, he looked around. Other than the wet blood, the clearing seemed much too peaceful to have borne witness to such atrocious events. There were no signs of any creatures. No dragons, no fish-things, nothing. He'd recovered enough that he smelled the stench of the creature all over him, felt the soggy clothing where its blood had mingled with his sweat.

He was *alive*, dammit.

Then he noticed Esmeralda. She was just standing there, fiddling with something. He peered at her, confused, until he realized she was tying a sling for the baby. She did it silently, without questioning whether they were safe outside or if he'd put her baby into mortal danger by leaving the tunnels. All he'd really had to do was to shut a door and hope none of the little dragons tried to break it down—he'd already seen that the fish-people couldn't decipher doorknobs. They would have been safe in that room. Instead, he'd run into one of the creatures, nearly gotten them all killed and, to make it worse, had then lurched outside where they already knew the big dragon waited.

And yet she'd followed without complaint, without question of any kind.

The forest chirped at them from all sides, exuding tropical peace, but all he could think of was the hope that he would be worthy of this woman's trust.

But even as he thought it, he knew he wasn't worthy. He should return to the house, get in the bedroom and close the door behind them. That would be the safest thing to do.

He refused, though. He'd nearly been killed too many times to count in there. He'd maimed a dumb creature who was probably just as confused and frightened as he was. They would walk away from here. Climb trees if anything found them.

And then he remembered Amber and Gaar. They were still inside with the Colombians who wanted to take them hostage, Philippe's people who probably wanted to kill off any witnesses by now and the French commandos… God only knew what the French commandos wanted.

He sighed and turned back to the door, knowing he was going to regret it.

***

"All right," Philippe said. "The next step is to program the right place for this egg to hatch. The lid on top will open when the creature starts moving." He pointed towards the shut line on top of the oblong. "We'll want to open it in an unoccupied cage in the animal pen, and reprogram that one not to let it out until we decide it's ready."

He donned a set of heavy gloves and walked quickly around the incubator, pulling hoses and pipes away from the casing, their work done. Fluids dripped onto the floor and he stared at one foul-smelling pool of brown sludge for a couple of seconds before smiling. "We'll leave the mess. It's not like anyone is going to be using this lab again, anyway."

Suddenly, Chapeau came into the room, making his characteristic bark-like sound of joy at seeing him. Philippe bent down and patted his head. "So that's where you are. I was beginning to worry about you. No. Don't eat that. It's probably not bad for you, but you'll smell awful."

Cora's eyes looked like they were about to pop out of her head as she stared at his tiny pet. "Ah, this is Chapeau. I'll introduce him to you properly once we have this cylinder out of here."

There was a short ladder stowed under one of the benches, and he pulled it out and set it beside the cylinder, trying to position it so that he wouldn't have to get down and move it in order to reach all the pipes. Of course, he got it wrong, and one little one was out of reach. He sighed in annoyance and climbed down, then decided not to bother. It was just a small pipe, a piece of plastic tubing carrying water for the mist system that kept the interior of the incubation pod at the right level of humidity. There was no real reason to bother with it; it would snap right off as soon as the heavy piece of equipment moved. He smiled at the thought of someone attempting to use the machinery and having it overheat because of insufficient water flow to the interior. It would serve them right.

Cora was watching the cylinder as if it would open up to reveal the seven wonders of the world all at once. Her eyes were wide and, for just a single moment, Philippe's heart warmed to her. Perhaps she was, after all these years of searching, the person who he could open up to. It's too bad she was about his own age, and wouldn't represent the next generation, a successor able to continue his work, but she had the right look: the expression of a child watching a magician with no cynical questions about whether it was all done with wires or whether the rabbit was there all along. She was fascinated because she wanted it to be real.

Yes, he knew that feeling. In him, however, there was another. He felt the first stirrings of the nerves. The same sensation he'd felt in his student days when a teacher was about to give out exam results: a sour, jumpy feeling in his stomach. It was a legacy of the early days, with all their failures and frustrations; this was the way he'd felt whenever he was decanting a new specimen, especially if it was somehow fundamentally different from things he'd done before. Lately, he hadn't suffered too many catastrophes, but the possibility was always there.

He shook it off.

"Now, help me spin it around. Watch out, it's very heavy." Two locks kept the incubator in place, solid damped mounts that wouldn't crack—or, worse, damage the equipment—under constant vibrations. He pulled the levers that released the rubberized clamps and, with Cora's help, they rotated the cylinder so that the tracks underneath it were aligned with the shallow depressions that led to the external door. Once rotated, they pushed it onto the track, from where the motor that ran the wheels could be automatically powered via the electric rails.

The cylinder thumped.

"Damn," Philippe said. "We must not have aligned it correctly. Let me look." He hoped it wasn't off by too much. If the wheels had gone off the rails, the cylinder was much too heavy for them to reposition by hand. They'd need to go to the garage to retrieve a crane… an operation which was completely out of the question.

He peered below the cylinder. It looked like everything was in position. Maybe the gap had caused something to move… or the final line had let go. He looked up, but it was still there, stretched taut but not snapped off yet.

It thumped again. "Do you see anything moving?" he asked Cora.

She didn't reply, and he looked up to find her staring at the incubation chamber.

"Cora?"

"I think it came from inside," she said.

"Oh." He should have thought of that himself. Even if it wasn't yet ready to hatch, a creature that big would have a lot of inertia as they moved its metal womb around from one place to the other. "All right. We'd better get it moving again, don't want it to hatch in here, do we?"

Cora remained silent. Maybe she *did* want the thing to hatch in there, to watch the process unfold fully. But Philippe most certainly didn't. He'd already been attacked by creatures he'd expected to love him as a benevolent master… he wasn't planning on being around when something he'd designed in a fit of rage for the express purpose of causing pain and mayhem saw the light. He was an idealist, not an idiot.

"Push it that way," he ordered.

They did, and it began to roll.

Then it stopped. The line, the one he hadn't disconnected, refused to snap, and the entire thing was snagged on it.

"Damn. Those lines break off every time I want them to stay on, so of course, as soon as I want one to break, it turns out that was the only one that actually went through quality control. Let me get the ladder."

He walked back to where he'd left it, and decided to cut the line instead of trying to unscrew it in its current, tensed position. That meant grabbing a knife or some kind of shears from the bench.

The cylinder thumped again.

Philippe rummaged in a drawer of random implements for a few moments before he found a pair of ordinary scissors which would probably do the trick. Then he had to untangle them from a length of wire that he'd used to tie stuff together back when he was building the plumbing.

Chapeau danced around his legs, intent on tripping him up.

The thumping had become continuous and, before he could even take two steps toward the cylinder, it sprung a leak. A thin stream of clear, yellowish fluid began to pour down onto the floor. Chapeau ran to investigate, but Philippe was too busy to scold his pet.

The thumping centered around the leak. The stream turned into spurts, pulsing in time with the thumps.

As Philippe watched, something tore through the metal of the tank. Something black and shiny.

He should have known immediately what it was. The only black, shiny thing in that tank was the creature's chitinous exoskeleton.

And the only things that could cut through metal were the powerful, scorpion-like pincers.

But he only understood when one of the claws emerged in all its glory and dripped yellow mucus-like liquid all over the floor, to splash at Cora's feet. She didn't even try to save her shoes, still transfixed by the sight.

The claw tore into the metal again, cutting it apart as if it was made of paper. The skin of the incubation chamber suddenly collapsed outward, spilling the remaining fluid in a slick mess of slime and stench. Philippe gagged, and Cora was actually knocked to the ground when the yellow wave hit her feet.

She pulled herself up, unhurt, but immediately fell on the slippery fluid again.

The beast unfolded itself from the incubator exactly like a baby bird emerging from its egg. And like a bird, it was hard to believe that something that big had been in a tube that small. Its legs seemed to fill half the room, and the pincers... he preferred not to think about those.

Cora was up again, and Philippe immediately knew it was a mistake. Her struggles caught the monster's attention, and it advanced towards her. Some of the legs slipped and slid on the wet surface, but there always seemed to be plenty more to keep it from falling.

Finally, Cora reacted. Realizing that she couldn't run in that frictionless goop, she picked up a chair—the only thing to hand—and held it menacingly between her body and the monster.

The creature didn't even bother to bring its pincers to bear. A careless—almost contemptuous—swipe of its nearest leg sent the chair flying into the distance to shatter a collection of beakers on a benchtop.

Philippe wanted to yell at her, tell her to run away, but doing so would only alert the creature to his own presence. There was one thing he could do, though: open the door in front of it, the one the tracks would have taken the incubation chamber down had the cylinder not jammed. That led to a tunnel into the holding area... but more importantly, it led away from the lab.

He inched towards the controls, hoping the compound eyes designed to see everything wouldn't see him.

Fortunately, the insect's attention seemed to be fully focused on Cora. The same leg that had knocked away the chair now swept her feet out from under her. She fell onto the slimy floor. The liquid had flowed all over the lab, and was now a film that covered everything as opposed to liquid with real depth.

The creature placed its leg on Cora's stomach, effectively pinning her to the ground.

Philippe reached the door controls and toggled the tunnel entrance. The door opened upward with a deep, grinding sound to reveal a dark tunnel beyond.

Please go in there. Ignore the little human behind you. It's a nice, dark, dank place, ideal for a crawling critter like you, Philippe thought at the creature.

The creature twitched its head, interested at the motion, and Philippe thought it would have entered without further ceremony if it hadn't been for Chapeau. In a brave, doomed effort to protect its master and the lab, the tiny creature gave its strange, barking war cry and bit down hard on the leg nearest it.

The creature shrieked, and now it did bring the pincers into play, snapping down with lightning speed and cutting his pet in two.

Philippe felt nothing. He hadn't even had time to grow truly fond of this one yet. Chiffon had been another matter... but Chiffon was gone.

Then the monster moved, much quicker than a thing equipped with the notoriously slow-learning human brain should have been able to. In fact, it should have taken it hours before it could even control its limbs effectively... but this one seemed to have been born with a reptile's ability to move around with no problems from the very start. Interesting.

But this wasn't an academic problem. It was a real live creature twice his height running amok inside his lab. He stayed perfectly still, hoping it couldn't see too well yet.

The creature appeared to shrug and pressed hard on the leg holding Cora down. It pierced the skin effortlessly. Her scream echoed in the confines of the lab and blood burst from the gaping wound in her stomach.

Only then, damage done, did the arachnid monster skitter over to the open tunnel entrance. It paused for a couple of moments, but it must have liked what it saw because it dove inside and disappeared into the darkness.

Philippe hit the button that closed the door behind it, but he didn't breathe again until the reinforced concrete had sealed the entrance completely.

CHAPTER 22

The door was being stubborn, and Brown was sweating from the heat and the tension. The fact that he hadn't slept in nearly two days and that his last energy bars had been depleted hours ago wasn't helping his ability to concentrate, but the thing that worried him most was the guard he'd released. He had visions of the man returning with one of the revolutionaries' AK-47s. After all, he presumably knew where they'd been stashed.

Hopefully, the man would evaluate the situation and understand that things had changed and that, whatever happened next, he would no longer be in the employ of his former master. In his place, the right thing to do was to grab the gun first, but then run, not bothering to return in a fit of misguided loyalty.

The lock was very different from the one on the door separating the animal enclosure from the maze of tunnels—that one had been a modern technological marvel while this one was a brute force electric item, meant to be unlocked only from the inside. As such it should have been easy to open; a jolt of electric current would be enough, whether it came from a battery or from a moving magnetic field.

That very lack of subtlety worked against him: the thick door was getting in the way of his attempts to manipulate the fields in the way he needed. He'd found where the wires went, but was having all sorts of trouble reaching them with his magic door opener.

He'd been trying for more than two hours when, unexpectedly, the door opened.

"Finally, you bastard," Brown said. He stood slowly, working away the kinks from contorting himself into a sort of human antenna against the wall. Once past the door—he didn't want that heavy thing to close on him and crush him-he proceeded without hurry, stopping to check each room for any sign of ambush. Philippe knew he was coming; this door was always going to be alarmed, so it was best to be careful, even if that meant sacrificing speed. Slow and steady was his best insurance against ambush. He knew it well.

That didn't make it easy, though. Every second he lost was a second his quarry had to destroy evidence and clear records. He wanted to finish this job right.

But not at the cost of his life, so he clenched his teeth and cleared yet another room that turned out to be nothing but a walk-in storage closet.

A ninety-degree corner ahead merited extra caution, so he stopped a couple of feet away and planned how to approach it.

Which meant that he was standing there when Philippe rushed around the corner and bowled him over. They fell to the floor in a tangled mass.

Brown recovered first and grabbed Philippe's legs as the man attempted to get away. "You're not going anywhere," he said. He showed the man his pistol, just to emphasize the point.

The Frenchman looked at him with wide, terrified eyes. "You're the man they call Brown, yes. You were outside." He slapped himself in the forehead with his palm. "How could I forget you were outside? I forgot."

Well, that solved the mystery of the suddenly opening door, anyway. "Well, we're going back in."

"It's no use. The lab is ruined."

"You destroyed the records?" Brown's heart sank, until he noticed that his captive was carrying a leather briefcase that looked like it had come directly from the seventies. Dog-eared sheets of yellowed paper, obviously packed in a hurry, peeked out from below the flap. "Then I'll take those."

Philippe shrugged and handed the briefcase over. After his short lapse into terror, the scientist had quickly gotten hold of his emotions again. A hint of the smile that adorned his features in all the photos reasserted itself after he climbed ponderously to his feet. "Do you mind handing me my cane?" Philippe pointed to a dark cylinder lying a few feet away.

"Can I trust you not to try anything stupid?"

"I'm too old for violence. Just hand me my cane."

Brown took the opportunity to study the man's features. He was much older than the pictures. That was logical enough considering that the newest of the images was from a decade ago, but there was something more. The man was tired and he was in pain. He was also tanned by a decade of tropical sun... but that only served to highlight eyes that seemed to burn with a desire to live. Brown had never seen a look that intense, which transformed otherwise nondescript brown eyes into orbs that seemed like they could look right through you.

He handed the man the cane.

"Thank you," Philippe said with a polite nod.

Brown gestured towards the lab. "You first."

"If you value the integrity of your shoes, I wouldn't go in there. It's quite... smelly."

"I insist."

"Ah. So that's how it is. All right." Philippe led the way, a slight limp highlighting why he needed the cane. That was comforting, but Brown still kept a close watch on him. This man had eluded the French government for more than a decade. It wouldn't surprise Brown to discover that he had a trick or two up his sleeve. A sword cane was a gentleman's solution... and this man was the perfect tropicalized gentleman, the perfect definition of a suave expatriate. A man who would wine you and dine you and then cold-bloodedly have you murdered.

The lab was a mess.

"You destroyed everything?" Brown said.

Philippe laughed. "I destroyed nothing. I didn't even stop to erase the records of what I've been producing here from the computers."

Brown looked around at the demolished tank, the foul-reeking liquid on the floor, the loose pipes and fixtures. His eyes settled on a prone form, a woman lying in the gunk... Cora, blood from a deep abdominal wound mingling with the yellow liquid to turn the floor around her orange.

"What happened here?"

"A miscalculation."

"One hell of a miscalculation."

"A small miscalculation, actually, albeit one with large consequences."

"Yeah, I'd say." Brown didn't feel much for the woman on the ground, other than a pang of regret at having wasted his time in rescuing her from the revolutionaries. If he'd hurried, maybe he could have beat the crowd to the complex, and he'd now have Philippe under lock and key and all the files safely protected from interference, both of the human and monstrous kind. Instead, everything was a clusterfuck of the most serious proportions. "Do the computers still work?"

"I haven't touched anything."

Brown indicated a chair in the yellow gunk, situated where Brown could see him while still checking the nearest terminal. "Sit there and don't move."

Philippe sat.

The machine was a desktop running what looked to be a database program lifted from a bureaucracy that hated its employees. Yellowish-white fields on a grey background. As he studied it, he whistled softly. "I haven't seen FoxPro in use for a long time. Not even a modified version like this one."

Philippe raised an eyebrow. "Ah. They sent someone with a brain," he said. "I thought you were just more muscle, like those guys in black getting themselves eaten by the dragons." He sighed. "In answer to your question, I wrote that program myself because I needed something simple enough to automatically interact with the rest of the equipment without getting bogged down—the machines here need to work in real time, precisely coordinated. The processing power and memory you need to run that database is negligible, while the computers, as you can see, are brand new. A perfect combination."

"And you still couldn't stop the thing from running around and killing people in your lab." Underneath the sarcasm, however, Brown was pleased. As Philippe had said, the computer was apparently untouched. The French government would have all the evidence it could possibly want... and that wasn't even counting what might be found in the briefcase that Philippe had attempted to abscond with.

"That might be as you say, of course, but I wouldn't go as far as to say that anyone was killed here. Not yet, anyhow."

"What?" Brown whirled around to see Cora, bloodied and mangled, but quite obviously alive, standing before him with a determined look on her face. Her arms were held above her head and Brown had the barest instant to look up and realize she was holding a fire extinguisher in the air before the heavy red lump crashed down.

Everything went black.

***

Max stood stock still, wondering why the forest had suddenly gone still. Finally, as the sounds around him returned to normal, he concluded that it must have been his imagination, or simply a passing lull in the forest background noise.

But Amber and the guy had caught on that something must have been wrong. They were observing him, sullen resistance replaced by concern.

"Don't be afraid," he said. He brandished the pistol in his hand. "I've fired this thing twice. Each time, I killed what I was aiming at. The most recent was one of the juvenile dragons who made the mistake of chasing me in the hallway. So, you understand, there's no need to be afraid. I can protect us from anything this jungle might have in store."

The young woman—he thought her name was Amber—looked up sharply. "And the first bullet?"

Max waved the memory away. "That's not even worth talking about. It took the life of a traitor, nothing but human refuse. A waste of a shot, and it makes me wish I could do what the Chinese do and bill his family for the cost of the bullet. He was nothing."

"Like Liliana?" she replied angrily.

"I don't need to justify my actions to you. Traitors get what they deserve."

Amber's eyes smoldered. "I doubt she was a traitor. I might not speak much Spanish, but I was watching you. You didn't kill her for anything other than jealousy. You don't like powerful women, do you?"

Max laughed and holstered the gun. "Oh, I respect power wherever it might be. I simply don't allow insubordination, regardless of gender." He smiled at them meaningfully. "Now, I suggest we walk."

"We have no water, no food…"

"We'll find all that. This is a jungle, not a desert. And if food is hard to come by… well, we can all do with a bit of a diet. Emaciated hostages always make people sit up and take notice. Now move."

Still angry, the woman led the way, with the young man, who'd not said more than three words since they'd been captured again, falling in behind her. It wasn't hard to tell who wore the pants in that unlikely duo—but then again, a woman as beautiful as this young academic, even under the grime of several days, could always do what she wanted with a dumpy little guy like him.

As he enjoyed the view from behind, Max smiled to himself. She'd find him a very different proposition. The situation might not be ideal, and his English wasn't as polished as he'd prefer it to be for this particular challenge, but she would come around. They always did. Power, conviction, knowledge: those were the true aphrodisiacs in a place like the Darién Gap.

The trio walked for a few minutes. Unexpectedly, it was the little guy whose name Max hadn't even bothered to learn, who broke the silence. "Listen," he said.

Max nearly told him to shut up. If there were any strange sounds in the forest, he would have picked up on it well before any of these city children would. But he stopped and cocked his head. Nothing sounded out of place. The insects buzzed the way they were supposed to, the birds flew overhead. The leaves rustled.

"What?" he asked the man.

"It's a screech, far away."

He strained his ears and… there, just above the threshold of hearing. A whine sounded. Reminiscent of the sound of a jet engine, it reminded him of that long night, trying to sleep on the plane from Bogotá to Bangkok before the tedious overland trek to the steppes.

But it wasn't an airplane engine. It was an animal sound. "Some kind of bird," he said with a shrug. "It's definitely not a dragon. Those make a loud roaring sound. I don't think it's one of the fish-men either. I haven't heard them make much noise at all." He smiled and held up the gun again, as a reminder that he was not exactly defenseless. "And if it is, we know how to deal with it, don't we?"

The young woman rolled her eyes and they got back on the trail. This close to the coast, there were actual animal trails to follow, or perhaps they were simply run-off courses that carried water during the wet season. Either way, they made the going much easier than in the denser, machete-obligatory jungle where his unit had been stationed for the previous year.

This time, he heard it first. The jungle went still, and his blood froze in his veins. He beckoned for them to come closer. "There's something coming this way," he said.

"What?"

"I'd say it's one of the dragons," Max replied. "From the sound of the forest, I think it's over there, so we want to go that way."

They moved in the direction he pointed, stopping every few dozen meters to listen to the jungle around them.

"I think we lost it," Max told them. "Keep going."

The afternoon was advancing, and Max knew that night fell extremely quickly at this latitude. He looked up at the sky and estimated it was probably around five o'clock. "Listen. The best thing to do is to get to the coast as soon as possible. That will help us in two ways: first, we'll be able to see anything coming at us over the open sand. Secondly, we'll be able to build a fire. The animals in the forest are all afraid of fire."

"Even the dragons?"

He gave Amber a level look. "I know as much about the dragons as you do, but I wouldn't be surprised. They're reptiles, so they should act like reptiles. In the worst case, at least we'll have a clear shot at it if it doesn't frighten easily… and the fire will give us light to see it by."

She sighed. "All right, which way?"

"That way."

The man spoke again. "That's the direction the dragon was coming from."

"We've gone around it by now. Come on."

They started again, and made good progress in the direction of the coast. An hour before dusk, Max knew they would make it. He could smell the sea on the air, and even thought he could hear the soft beat of the waves on the sand. He expected the jungle to thin out and give way to coastal vegetation around every twist and turn. It was only a matter of a few hundred meters more.

And suddenly, the jungle went quiet again. A loud crash reached them from somewhere to the right and behind them, much too close for comfort.

Max forgot his years of training, his easy knowledge of the jungle. All he wanted was to get out from among the trees that hid the thing stalking them. He realized they must have unwittingly crossed paths with the dragon. He knew that had to be the right answer, but the frozen ball of fear in his stomach shouted the rational part of his being down. The primal part of him was convinced the creature was following them, that it had one desire, and one desire only in that walnut-sized reptilian brain: to eat them alive.

"Run!" he said. The word emerged in a hoarse whisper and, to his ear, expressed the enormity of the terror he felt.

If the hostages noticed, they were too busy with their own panic to make any comment. They ran as if they'd been primed to do it their entire lives, with no thought for stealth or strategy; all three of them barreled through the underbrush with more noise than a troop of elephants.

But not more than the dragon. A roar followed them between the trees, and the sound of something big tearing away the obstacles in its path echoed through the trees. Max was surprised at how quickly a couple of academics managed to move when sufficiently motivated, but soon the man, initially out front, began to flag.

First Amber shot past him, taking it upon herself to open the path through the underbrush. Then, when it became clear that the smaller man would never make it, Max followed her. Even at this late date, he felt a pang for losing one of his hostages, but a good commander needed to know when to sacrifice for the greater good. Keeping Max from being eaten seemed to be the greatest good possible, so he'd happily sacrifice an American academic to the dragon's stomach.

So he derived a certain satisfaction in listening to the man fall back further and further, and he actually found himself straining his ears for the sound of crushing bones, or the sound of a dying scream.

None of that happened, but there was a new sound. The jet engines they'd heard earlier had come back, but much closer and somehow different. Louder, but higher-pitched, not a jet engine but the beeping from the hearing tests the Comando sometimes ran on the rural population in their guise as concerned humanitarians. The ones that would get slightly softer with each application until the threshold was reached below which the subject simply couldn't hear anything at all.

Well, no one would have trouble making this one out unless they were stone deaf. It was loud, and getting closer. Even in his terror, with the much more pressing sound of a charging dragon commanding his attention, Max began to look upward for a helicopter or one of those drones the Americans used to kill terrorists in the Middle East.

He saw nothing, but suddenly stumbled. As he desperately dragged himself back to his feet, he realized that the packed dirt of the trail had turned to sand. The trees disappeared.

Now, the beach that had seemed a safe haven was simply a killing field, a place where they would be visible to the thing behind them for miles, where they didn't have the cover of trees to hide behind, and where the sand would slow them to a crawl.

Max realized he was going to die.

"Amber, wait," he called.

She was twenty meters ahead, and turned her head. The motion, combined with her pell-mell sprint, caused her to tumble forward. He caught up.

"It's no use running here. We have to try to shoot it," he said.

"You shoot it. I'll run."

And she did.

"Fine," Max said. He turned to face his oncoming death. The jungle shuddered and heaved, as if giving birth to his darkest, deepest fears. The dragon powered out, covered with the detritus of its mad career through the trees, its scales scratched and bloodied.

He got into his shooter's stance, something he hadn't done since basic training years and years before, and took a bead on the monster.

CHAPTER 23

Too many thoughts came through at once. He could feel the sudden wrongness, the unfamiliarity of the shape that told him the body around him wasn't his.

It wasn't a new feeling. Luca's job involved getting downloaded onto people's minds for money.

But this didn't feel like a job. For one thing, the last thing he remembered was having his mind backed up in preparation for a project in New York. He was to be imported onto a hugely overweight billionaire… He expected to wake up in an apartment he already knew perfectly well. His work environment, when waking from the transfer, invariably involved antiseptic rooms and comfortable beds.

His eyes, however, told a different story. He was in a lab of some sort, which was unusual. Worse, it looked like it had been bombed. Instead of the nurse and upscale amenities he remembered agreeing to, a man he'd never seen before stood over him.

Luca tried to move his head to get a better look at the guy, and realized he was lying on a hard surface, not a bed, but—judging by the height, at least—one of the lab's work surfaces.

The man peering down at him with a look of extreme interest was tanned and handsome, wearing a white suit.

"Can you hear me?"

It felt like someone had hit the back of his head with a baseball bat. His ears rang and pain shot through like lightning every time he focused his eyes. Did he have a concussion? He didn't know.

Worst of all, though, were the screams of terror he heard in his own thoughts. A muted, but still audible undercurrent that made it difficult to concentrate and impossible to string more than a couple of thoughts together.

He knew someone had asked a question. He thought he knew the answer. But how to put it into words? It took concentration to learn to use a new body, and that appeared to be an utter impossibility right then.

A growing horror then started gnawing at him and he realized that it wasn't coming from an alien source like the strangely unconnected thoughts assaulting his reason. No, this was his own subconscious fear welling upward to impose itself.

But why? He couldn't think straight, much less try to analyze his feelings. What in the world could be causing him to panic? Other than the blow to the head, he seemed to be all right, physically. He tried to move a hand, and that worked well enough. He could turn his head, wiggle his feet. He seemed to be in reasonable shape. He just needed to learn to use the new body and get something for the headache.

Then he froze. The voice in his head. He wasn't imagining it. It was really there. Someone had uploaded him onto a body without shutting down the previous owner first. That guaranteed a slow descent into madness, it had been his one major fear ever since he started working for the Russians.

The upside of the career he'd chosen was that he would become a millionaire very quickly. This was the downside.

"What did you do?" he tried to say, but the words were slurred, incomprehensible even to him. It was as if the other mind sharing his head was fighting him every step of the way. He concentrated, blocking out the panicked yells of the overwritten consciousness and tried again. "What. Did. You. Do?"

The man in white peered at him. "Who is this?" he asked.

Luca tried to answer, but the words wouldn't come. A part of his mind refused to let them out. Finally, a colossal effort yielded a result. "Luca. My name is Luca. Who are you?"

The man in white smiled. "That is immaterial right now. Can you sit?"

With help from the mysterious figure, Luca managed to get seated. His guess that he was on one of the lab's work surfaces proved correct. His legs dangled below him. They were reasonable legs, much thinner than the client he was supposed to be transferred into. "Where am I?" he said.

"You're at the Darién Gap."

Luca attempted to fit that information into anything that made sense, but he couldn't. Was it a hospital? A city? He was pretty certain it wasn't a country. His confusion must have shown on his features because the man continued speaking. "You're in Panama. The Darién Gap is a jungle, the most impenetrable one in the Americas. It's a break in the Pan-American Highway, the road that runs all the way from Patagonia to Alaska, except for about a hundred kilometers. We're right in the middle of that hundred kilometers."

"I'm supposed…" he paused. It was getting easier to speak, but it still wasn't easy by any stretch of the imagination, and he had a hard time putting ideas together. "…to be in New York."

"You never made it." A pause. "Or maybe you did, but this copy of you never made it. You're here because you annoyed a man named Anton."

Anton did this to me? The thought came as both a logical answer and a betrayal. Logical because Anton controlled the technology that allowed the transfer of a mind from one body to another, and also because Anton, despite all his civilized veneer was essentially a Russian gangster, a guy whose code of honor had a strict set of rules for dealing with disobedience. Punishment started with the removal of fingers—with a set of pliers—for small stuff, and went from there. A part of Luca, the part that was still capable of rational thought among the cacophony wondered what he'd done to earn this particular bit of cruel and unusual treatment.

Betrayal… well, how could he not feel betrayed? He'd generated millions for Anton and Anton's bosses over the years they'd been working together, and Anton himself had always treated him affectionately.

Then, from the maelstrom of muddled minds, a thought emerged. Luca wasn't even sure if it was his.

"Am I the one who's being punished?" he said. "Or the poor bastard you loaded me onto?"

"I'm afraid we don't have time for philosophy. Suffice to say that a backup of your personality has been donated to science. It's in that black briefcase-looking thing over there."

Luca looked and saw a transport memory case like the one he'd used countless times. Most countries in the world—and every single religion he could think of—would have been appalled if they'd learned that people were swapping minds around like trading cards, so they travelled disguised as computer memories. No one who wasn't an expert would be able to decipher the enormous amounts of data within.

The man kept speaking. Now that his brain was working again, Luca identified an accent. Probably French. "As for your host, he isn't being punished. I needed a way to incapacitate him to keep him from coming after me. I decided that this was better than just killing him." He paused for a moment, and his look lingered on something lying on the floor. Luca turned his head to see a woman with a huge hole torn in her stomach lying beside a first aid kit and a fire extinguisher in a pool of congealed yellow fluid. Her eyes stared lifelessly at the roof. "There's been too much death already."

"Who is he?" With the question, a wave of uncoordinated images and unconnected names emerged, unbidden in his mind. Were these the man's memories, suppressed under the overlaid personality? Luca had no way to know. All he knew was that, unless he learned to get this under control, there was no way he could function.

"I'm not actually sure. Everyone kept referring to him as Brown, but we were never formally introduced."

Brown. Yes, that word stuck to mind beneath, but there were others. Sked. Krine. Most of the man's memories, at least the ones Luca could access, seemed to center around images of computer screens and office buildings paneled in grey cloth. Punk music. And a woman. Too thin, too pale, dressed in black plastic. Judging by how often she popped into his head, she must have been important to this guy.

"All right. Brown." Luca shook his head.

The man was eyeing him curiously. "Tell me something. Can you use this body? Are you in control?"

Luca tentatively slid off the bench and took a couple of short steps. Dizziness caused him to lean back on the flat work surface. "Yes, I'm a bit nauseous now, but that's normal when you transfer to a new body."

"Do you do this often?"

"I do it for a living."

"Fascinating," the man said. "As a scientist who never imagined this might be possible, I'd love to speak about it at greater length, but I'm afraid I will be leaving shortly."

"Alone?"

"Of course. I really couldn't take you, of all people, with me, and I'm afraid that a woman who was becoming interesting… didn't make it through this particular ordeal." He nodded towards the corpse that Luca had been doing his best to ignore. "It's a pity. We could have done great things together. Perhaps it's fortunate that I didn't manage to get to know her better."

The man reminded Luca of an aging Italian mafia Godfather from any number of Hollywood films. A perfect gentleman—polite, suave, soft-spoken—but one that couldn't speak without displaying an utterly callous side that chilled the blood. There was warmth in the man, a palpable personal magnetism, but there was no personal connection. A perfect sociopath.

Luca had known quite a few of them in the course of his professional life.

"And what can I do? Are we in the jungle? This doesn't look like a jungle."

"Well, that depends on you. If my suspicions are correct, half the French Army will be here in a few hours. If you tell them that you're Brown, and that you managed to capture these computers intact, they'll be very happy with you and likely give you a lot of money. Can you access Brown's memories?"

"Some of them. It's chaotic, like trying to have a conversation in a noisy, crowded room. Normally, the host's mind is backed up and then suppressed before the transfer. What you did is insane. Or at least, it's making me insane."

"So, so fascinating. Well, maybe you should tell them you were hit on the head by a fire extinguisher. That's not only something that the bump on your head will bear out, but it would also explain any confusion you might be experiencing. Also, it's true. They'll be happy enough not to ask any questions. Unfortunately, I'll be taking your weapons with me. And how is Brown in there? Is he angry at me?"

"He's terrified. I think he's trying to regain control of our body, but he can't. Wherever your little machine relegated him to, it isn't somewhere where he can do anything."

"So he's still alive?"

"He's conscious of what's happening to him."

"Ah." The other man reflected, apparently thinking about the information for some moments. "Perhaps that is for the best. The reason he came here was to capture me and send me off to rot in a French jail for the rest of my life. I find it poetic justice that he now has to spend the rest of his days locked up while a random stranger lives his life." He picked up a cane that had been lying on the chair next to him and limped to the body of the woman on the ground. Kneeling, but careful not to get any of the yellow fluid on his white suit, he bent close to her face. "Dr. Gomez, I'm truly sorry it ended this way," he said. "I meant it when I told you that I have been trying to find someone who shared my vision. I will never get to know if you would have stayed the course, but at least you showed me that it's possible for someone to understand my fascination with what I do. Thank you." He kissed the woman's forehead and straightened with a soft moan. Turning back to Luca, he said: "What do you think you'll do now?"

"I... I have no idea."

"I suppose that makes sense. Well, don't forget that the briefcase there holds a copy of your mind. You will want to take care of that. If the French get it…"

The man in white hobbled to the back of the lab, pressed his hand against something that looked like a perfectly innocent wall and stepped through the sliding panel that unexpectedly revealed itself. It closed behind him, leaving Luca alone in the lab.

The voices in his head were screaming for his attention, but he beat them back savagely. There were more pressing matters on his mind.

He walked to the black briefcase, noting that the nausea had subsided somewhat. Once there, he opened it to reveal a black plastic prism about the size of a shoebox. He looked around the room to find something he could smash it with. Nothing presented itself, but the fire extinguisher. He shrugged. It wouldn't be elegant, but it would do.

He raised it above his head and brought it down, hard. The casing snapped with a satisfying crack to expose a series of circuits and hard drives within. He removed each element and smashed it to a pulp. Then he threw it into the gunk on the floor.

Only when he was done, only when there was one less copy of his mind in the world, one less possibility of waking up to a nightmare like the one he was living, did he stop and listen to the pleading of the ghost trapped inside his mind. The man, Brown, had calmed down considerably.

Listen, he was saying. *Please listen.*

"What do you want?" Luca said, aloud. It was just too confusing to think to himself.

We need to get out of here.

"Why? You heard what that man said. The French are coming."

Yeah. Well, my agreement with the French was to turn Philippe over to them.

"We got his computers."

Not good enough.

"So what will they do?"

Best-case scenario? They'll leave us in this jungle to rot and won't pay a cent of my fee. Worst-case? They'll take us with them and forget us in some dungeon somewhere. We're very, very inconvenient witnesses right now.

Luca stopped cold. Either the guy in his head didn't quite understand just how thoroughly fucked he was by the situation or he had already gone mad. It was impossible to tell which it might be. "Why would you help me?"

Because you know the people who built that black box you just demolished. I wish you hadn't done that, by the way.

"Do you think you can get your body back? I hate to tell you this, but I don't particularly want to give you the body back. You should keep in mind that I'm not a real person... I'm just a copy someone stored on a drive in case the real person had a problem. The real me is probably having sex with some pretty girl somewhere. Or maybe the Russians caught him for whatever it was he did—I have no memory of that—and cut him into cubes before feeding him to the pigs. Your body is all I have."

The sound of laughter echoed in his mind. Perhaps it was only Luca's imagination, but the person doing the laughing didn't sound like a well-balanced example of the breed.

Then let's make a deal. You can have my body if you upload me out of here and pay for my entry into one of the playgrounds.

"You know about the playgrounds?"

I thought they were a myth... until I saw your black box. They're real, aren't they?

"Yes." That was where Anton loaded his clients' minds while they waited for Luca to do the jobs he was hired for.

And anyone can get in?

"For a price."

Good, then we have a deal.

"No we don't. For starters, I don't have the money."

I'll show you where to get it.

And suddenly, his memories—well, Brown's memories, actually—came to the fore. The computers he'd seen earlier turned into hacking sessions... blasting through a firewall, coordinating a diversionary DDoS attack while hitting a secure site elsewhere with pre-packaged encryption breakers. This man could get what he needed, that was for sure.

Luca felt something else, too. He felt that Brown's memories, as he scanned them, became shared memories, that he was learning along with this man.

"All right. We'll try it. I could do with a body and, no offense, but I'm not sure having you in here will work out. But I have a condition."

What is it? I'm asking out of curiosity only. I accept, of course... I'm not in much of a position to negotiate. The voice in his mind chuckled.

"I want you to help me find every other copy of my mind out there and erase it. These bastards can do whatever they want to me if they have it."

All right.

"Good. What next?"

They walked—a bit unsteadily as Luca still struggled for complete mastery of his host body—to a room full of computer monitors. The monitors showed dozens of rooms and corridors, and it looked like another room had a dead body in it. Some of the bodies were deformed, impossible to identify as human.

All right. I suppose we're going out the front door. That's dangerous as hell unfortunately, but we don't have much choice.

They walked up the corridor. Just inside the outer door of what seemed to be a luxurious jungle cottage, Brown had Luca pause to look out the door. The coast was clear.

"Brown!"

The voice came from the door to Luca's left. He turned.

"Brown!"

A man and a very young woman, no more than seventeen or eighteen, peered out from the bedroom beyond. "What's going on?"

Tell him you're going outside to have a look and that the French will be here soon, and that he needs to join them as soon as he can. They won't shoot him. He's an important American professor.

Luca relayed the gist of it as well as he could. To his surprise, the other man didn't challenge him, and just nodded at the instructions before going back inside.

Out of earshot, Luca asked the question that had been nagging him. "What about us?"

We run towards the coast. And if you hear anything strange or out of place, climb a tree as fast as you can. I'll explain as we go.

CHAPTER 24

Gaar felt the dragon shoot ahead of him, but he never saw it. Leaves from its passing pelted him in the side and in the head, and a branch thicker than his arm was tossed into his way as if weightless. He tripped over it and crashed head over heels onto the ground.

Then, like a freight train in a tunnel, the creature was gone, and its absence left an emptiness that was impossible to believe. It emerged into the sunny beach ahead and paid no attention to the man it had left lying on the sandy floor of the jungle path. He thanked whatever spirits watched over hopeless cases in tropical jungles.

Gaar picked himself up and looked through the last row of plants before the beach opened up in front. He saw what he expected to see: the dragon was intent on chasing down Amber and the revolutionary, closing the gap steadily now that it was out of the woods.

For a single unworthy moment, he considered using the situation to his advantage. This was the chance he needed: while the dragon was distracted, he could slip away unnoticed. A hundred meters into the jungle was really all he needed, once he put that much vegetation between himself and his pursuer, he might as well be in a different country. He could be gone in a minute, utterly safe in two.

He hesitated for a second, his feet about to take him away without asking his conscience how it might feel.

But he stayed long enough to see something that made it impossible to leave. Instead of running for his life like the scared rat he was, the would-be revolutionary turned and, as Gaar watched open-mouthed, stood his ground facing the dragon. He raised his pistol—such a puny, tiny thing—and fired.

Incredibly, the dragon faltered. Had the man managed to hit something vital?

No. The monster reared onto its hind legs and screamed in fury. To Gaar's horror, however, it avoided the man with the gun in much the same way a human might have given wide berth to a bee after being stung: it ran around him and bore down on Amber's fleeing form.

Max shot after it a few more times, but the dragon either didn't feel the impacts or paid them no heed. It concentrated on the quarry ahead of it. Amber, meanwhile, stumbled and rolled, then got back up… but she'd lost much of her advantage.

It was too much for Gaar. Abandoning his idea of fleeing while the fleeing was good, he found himself doing something he never imagined he'd be brave—or stupid—enough to do: running after a man-eating monster fifty times his size. What he would do once he reached it was a problem to consider later. Right now, he had to catch up. Reaching Amber was paramount, even if it just meant that they would die together.

He ran with all his might. Despite already being tired from the run through the woods, and despite the sand that made going difficult, he redoubled his pace. And he was closing the gap to Amber, even as the dragon did so as well. That knowledge gave him wings.

About fifty meters from his quarry, time ran out. The dragon caught up with the running woman and, with a casual swat of its front leg, knocked her to the ground. An instant later, the creature's massive head bent towards her and came back up bloodied and tugging on entrails.

Just like that, without ceremony, the light in Gaar's life was extinguished. The dragon continued to feed, tearing the carcass—he could no longer think of that lifeless hunk of meat as the vibrant, stunning, smart woman he'd idolized—to pieces. He fell to his knees and watched numbly as the grisly feast proceeded.

After some moments, he realized that someone was standing beside him. Max. The piece of shit who, with his insistence on taking them hostage, had killed Amber as surely as if he'd pulled the trigger himself. The Colombian looked on with a gaze of bovine incomprehension.

Gaar, panting, pulled himself off the ground and closed the gap between them with two strides. Then he did something he'd never done before: he punched another human being in the face as hard as he could, putting every ounce of weight behind it.

Max took two steps back and absently rubbed his cheek where Gaar's wayward fist had landed. He raised the gun in an equally offhand way and pressed the trigger.

The bullet hit Gaar's side. He swore he felt it bounce off of one of his ribs. It was a terrible shot, considering the range, but Max seemed to be fascinated, watching Amber become dragon food.

Gaar kept walking and Max pulled the trigger again. Nothing happened.

"Out of bullets, asshole?"

This time, the punch landed on the Colombian's nose and Gaar had the satisfaction of feeling bone crunch under his fury. For the first time in his life, he wasn't the one getting the crap beat out of him in a fight with another man, and even through the grief and fury, it felt good.

The guerilla fell to the floor and Gaar stomped on his gun hand, just in case he had more bullets somewhere. Then he kicked Max in the head. And again. A third time.

His opponent was beaten. Max looked up at him from the ground, bloody nose streaming, and tried to get up. He stumbled back onto the sand.

All of Gaar's anger evaporated. He felt nothing for Max now, not even the pity the pathetic loser deserved. He fleetingly wondered why anyone would dedicate their life to such a miserable cause when worthwhile pursuits existed everywhere in the world. Love for power? The feeling that he was the man with the gun in a world where people resolved their differences through conversation? It was pathetic.

"You poor piece of shit," Gaar said, driven by sadness now. "You killed her."

"I…" Max grimaced and probed his nose with a finger, gently. "I was trying to save her. I thought the dragon would come after me. If it came close enough, I could shoot it in the eye."

"You're a terrible shot," Gaar said.

"How would you know?"

"You could have killed me easily."

"I didn't actually want to kill you."

It suddenly dawned on them, apparently at the same moment, that the monster that had killed Amber was still just a few dozen yards away, and just as dangerous as it always was.

They looked in that direction. As if reading their thoughts, the dragon chose that moment to look back.

Max struggled to rise and Gaar offered no help. He walked slowly away, hoping the monster would go after the immobile target first, but not really caring.

A warm wetness at his side caused him to look down and he realized that he was bleeding from the gunshot. Maybe it hadn't bounced off bone after all, no matter what it felt like. He didn't probe it with a finger. He was sure that would have hurt like hell.

Whatever other damage the bullet might have done, it had definitely clipped a blood vessel of some kind. The red fluid flowed freely, down his side and onto his pants. Instead of heading back to the forest, Gaar turned to where the remains of what had once been Amber lay on the ground. The dragon was halfway between the dead girl and the soon-to-be-dead Colombian, so Gaar knelt.

There wasn't much there. A leg untidily torn off above the knee, complete with its boot. A huge patch of blood-wet sand. A couple of unidentified giblets. That was it.

"I'm sorry, Amber," he said. "I tried to help you. I swear I did. I would have given anything to be in your place." As he said the words, he realized they were true. He'd never been physically brave in his life, but Amber had made him transcend his history of being nothing but a doorstop for more athletic, larger kids to show how macho they were. "I wish you were alive to hear this. I wish I could have said goodbye. I wish I could have told you that I love you."

A sound from further down the beach made him look up.

"No! Por favor, no!"

Max had reverted to his native Spanish as the dragon bore down on him, his voice rising an octave from the usual gruff baritone he normally affected. The Colombian had managed to get to his feet, but he swayed woozily, unable to escape.

The wind picked up, and Max raised a hand to keep flying sand from his eyes.

The dragon targeted that raised arm. It closed its jaws around it but, instead of biting it off, lifted the hapless guerilla into the air and launched him upwards. Even though he was thirty meters away, the bone-jarring thump when he hit the ground made Gaar shudder.

Bone-jarring, but not fatal. Max was still alive and conscious. He got onto his hands and knees, tears flowing freely down his cheeks.

"Por favor," he pleaded, sobbing.

Unfortunately for him, the dragon was in no mood for mercy. It walked over, still cautious—Max must have shot it in a tender spot and—as if by way of experiment, bit off a foot. The crunch of bone being snapped away echoed like a gunshot.

Max screamed, and Gaar smiled. Reality was even better than his daydreams. In his mind, of course, it was Gaar himself who did the physical damage to the guerilla, but he'd never been quite as sadistic as the dragon. It never occurred to him to cut him to pieces while he was still alive.

Another darting movement of the dragon's head and another scream. This time, the already mangled arm that had been used to launch the man was chomped away.

Gaar laughed.

For the second time in less than ten minutes, he watched as one of Philippe's monstrous creations ate a man. Though he wished that the dragon would have kept toying with the man, keeping him alive like a cat playing with a mouse, it wasn't to be. The next strike disemboweled the guerilla who gave one final shriek and was silent.

The dragon didn't seem unduly worried about that, however, it consumed the body slowly, only casting an occasional glance Gaar's way, as if to say: "Just sit tight, I'll be with you shortly."

Gaar no longer cared whether he lived or died. Besides, he was feeling dizzy from the blood he'd lost. It was very clear now that the wound was serious, and would require equally serious medical attention… which he was unlikely to find in the middle of a tropical jungle.

He laughed again. All his life he'd been afraid to participate in sports or roughhouse with the other boys because he might get hurt. He'd always been terrified of pain, and would freak whenever he bled.

But here he was, dying of a gunshot wound, and not afraid in the least. He dispassionately noted his symptoms: weakness, dizziness, blood loss. It was a beautiful day for it: not too cold, not too hot, if the wind died down a little it would be like drifting back into the womb. And now another symptom of his impending demise: a high-pitched whining in his ears which got louder and louder.

A crashing sound from the direction of the trees drew his attention in that direction and he nearly added hallucinations to his list of ailments.

Unfortunately, the dragon's reaction—it looked up and then, startled, took a couple of steps back—confirmed what his eyes were looking at.

The… thing… that had exploded from the jungle was at least ten feet tall. It looked like a black widow spider, all shiny black legs and orange markings which blazed evilly in the pre-dusk light. Two scorpion-like pincers originating just beneath the eyes completed the look.

"What the fuck?" Gaar said. The terror of death returned and suddenly he was no longer a man slowly fading away from the effects of a serious but painless wound. Suddenly, he could feel every screaming nerve ending that surrounded the ragged hole in his flesh where the bullet had entered and the wrongness inside him.

He yelled in agony, but the two monsters ignored him.

Gaar wished he'd bled out earlier. It was one thing to drift into darkness, to go gently into that goodnight, quite another to be torn to pieces by one monster—let alone two. He shook.

The creatures, however, paid him no attention. They were watching each other intently, a study which soon evolved into something that resembled the dance of two drunken men in a bar circling each other, each unwilling to give ground but each also unwilling to throw the first blow until he was certain that he could win.

Gaar relaxed and the pain subsided. Maybe he would be able to bleed his life away peacefully after all.

The dragon roared and charged. The spider-creature skittered back, avoiding the furiously snapping jaws and letting the other monster flash past.

It didn't press its advantage, however. It just stayed out of reach.

The miss enraged the dragon. Once again, it reared onto its hind legs and bellowed thunder. Another attack followed, just as ineffectual as the first; the spider-creature didn't seem to be faster, just a hell of a lot better at predicting where the dragon would strike than the dragon was at identifying its retreat patterns. Looking at it, Gaar had the feeling that the spider was... smarter.

A lull in the battle gave him a few moments to consider what he was seeing. Though both creatures were the product of a mix of genes that defied categorization—at least if Philippe was to be believed—it seemed natural that the one that looked like a lizard should be smarter, all things being relative, than the one that resembled an insect. And yet, the evidence pointed in the opposite direction.

The creatures circled again, the dragon snorting and puffing, occasionally standing on its hind legs, while the spider-scorpion thing watched implacably in silence, giving no outward sign that it was locked in a life-and-death struggle.

No, Gaar realized. That wasn't quite true. The high-pitched humming sound emanated from the spider, which was interesting. While many insects buzzed to their hearts' content, Gaar was unaware of any spiders that made noise.

Which brought the lesson home. This wasn't what it seemed. Nothing that Philippe designed worked how one would expect. The fish-men were just dumb animals, less intelligent than monkeys. The spider-thing looked smarter than anything else in the forest, and it buzzed like a swarm of bees.

But the Frenchman's worst crime, of course, was that the dragons, otherwise so perfectly made, seemed completely incapable of breathing fire. Even a mad scientist should have known better than to allow an atrocity like that.

He realized he was slipping out of consciousness, and suddenly didn't want to die. He forced himself to concentrate on the combatants, to stay awake and savor life just a few moments more.

The dragon appeared to be working itself into a fury that would allow it to attack the spider. It stomped each of its feet in turn, reared up like a horse and bellowed, all under the impassive gaze of its opponent.

Then the dragon charged again. This time, as it sidestepped, the enormous black ball brought its pincers to bear. First blood, in the form of a long gash running across two thirds of the dragon's length, was awarded to the spider.

But the dragon had learned from its prior errors as well. Halfway through its lunge, it suddenly jumped to the side and, whether from premeditation or mere chance, managed to grip one of the spider's legs in its jaws. The appendage, so tiny looking compared to the massive dragon's head, snapped off loudly.

"Second blood—Dragon!" Gaar exulted. He felt quite woozy by then and closed his eyes.

When he opened them again, the two beasts were grappling. It was obvious that several rounds had been fought while Gaar had tuned out: scratches, gouges and blood marred both creatures. The spider's left pincer appeared to be out of action, bent at an unnatural angle.

The dragon was concentrating on getting at the spider's legs. It was a smart strategy and, as well as Gaar could see in the distance and in his confused condition, at least two, possibly three of the legs were broken.

But the spider had plenty of legs left, and it was using them to good effect, still moving around and making the dragon miss most of the time.

Then, unexpectedly, it stumbled back, exposing a single leg on its right side to attack. The dragon pounced.

It was the reptile's last mistake. The unhurt pincer shot out, almost as if the spider had fallen back on purpose and was anticipating the next move. Working like a knife as opposed to a pair of scissors, it plunged deep into the dragon's underbelly, burying all the way to its second joint.

The dragon writhed in pain, a strangely silent affair, considering how much noise it had been making just moments before but, as Gaar watched, unable to look away, the pincer emerged from the other side of the dragon's flank.

Now, pierced all the way through, the monster screamed. But it was destined to be a short-lived sound. The pincer retracted into the dragon's body and did something that cut the sound off mid-cry.

The now-silent dragon attempted to bring its head to bear, to take its enemy with it to whatever hell awaited these monsters, but it was a spent force. The few movements it managed were weak… and got weaker by the second.

Gaar felt a strange kinship with the vanquished creature. Monster or not, it was seeping into death the same way he was, and he suddenly found himself rooting for the dragon.

Like most underdogs, however, the dragon did not suddenly resurge to win the fight. Instead, it took a couple of faltering steps and fell onto the sand, never to rise again. Its chest heaved a few times before finally lying still.

The spider made no overt victory display. It just extracted the pincer and, with fastidious care, wiped it on the sand at its feet. Then it stood there, the very image of a monster considering its next move.

It didn't take long to decide. Moving to the dragon's head, it applied the pincer to the defeated reptile's neck. Methodically cutting and thrusting, it worked and worked until, with a mighty pull, it managed to separate the dragon's head from its body.

Gaar wondered what instinct could have driven that particular behavior. Was this a trophy? Was it a symbol?

No. The spider simply abandoned the head where it lay and, wiping its still-working pincer again, lay on its abdomen to rest, holding its mangled legs in the air where it could put them in its mouth—itself a monstrosity of enormous mandibles rendered less notable by the fact that the creature had other, even more horrific, features—and cover them in a white, gooey saliva.

Once it finished, it stood and looked around. When it saw Gaar, it stood perfectly still.

After some moments during which the spider shifted its weight among its many legs, changing the angle in which it looked at him. Then, ponderously, it advanced towards Gaar.

He smiled at it. "It's too late, my friend. I'm already dead."

The spider gave no sign that it had heard him. It kept moving.

Finally, it arrived, towering over the kneeling man.

"Man, you're a big bastard, aren't you?"

He looked up at it unflinching. Even in his diminished state, he could tell that he was close to blacking out. His vison was tunneling, with more and more darkness around a tiny area of light and visibility. That area was filled with spider.

He watched the enormous pincer come down and open in front of him, right below his chin.

He saw the pincers begin to snap together, felt them bite into the soft flesh of his neck, but never saw them finish. The darkness got him first.

CHAPTER 25

John watched Brown walk out and wondered what was wrong with the man. The other man's advice was probably good, but John had a sense that he was preoccupied with something, perhaps not all there. For a man who'd claimed to be working closely with the French to apprehend a fugitive from the law, he suddenly seemed in an enormous hurry to get out before they arrived in numbers.

Also, he didn't have a fugitive with him.

"Let's find out what's going on," John said.

Esmeralda, no comprehension on her face, simply nodded and began her ritual of tying the sling around her body and placing the baby snugly inside. The little guy had nodded off, and no amount of pulling to put him into place seemed to disturb him much.

They set off down the hallway, and he kept his cleaver gripped firmly in his hand, but there didn't seem to be much of anyone around. They skirted the dead bodies until they reached the entrance to the dining room. Once there, John ducked inside and, keeping his eyes firmly averted from the body of the murdered revolutionary woman, he picked his pith helmet—abandoned in the excitement—off the table.

Then they followed the open doors—on the assumption that that was the way everyone went—into what appeared to be a garage. At any rate, the place was full of cars.

One of the cars, an SUV from a couple of decades before, had one door open and a man was trying, without much apparent luck, to bump-start it. His legs could be seen sticking out from the open door. For a second, John wondered whether he might also be dead, a discarded body half-in and half-out of the car, but it soon became clear that he was working, and standing on the legs, pushing the heavy vehicle forward.

When they walked in, his head popped up from under the dash, and John recognized one of Philippe's servants. The man said something in Spanish, but John just shook his head. Esmeralda, on the other hand, seemed to come alive. They held a long conversation and beckoned for John to approach the car. The man was pointing to the battery.

"You want me to push?" John said, mimicking the action.

The man nodded.

"But that car has been here for years. It's probably all seized up. And I don't even want to think about what the gasoline has turned into."

The other man shrugged and made the pushing motion again.

John pointed to the blank wall in front of them, paneled in grey cloth. "Even if that thing does start, which I doubt, you can't drive it out of here. They must have blocked off the garage when they remodeled this place."

This time, the guy must have understood, because he laughed and, pointing, ran over to the far wall, where he pulled on the paneling. To John's surprise, it slid aside to reveal a darkened tunnel on the other side big enough to drive any of the vehicles through.

"It's worth a shot, I guess."

But though they spent nearly fifteen minutes—and all their energy—pushing the SUV in an attempt to bump-start it, they ended up with nothing to show for it but copious quantities of sweat.

"We're going on ahead. Want to come with us?"

The man shook his head and pointed at the car.

"Suit yourself." John headed for the only regular-sized door out of the garage. He wanted to find his students, and there was no chance they would have discovered the hidden tunnel.

Just as they were about to leave, the servant called out to them and walked over, holding some kind of machine gun. He handed it to John wordlessly and returned to the car.

"Thank you," John said. He understood both the utility of the gun and its significance: old enmities and alliances had been set aside, and now it was humanity against the stuff in the tunnels.

At the sight of the gun, Esmeralda became excited, chattering away in rapid-fire Spanish of which he understood even less than usual. She pulled the gun out of his hands, expertly removed the magazine, checked to see if it held any bullets, nodded in satisfaction and slid it back.

"All right. You carry the gun then." He smiled at his own joke; she'd made no move to return it.

The door led into a dimly lit maze of corridors where they found a couple of human bodies—the other servant and one of Esmeralda's former comrades at arms—several dead fish-men, and the bullet-riddled carcass of one of the juvenile dragons before arriving at a door that opened into the animal pens.

John breathed a sigh of relief: there was no sign of the students in those hallways of death. Of course they hadn't been in every turning of the maze... but not finding bodies meant that hope still lived.

He hesitated at the door but Esmeralda simply walked past him into the enclosure slinging her machine rifle onto her shoulder, ready to use should the need arise.

She led the way between the enclosures, wordlessly skirting the mangled pieces of black-uniformed soldiers, and out the hangar door.

John's heart skipped a beat as one of the fish-men limped into the clearing. He gripped his cleaver tightly. Before it could advance, however, Esmeralda pointed her gun at it and, when it didn't back away, she shook it like a spear. The thing disappeared into the trees. Apparently, even the dumbest of creatures had the capacity to learn, albeit slowly.

She turned to him, pointed at the baby and put a finger over her lips. Then she smiled.

John was stunned. Here, he'd been racking his brains trying to think of a way to protect this young woman and her tiny child when maybe the answer was to let her loose in the jungle with her rifle. She definitely acted like she could take care of herself... and she'd already proven beyond any doubt that she could take care of her baby.

"But where do we go now?" he asked himself. "There's no one around."

A hollow, hopeless feeling installed itself in the pit of his stomach, the sudden conviction that he would never see his students again. Night would fall soon—the shadows of the trees already covered the entire clearing in front of the complex—and the night belonged to the animals, not to humanity. Even if they were still alive, he was certain they wouldn't see dawn.

Nevertheless, he wouldn't stop searching for them until he knew, one way or the other, where they were and what had happened to them.

Trees rustled on the far side of the clearing and John looked up to see two figures approaching. His heart leapt, but disappointment followed almost immediately: two of the French soldiers were approaching, guns at the ready.

They looked as though they'd been in a fistfight. Their uniforms were spattered with blood, and the man John believed was the leader had an enormous purple bruise on the side of his forehead.

The two duos stood across from each other, eyeing one another with mistrust. Finally, the officer lowered his rifle and walked over to where John and Esmeralda stood waiting.

"Is anyone else still alive in there?"

"One man, a servant. He's trying to fix a car."

The soldier looked around and his thoughts were clear as if John had been inside his head. How the hell was anything going to drive through this jungle? The gaps between trees would make it an impossible proposition unless one carried a chainsaw around as well. "And a man named Brown? Did you see him?"

John thought about the confusion on Brown's face when he'd encountered the man and the apparent urgency to get the hell out of Dodge. "No. I'm sorry." He paused. "If it's any consolation, I didn't see his body anywhere, either."

The soldier gave them a stereotypically Gallic shrug. "I don't really care, one way or the other. I'd never met the man, but since my orders were to rendezvous with him, I would have preferred for him to survive. It's an inconvenience that he probably got himself killed. More for him than for me, of course." Then his eyes hardened. "What about Philippe?"

"He disappeared from the dining room just before you arrived, and I haven't seen him since." At least this was a question he could answer with absolute conviction. He wondered where Cora might have gotten herself off to, but again, he wasn't very hopeful on that score. While he was sure the students were dead, he had a feeling that Cora had run off with the suave French scientist, mad or not.

"Damn. We haven't seen him out here. We'll need to sweep the complex thoroughly." He spoke into a radio in French. "We'll have a helicopter full of troops here in a few minutes."

"I hope they come loaded for bear," John remarked.

The Frenchman nodded back grimly. "They will be adequately armed. As you Americans would say, we've learned our lesson the hard way."

"And what about us?"

"You will wait."

"I'd rather leave. Do you mind if we walk off into the jungle?"

"You will wait."

The man was adamant, and it really wasn't worth making an issue out of it. John definitely wasn't in any hurry to attempt a jungle crossing, and getting into a firefight with other humans as opposed to saving their ammunition to fight the monsters didn't feel like the best use of their resources.

On the plus side, the French commandoes didn't attempt to disarm them. They established a defensive position in the hangar, even giving Esmeralda responsibility for part of a field of fire.

"What did you see out there?" John asked.

"Not a lot. We found one of the fish-things, but it ran away. Other than that, no one, and nothing. Two men just isn't enough to cover the area around here effectively."

The unmistakable sound of a helicopter overhead cut into their conversation. They watched a rope disgorge another half-dozen men dressed in black like the first group. Two of these guys were carrying shoulder-mounted RPG launchers. The rest were carrying shells for the tubes.

"Not taking any chances, huh?"

"We're soldiers, not idiots. None of us signed up for a suicide mission." He looked grimly out into the jungle. "Also, we want revenge for our fallen."

John thought they were probably out of luck, and that their human quarry, at least, was out of reach. Philippe was probably long gone, but he didn't get a chance to discuss it as the officer, leaving them with one of the RPG guys, went back into the complex. Night fell and the lights went on automatically.

They slept in turns, fitfully, with nightmares. John sat cross-legged on the ground and let Esmeralda lay her head on his lap. She spoke in her sleep, but never moved, holding her child in her arms. John felt admiration for the woman.

The night passed without incident, except for one of the fish-men, possibly the same one they'd encountered before, who entered the hangar door a couple of hours after dusk. Staying as far away from them as it could, it wandered in among the enclosures before selecting one and walking in. The bars closed automatically behind it.

The light of dawn woke John from the first deep sleep he'd managed all night. The French soldiers were brewing coffee, and the officer was back.

"Did you find what you were looking for?" John asked, taking a sip of the proffered brew. The soldiers treated them with the utmost respect, probably feeling that anyone who had managed to survive conditions that had killed four of their number had earned a measure of respect. The combination of one girl with an AK-47 and one six-month old baby seemed to be particularly amusing.

"Yes. Brown left us a note. He couldn't find Philippe, but at least the computers are all intact."

"Any idea where he went?"

"We didn't find him, but I suppose he probably tried to leave through the front door and got himself eaten." His face turned somber. "I'm afraid we also found the body of a woman. Greying short hair, in her late forties."

"It's probably Cora. I'd like to see her to be sure."

"No need to go inside. We brought photographs. She died of a massive abdominal injury."

The soldier handed him the phone. The zoom showed Cora's face, mercifully concealing whatever had killed her. She looked at peace, but very, very tired. Well, wherever she was, she was resting now.

He waited for the hammer-blow of grief. Cora was a colleague who he liked and admired. They'd been friends for nearly two decades. But nothing came. Her death affected him much less than that of Stephane—and even less than the fact that he had no idea where Gaar and Amber might be. Her actions of the past day had distanced him, disgusted him, even. She'd sided with the wrong man... the people who were always bandying about alarmist Frankenstein scenarios whenever a new development came along were right in her case. She would happily have continued breeding monsters with the Frenchman, regardless of the consequences, holding science a higher God than morality.

It was a blow. He'd always felt that he would also put his research before any other considerations... but that was before he arrived in Panama. Maybe there *should* be a moral policing of basic research.

Every cell in his body rebelled against that idea, however. You couldn't put that sort of decision in the hands of people who could never understand how important basic science was. Perhaps it was better to let the bad apples do their worst... and find solutions to the problems once they arose.

He would need to think about it.

"I'm not sure if I'm supposed to tell you this, but Paris has been speaking to Panama City. We're expecting a contingent of the local military in about an hour. We will hand the whole place, and you and the girl, over to them after destroying anything that might be embarrassing to France. Also, if anyone asks, we were never here." He looked pointedly at the weapon Esmeralda was carrying. "I would get rid of that thing if I were you. It will only cause awkward questions. No one in the Western Hemisphere uses AK-47s for their regular army. Only the insurgents and drug armies still use them."

"You tell her."

They found a soldier who spoke Spanish, and they explained the situation to Esmeralda. Finally, after the rifle had been disposed of, she turned to the man and spoke at length.

The young soldier translated. "She wants to thank you. She says she never knew her father, but she hopes he would have been something like you."

Tears welled up in John's eyes as he imagined what her life must have been like before they met. "Tell her that this is just beginning, and that whatever happens now, she can count on me to protect her. To protect both of them."

Esmeralda listened to the translation and then hugged him tight. Moments later, they were crying into each other's shoulders.

Only the baby was quiet. It looked at one, then at the other, and laughed.

EPILOGUE

It was a flat, dusty town with its back to the sea. The European seated at a table on an outdoor terrace in a bar by the national road wondered why anyone in Africa, with a coastline awash in wonder and natural beauty would build a town that far from the blue expanse.

Especially this town. Ouidah's glory years, a century and a half gone, had owed everything to the slave trade. The Portuguese had sold human cargo to all comers without discriminating against origin or religion: British gold, to them, was as good as that of Zanzibar. Christian acceptable as Mohammedan. Every unfortunate sold in the marketplace was shipped off on the Atlantic, to new and terrifying homes in the Americas or in the East.

It would have made sense for such a town to have been constructed right up against the source of its wealth, and yet nearly a kilometer separated the edge of the town from the sea. Perhaps it was a question of defense. Being too close to the sea might have made the town, and its once-strategic trade, vulnerable to assault by unfriendly powers. Portuguese dominion of the seas had, after all, been a fleeting thing which was the mere ghost of a memory by the 19th century, and the British had not been known for their patience or for using diplomacy when red-coated troops might serve equally well.

In the end it had worked out for the best. The wide-open stretch of sand between town and water was perfectly adapted to Ouidah's new claim to fame: the dusty town was home to the world's largest voodoo festival.

From what had been on display over the past two days, the festival mostly took place in the town proper, but on the final night those sands became a dreamlike stage where fire and alcohol and rhythm and sweat-covered bodies blended into something that, even the following morning, were an impression as opposed to a memory.

The headache from the terrible alcohol he'd drunk too much of without knowing what it was, on the other hand, was all too real. He grimaced into his glass of Coca-Cola—one liquid that was usually safe to drink anywhere on the planet—and wondered why he'd bothered coming to the meeting at all.

Maybe because it was the only thing he remembered clearly from the alcoholic haze of the night.

A tall, thin woman, skin as dark as the night and hair cropped short, walked in, and Philippe felt his heart quicken. She had remembered. Unlike the previous night when she had been dressed in ceremonial robes, she was now dressed in a European style: a dark suit over a white button-down blouse. She laid the hardcover book she was carrying on the table and sat down facing him. He half-rose, a sign of respect, before re-taking his seat.

"Good afternoon," he said.

She smiled to reveal perfect white teeth. "How are you feeling today?" she said. "Not many tourists can drink the amount of sodabi you were consuming and come out of it without some consequences." She spoke English with a crisp, upper-class British accent which his French blood almost instantly wanted to declare war on.

Instead, he smiled. "Is that what it's called? Well, you can add me to the list of its victims. I feel like death."

"You look fine," she replied.

"That's because I got up at two in the afternoon and took a shower. I couldn't move at any reasonable hour. And here, you look as if you've been up and around all day... you weren't exactly stinting on the... sadoba?"

"Sodabi. I'm the director of the art museum," she replied. "I don't have the luxury of sleeping all morning."

"Art museum..." he left the words hanging there.

"It's the only job for a post-doctoral researcher in the entire town. They insisted I should take it, and they weren't really concerned about the fact that I couldn't tell African art from... well, from anything. I'm a sociologist, not an art critic. But they don't care. Apparently, I'm something of a celebrity because of the voodoo stuff."

"Voodoo stuff?"

"I'm the foremost expert on the rites of West African Vodun in the world. And, unless you were really drunk last night, you could probably tell that this city is pretty obsessed with voodoo for a few nights a year."

He felt the disappointment rise. "Last night, you gave me the impression you were a different kind of scientist," Philippe replied.

"I have more than a passing interest in biology and genetics."

So, she remembered their conversation. "I didn't catch your name."

"My name is Angelique, Philippe."

He tried to remember if he'd told her his name, but the night was a blur. He only remembered speaking of his experiments, and of the imperative need that they should meet the following day.

"Well, Angelique, if you aren't a geneticist, I really don't have much to say to you that you can't read anywhere else, and probably in terms you could understand better than if I explained them to you."

The woman scowled at him. "Don't patronize me. I understand a lot more than you might expect. And besides, I know exactly who you are."

She let that sink in. Philippe had told no one his true last name. And the security forces of Benin were not likely to have seen through his cover. His false papers were real in every sense of the word except for the name on the first page.

"And who do you think I am?"

In response, she leaned over and stole a newspaper from the man at the next table. His protest died on his lips as soon as he saw who it was that had pilfered it.

The newspaper was in French, and it had a terrible picture, distant and pixeled, of what looked like a huge spider in a forest. It was the same picture that had been making the rounds of every news wire on the planet for the past few days.

The headline read: *Photo of The Panama Horror*.

"This is who I think you are."

He was about to issue a blustering denial, but the dark, impassive eyes held his own.

"Are you *Sûreté*?"

A laugh. "No. By no means. You're safe with me."

"Then how?"

"We have a friend in common."

Who knew he was there? Park Sun-Lee could probably find him if he set his mind to it, but the Korean and his Russian backers had no reason to do it. They would wait until he was on his feet again before using him further; the response to his report about the mind download had made that perfectly clear.

Brown? If he was some kind of hacker, as Philippe suspected, he might have been able to backtrack the long chain of false identities and apocryphal documentation Philippe had used to cover his tracks. Maybe. But if it was Brown, if the original personality had somehow wrested control of his body back from the man who'd been overlaid onto him, he wouldn't have sent this woman to talk to him. Brown's message would have been delivered via a knife in the back in a dark alley. Or just with a visit from the French military.

Either scenario would have required that Brown take things personally. There was no room for personal feelings in the shadowy world they both inhabited. It was business. Had Brown's business gone as planned, Philippe would now be in some maximum-security French prison. But it didn't, and Brown had suffered the consequences. There should be no hard feelings.

But if not them, who? The woman, who seemed to be about in her mid-thirties, was grinning.

"You won't guess."

"Then tell me."

"I was in Gabon."

"No one in Gabon knows I'm here." But a ball of ice was forming in Philippe's stomach. It was true that no one in Gabon knew he was there, but a lot of people in Gabon knew who he was.

"I didn't say they did. I just said I was in Gabon. I was doing research into the beliefs of the different populations in the Gabonese jungle, especially concentrated on the National Parks, where life goes on without too much interference from the outside world." She gave him a significant look. "I believe you're familiar with the area. I tracked down one specific instance of spirit-worship, several lakeside villages who hated each other but also worshipped the same set of forest deities: an imp and a dragon who supposedly lived on a haunted spit of land where nobody went. An unusual combination, and worthy of study, don't you think?"

"No…"

"I went there. I'm not superstitious… You can't be if you want to study, seriously study, the belief systems of the world from a sociological viewpoint. So I went. And you know what?"

Philippe shook his head, not trusting himself to speak without betraying his deepest, darkest fears.

"The religion, the superstitions… they were true. There was a tiny imp there, and a dragon… except there was nothing supernatural about either."

"Poupée… she's still alive?"

"Yes. And so is Harold. He's too big to move on land anymore, but those mangrove swamps are perfect for him."

Philippe drank. His drink was Coca-Cola. That wasn't the right thing to drink during this conversation. He ordered a whisky on the rocks and Angelique waited with him in silence. He took a long drink and, fortified, nodded for her to continue.

"Poupée told me all about you. She showed me pictures. I think she came to regret what happened between you. She thinks you're dead."

"I know. I nearly was. She made sure of that."

"She told me what she'd managed to piece together about your experiments, about what you'd done. She also made me promise never to tell anyone she was real, to let the outside world think the villagers were just people with vivid imaginations. I convinced her she could trust me."

"That's obvious by the fact that you're alive."

"Yes. But she might as well have killed me, because she left me with an obsession. So many people talk of changing the world... and none of them ever do. But you did it, at a genetic level... the very building blocks of life. It's as close to being God as anything I'd ever seen."

He laughed. "It's nothing at all like being God. God doesn't get attacked by everything he touches."

"It's just like being God," she said, the fervor of true belief in her eyes. "And I wished I'd been able to meet you before you died. I... I even made a few offers to the Gods of Vodun that I might be able to communicate with you along one of the dark roads."

Philippe squirmed uncomfortably at that, but said nothing. Death, he thought, should have been a sufficient barrier against stalkers.

"When I saw you last night, I thought you were a spirit, brought for the festival. I recognized you immediately. Then I thought I must have let my obsession drive me insane. It took me the longest time to realize you were actually there."

"What do you want from me?"

"Teach me."

He studied her. It was too much coincidence, he thought. Just as he was beginning to set up operations in Africa again—America, even the jungles, was just too officious and full of snooping governments—a woman with an impossible story came to beg him to take her under his wing?

It was the perfect setup for betrayal. She wanted his secrets. The Cubans had probably sent her. Or maybe some faction he wasn't aware of. Maybe even his Russian allies, tired of waiting for results.

"Why would I believe that?"

"Because it's true." Her eyes held the same expression as Cora's: wonder at what was possible, a burning desire to be part of it.

"No."

"I…"

"No. Just go."

She nodded curtly, pain written in her face, and stood to go. In her haste, she left her book on the table.

"Wait, you forgot this." He picked it up and closed the gap.

She turned and he saw that she was crying.

"Your book." He happened to glance down at the cover. *Pride & Prejudice*. He'd lost his own copy back in Gabon. Presumably, it had been eaten away by the swamp by now.

Poupée used to bring it to him. She loved it when he read out loud for her about Mr. Darcy.

Philippe sighed.

"Listen, perhaps I was too hasty. I can show you a few things, and we can go from there."

Angelique beamed, and he wondered how long it would take her to betray him, too.

THE END

CHECK OUT OTHER GREAT HORROR NOVELS

BLACK FRIDAY
by Michael Hodges

Jerrid the kleptomaniac, Chike the unemployed IT guy, Patricia the shopaholic, and Jeff the meth dealer are trapped inside a Chicago supermall on Black Friday. Bridgefield Mall empties during a fire alarm, and most of the shoppers drive off into a strange mist surrounding the mall parking lot. They never return. Chike and his group try calling friends and family, but their smart phones won't work, not even Twitter. As the mist creeps closer, the mall lights flicker and surge. Bulbs shatter and spray glass into the air. Unsettling noises are heard from within the mist, as the meth dealer becomes unhinged and hunts the group within the mall. Cornered by the mist, and hunted from within, Chike and the survivors must fight for their lives while solving the mystery of what happened to Bridgefield Mall. Sometimes, a good sale just isn't worth it.

GRIMWEAVE
by Tim Curran

In the deepest, darkest jungles of Indochina, an ancient evil is waiting in a forgotten, primeval valley. It is patient, monstrous, and bloodthirsty. Perfectly adapted to its hot, steaming environment, it strikes silent and stealthy, its chosen prey: human. Now Michael Spiers, a Marine sniper, the only survivor of a previous encounter with the beast, is going after it again. Against his better judgement, he is made part of a Marine Force Recon team that will hunt it down and destroy it.

The hunters are about to become the hunted.

CHECK OUT OTHER GREAT HORROR NOVELS

DEATH CRAWLERS
by Gerry Griffiths

Worldwide, there are thought to be 8,000 species of centipede, of which, only 3,000 have been scientifically recorded. The venom of Scolopendra gigantea—the largest of the arthropod genus found in the Amazon rainforest—is so potent that it is fatal to small animals and toxic to humans. But when a cargo plane departs the Amazon region and crashes inside a national park in the United States, much larger and deadlier creatures escape the wreckage to roam who reproduce at an astounding rate. Entomologist Frank Travis solicits small town sheriff Wanda Rafferty's help and together they investigate the crash site. But as a rash of gruesome deaths befalls the townsfolk of Prospect, Frank and Wanda will soon discover how vicious and cunning these new breed of predators can be. Meanwhile, Jake and Nora Carter, and another backpacking couple, are venturing up into the mountainous terrain of the park. If only they knew their fun-filled weekend is about to become a living nightmare

THE PULLER
by Michael Hodges

Matt Kearns has two choices: fight or die. The creature in the orchard took the rest. Three days ago, he arrived at his favorite place in the world, a remote shack in Michigan's Upper Peninsula. The plan was to mourn his father's death and figure out his life. Now he's fighting for it. An invisible creature has him trapped. Every time Matt tries to flee, he's dragged backwards by an unseen force. Alone and with no hope of rescue, Matt must escape the Puller's reach. But how do you free yourself from something you can't see?

CHECK OUT OTHER GREAT
HORROR NOVELS

MONSTROSITY
by Tim Curran

The Food: It seeped from the ground, a living, gushing, teratogenic nightmare. It contaminated anything that ate it, causing nature to run wild with horrible mutations, creating massive monstrosities that roam the land destroying towns and cities, feeding on livestock and human beings and one another. Now Frank Bowman, an ordinary farmer with no military skills, must get his children to safety. And that will mean a trip through the contaminated zone of monsters, madmen, and The Food itself. Only a fool would attempt it. Or a man with a mission.

THE SQUIRMING
by Jack Hamlyn

You are their hosts.

You are their food.

The parasites came out of nowhere, squirming horrors that infested the human race. They turned the population into mindless pack animals, psychotic cannibalistic hordes whose only purpose was to feed them.

Now with the human race teetering at the edge of extinction, extermination teams are fighting back, killing off the parasites and their voracious hosts. Taking them out one by one in violent, bloody encounters.

The future of mankind is at stake.

And time is running out.

www.ingramcontent.com/pod-product-compliance
Lightning Source LLC
Chambersburg PA
CBHW031953170626
46807CB00006B/2472